TH
SW

By the same author:

THE PALACE OF FANTASIES
THE PALACE OF HONEYMOONS
THE PALACE OF EROS

THE PALACE OF SWEETHEARTS

Delver Maddingley

First published in Great Britain in 1992 by
Nexus
332 Ladbroke Grove
London W10 5AH

Reprinted 1994

A catalogue record for this title is available from the British
Library

ISBN 0 352 32823 1

Typeset by TW Typesetting, Plymouth, Devon
Printed and bound in Great Britain by
Cox & Wyman Ltd, Reading, Berks.

To
the author of
Adventures of a Naked Girl

ONE

A CASE OF MISTAKEN IDENTITY

Inside the leathers his cock hardened. The girl struck him as dazzlingly pretty standing there, slim, fair-haired and surely eighteen. Already he felt he had fallen on his feet.

His suppositions about what lay ahead of him had been of the vaguest as he set out from his temporary digs in the village. On this hot Monday afternoon in late May he was looking for likely skirt, having been deprived of female company for the past eighteen months, for reasons he preferred not to dwell on. A promising-looking signboard half a mile back up the road had caught his eye, so he had pulled up to read it:

CUNLIP COLLEGE
(Residential, 16–18)
for the Daughters of Professional Men
ACADEMIC & FINISHING:
RAPID RESULTS GUARANTEED
Principal: Miss Mary Muttock, M.A.
FIRST RIGHT

Below, in fresher paint, the words 'OFFICIAL RECOGNITION APPLIED FOR' had been added. The girls wouldn't need to be academic to please him, he mused, as long as they were ready for finishing. He observed a more blatant addition to the sign: some joker had inserted a 'T' between the two middle letters of 'CUNLIP'. The crossbar of the 'T' consisted of a pair of bollocks, and the upright was a dangling, dripping dick.

Kicking down into second gear, he had leaned into the sharp bend and revved up with an impressive, throaty roar to hurtle down the tree-lined driveway. Loitering girls scurried squealing to the kerbside as he kamikaze'd towards the drab, brick building. His front forks plunged and reared up again as he stopped dead at the foot of the stone steps leading down from the main entrance. He killed the 750-cc engine and at that moment his

1

prospective skirt, or regulation pale-blue dress, appeared at the door. For some reason the girl looked annoyed with him, but that only increased her appeal. She was cock-stiffeningly pretty, and he winced slightly as he swung his leg over the mean Suzuki to dismount. Then he hiked the machine up on its centre stand and raised his visor just a little, grinning at her.

With a distracted air, this charming stranger returned the grin momentarily before resuming her air of annoyance and approached him. But instead of eyeing him to size him up, as they usually did, she laid a hand on his elbow and steered him up the steps.

'You're nearly too late,' she complained, to his astonishment. She spoke like someone in a forties or fifties British movie. 'Keep your mouth shut and if we're lucky no one will notice you. It's all set up, and she'll be starting any minute now.'

He followed her at a brisk pace through the entrance hall, up a staircase and along a carpeted passage. At one point as she hurried along she uttered some words he could only just hear: 'Wednesday evening, like we said. And don't be late.'

They rounded a corner and passed three startled girls who sat outside a door inscribed 'PRINCIPAL'. Then, just around another corner, his new companion opened a smaller door and pushed him into a dark cupboard.

'There,' she said. 'I managed to get all that gunge out of the keyhole. Put your eye right up to it, and you'll see most of the room quite easily.'

This cupboard, it seemed, was merely a space between two doors. He dropped to his knees, and in his eagerness to apply his eye to the hole in the door in front of him, banged his helmet, which he had forgotten he was wearing, against the wood.

'Bloody idiot!' she scolded. 'If Muttock hears anything the game's up. Here, take this.' She handed him a large manila envelope. 'Last Wednesday's – they came back quickly,' she said. 'I put yours and mine together. They look quite randy.' And she was gone, shutting the outer door behind her and leaving him in darkness.

Trying to control his shaking and to keep quiet, he tugged off his helmet and set it on the floor, along with the package the girl had given him. As soon as his eye became accustomed to

2

the slight draft blowing through the keyhole and to the brightness beyond, he focused on an unexpected sight. No more than four feet away, and directly ahead of him, the sunlight fell on a smooth, white bottom. Then a hand fell on it, setting it a-quiver.

The stern-faced, bespectacled disciplinarian wielding this hand was evidently Mary Muttock, the Principal of Cunlip College. She sat upright on a hard chair, the girl to whom the bottom belonged draped across her lap with her face hidden by a cascade of dark hair hanging to the floor. The girl's navy knickers had been pulled down round her knees. Her grey skirt was held up over her back by one of the Principal's long-fingered hands, while the other one administered several more slaps. Although he could distinctly hear the impact of palm on bum-flesh, it did not appear that the blows were particularly heavy or in any degree painful.

The girl, a dimpled brunette, got up, smoothed down her skirt and smiled. 'Thank you, Miss Muttock,' she said.

'Next time it'll be a bit harder,' replied the Principal in velvety tones. 'Send Emily Capstick in.'

Miss Muttock rose to her feet and took a draught from a glass standing on her desk. She was a tall woman with narrow hips and a prominent bust. Her appearance was prim and old-fashioned, her mouse-coloured hair being swept up in a tight bun, and her nose adorned with gold-rimmed half-moon spectacles. And this effect was heightened by the costume she wore under her academic gown: a high-necked, starched white blouse with long sleeves and a black skirt reaching to below her knees. Far from repelling the hidden intruder, this rather forbidding person excited his interest. At first sight he had taken her to be middle-aged and somewhat dehydrated, but now he judged her to be no more than twenty-nine or so, and very handsome despite the severity of her attire.

Her next victim entered, closing the door behind her. Emily was a well-grown blonde of rosy complexion. Plump was not quite the word for her; as a rule the Captain didn't find plumpness a turn-on. It would be fairer to say that her build just suggested a promise of yielding firmness. Hers appeared to be the kind of body that invited cuddling and pressing one's face into. Over her generous bottom the grey skirt was stretched tightly. It was, he supposed, shorter than the length prescribed

3

by whatever regulations operated in this draconian institution. It revealed the greater part of a delicious pair of thighs, their texture set off by the white socks pulled up to her knees.

'I've had a bad report from Miss MacDonald, Emily.'

'What did she say?'

The Principal consulted a note on her desk.

'It would seem you've been lifting your dress to the odd-job man. How can you possibly justify such lewd behaviour?'

'I've never had a man up me in my life – I swear, miss!' retorted the blushing girl.

'Control your vulgarity, you slattern! Miss MacDonald never accused you of – of having intercourse. But you were showing off your – your private parts.'

'Never! I was just scratching an itch and I didn't notice him till he came out from behind that bush, so there.'

'And came face to face with another bush. Yes, she says you had no knickers on.'

'It's this touch of thrush,' the tearful girl explained, deflated. 'It was Miss MacDonald who said I ought to leave them off till it cleared up.'

'Well, you won't need them for the next few minutes, young lady. Bend over the desk.'

Emily obeyed. The hem of her skirt rode up to the tops of her well-formed thighs, and the Principal tugged at the sides to raise it higher. But finding it too tight to shift easily in this posture, she instructed the girl to stand, unfasten it and let it fall to her feet before resuming her undignified position – a position, incidentally, which favoured the concealed biker's lascivious gaze perfectly. How he would have loved to press his cheek against those softer cheeks! Or to let his cock-knob grow big between them until it probed the velvet mound just visible between the slightly parted thighs!

Miss Muttock took a ruler from her desk and used the flat side to administer half a dozen gentle strokes, before concluding the punishment with a stinging slap from the palm of her hand. This at least provoked a yelp of pain and brought a rosy flush to the buttocks. Emily was dismissed, with orders to send in a girl called Cathy.

Cathy was a good-looking senior girl with medium-length dark

4

hair and a rather full bust under her crisp white shirt. Without waiting to be asked she removed her skirt and stood there in navy knickers and white socks. Far from seeming apprehensive, she gave the Captain the impression that the occasion was a pleasant, routine sort of affair for her. She smiled broadly at the Principal and began to unbutton her shirt. It dropped from her shoulders, revealing a lacy white bra through which small, dark nipples could be observed.

'Has that beastly German boy been touching them again?' demanded Miss Muttock as she stationed herself behind the girl and fondled these nipples through the bra. The long fingers worked at the lace and dragged it down until the breasts sprang out. Although generously developed, they were perfectly formed and in no way disproportionate to the rest of her body.

'He insists on a bit of heavy petting,' laughed Cathy. 'Last night I let him jerk off between my boobs, and I let him suck the nipples really hard. But I always keep my knickers on.'

'Now that's an outright lie! Believe me, Cathy, I have my informants. Let me inspect your thing.'

Cathy looked rather taken aback. But the Principal knelt in front of her and eased down the regulation pants until they were halfway down her thighs. She then made the girl part her legs, and subjected the dark bushy hair to a close inspection which unfortunately hid it from the watcher's avid gaze.

'Why,' exclaimed Miss Muttock, 'it's all caked up with these white flakes. How do you explain that?'

'That's just discharge. I always get it this time of the month.'

Her inquisitor examined the gusset of her knickers. 'These are perfectly clean,' she declared. 'If you had any sort of vaginal discharge, it would be running out and staining them. In any case, I can tell from the way it's all up here, round the base of your tummy, and not at all between your legs. That can only mean one thing: it's a sure sign you were interfered with last night. You haven't even bothered to wash it off.'

These observations subdued poor Cathy, who had entered the room with such a buoyant demeanour. She now began to sulk and spun round, bending forwards and thrusting her buttocks at her tormentor. The latter laid one hand on her pubis to steady her, and with the other administered a series of hard blows until the girl squirmed and begged for mercy. Only then did Miss Muttock desist from chastising her, but continued for a short time to squeeze the plump and hairy mound.

'You will have to comb all this dry stuff out,' she said. 'Don't let it happen again. Run along now, and send in the next girl.'

Out in the corridor, the Captain had been hustled along too briskly to get a proper view of the delinquents awaiting their chastisement. He now saw that the one who entered was rather younger and more petite than those already dealt with: a sixteen-year-old, radiantly pretty in her pale blue summer dress.

'Sit down, Nikki,' said Miss Muttock, 'and tell me what you've been up to.'

Showing no signs of embarrassment as she artfully contrived to sprawl on an upright chair, the girl grinned, clasped her hands behind her head and came right out with it: 'I've been frigging myself, miss.'

'Often?'

'All the time, miss.'

'Where?'

'Oh, everywhere. In bed, in the bath, in lessons, in the woods, in the long grass . . .'

'Only with yourself?'

'Only properly with myself. But I've been trying to get Susie Freemantle to do it with me. She's shy.'

By now, the observer no longer knew quite what to expect in the way of disapproval, anger or lasciviousness from this extraordinary and, maybe, more sapphic than draconian Principal. And indeed, her reaction was again quite different, but just as remote from anything he could have foreseen. First she opened the door to the corridor. 'Hold any calls, Grote,' the Captain heard her shout. When she closed the door again, she locked it.

'Unzip my skirt,' she commanded.

The girl moved behind her and did so. Miss Mary Muttock stepped out of her skirt, and stood, tall and elegant in black silk stockings and suspender belt, a veritable cliché of glamour. Her black panties were loose, lacy and transparent, shading rather than hiding a triangle of light brown pubic hair.

So far, all the events of this disciplinary session had taken place in full view of the keyhole. But now the Captain's luck seemed

6

to have run out. The splendid Miss Muttock threw herself into an armchair that had its back to him; all he could see was one of her arms and an outstretched leg, the white flesh at the top of the stocking just visible. Heaving herself up for a moment, she removed her panties and tossed them aside.

'Well, Nikki,' she said, 'show me how you do it.'

Nikki knelt between her thighs. He could see her head and shoulders, but only imagine what she was doing with her hands on the basis of movements of the Principal's leg, and the drumming of her fingers on the arm of the chair.

'That's right, darling,' he heard her murmur, 'put another one in. It feels so good.'

Nikki's activities became brisker. Her older lover reached her hands forward and deftly unfastened the buttons down the front of the girl's dress, which she then pulled open to reveal a bare, boyish chest, its immature twin swellings hardly noticeable from the front.

'Let's see if we can get these big,' she said and proceeded to suck the little pink nipples, first one, then the other, until to his amazement they stuck out like wet redcurrants.

Something else was sticking out now, but less like a redcurrant than a cucumber. He undid his zip fastener, and it leapt forward in the dark, its head hot and angry. As he made to reapply his eye to the keyhole, he lost his balance and fell with a crash against the inner door of his hiding place.

'Quick! Off you go!' he heard Miss Muttock cry, and then the sound of the study door being unlocked, opening and closing. Then, before he had time to consider his position, the door in front of him was unlatched and whipped open by the smiling Principal, her black gown hanging open.

Mary Muttock tried to run a tight ship. Until recently she had been in almost total control of the establishment, subject only to a Board of Governors swayed by pig-ignorant local worthies and dozy clerics. Their Chairman, Dr Winspur, was Reader in Morbid Anatomy at some provincial university, a man not easily shocked; he had shown her some favour. Lately, however, he had been preoccupied with the threatened closure of his department, now deemed a frivolous luxury the nation could ill afford.

So distracted was he by the turmoil on his own patch that he had not appeared at Cunlip College for many months, even to visit his daughter Melanie, one of the senior girls.

In the past, Miss Muttock had been able to rule the college with a rod, not of iron, but quite painful enough to keep her young charges in order. But in recent months the spirit of reform now rampant in the state education system had begun to insinuate its tentacles even into the operations of obscure academies like Cunlip College. There had been talk of inspections, curriculum reviews, audits, prunings and shakedowns. Dark murmurings about child abuse had faded away only when their perpetrators realised that all the students, backwards though some of them were, had reached the age of consent. Surveyors had been seen with large-scale maps; the beautiful and extensive grounds were clearly being viewed as prime building land, ripe for speculative grabs. Wherever she went, she felt she was being watched, watched by familiar faces she could no longer trust as well as by shadowy ones she had never seen before. Counter-intelligence seemed to be the only means of protection open to her and, accordingly, she had taken to cultivating favourites in a more serious and systematic way than formerly. These were drawn mainly from the ranks of the girls, but she had also formed a connection with dirty Derrick, a young layabout retained to see to odd jobs around the grounds and to fill in for the bedridden and moribund college porter. Derrick had some peculiar tastes that required satisfying (some of them involving the black leather garb in which he rode his motorcycle noisily round the grounds), but so did she, and their mutual backscratching had given both of them some amusement.

On the whole, what Mary Muttock had gained in the way of intimacy with young persons through these developments did not make up for the harassment. This irked and offended her, for she took some pride in her old-fashioned managerial methods (although management was not a term she used) and in the cultural régime she provided for her young ladies. The discipline of the classroom was more congenial to her than that of the marketplace. Her approach was founded on the experience of a dozen years in various capacities within the private sector of secondary education.

Precisely what scholarly or professional qualifications she possessed was a question the men in suits who had been seen around the place would be asking with embarrassing persistence. Her master's degree had been awarded by a Midwestern correspondence school of which the academic credentials were as insubstantial as its physical existence. The real estate of Cunlip College sprawled over broad acres, but the campus of Doodsville University was much harder to locate, as it operated out of a mere box number. Recently she had decided it would be prudent to take down the eye-catching certificate which had embellished the wall of her study. It had been good enough for the fee-paying professional men whose daughters were entrusted to her, but might provoke scepticism in visitors from the Department.

The dodgy degree was not her only connection with the United States; nor was the teaching world the only world of which she had professional experience. In her late teens, after an unrewarding spell shaking her charms about in a Los Angeles 'nude disco parlor', she had taken off with one of the clients and ended up in an establishment in the Nevada desert known as the Raunch Ranch. The Ranch offered a kind of security within a barbed-wire compound. It was one of those brothels where the bizarrely attired young ladies are confined in quarters luxurious and hygienic but decorated and furnished in a taste so loud and vulgar that even some of the punters (or 'johns') not already dead drunk (or 'impaired') on arrival were quickly reduced to nausea by their surroundings. Mary, however, had done well ('she done good') in this environment, and by the time she escaped with the help of a professional poker player from Las Vegas, she had accumulated enough bucks to get her back to her native shores.

Few traces of the imprint left on her by her American experiences were visible, except when she stripped down to her underwear and went into erotic overdrive. To achieve credibility of sorts in the world of private education, she had cultivated a primness of manner, a chaste simplicity of appearance and a wholesomeness of vocabulary that impressed the various interviewing panels she had confronted as much as the glowing references certain gentlemen friends were happy to provide. She had kept up an impressive front until those vicious reformers had begun to poke about behind the façade.

Meanwhile, pending the possible disruption of her world, she was determined to continue with her pleasant pursuits: a little teaching (geography, needlework, French and 'general studies'), the contemplation of her domain and its delightful inmates and, above all, the gentle curbing of the wilder excesses of both staff and students. It was while engaged in the last of these favourite activities that she had been alarmed by a crash behind the disused door, and had hurriedly dismissed the precocious Nikki.

Mary Muttock soon regained her ladylike composure. There could be no doubt that the disturbance had been caused by the odd-jobbing Derrick, who had given her notice that he meant to take a discreet look at this disciplinary session. She had agreed on condition that the girls' suspicion was not aroused, but now his clumsiness had nearly given him away. The stupid boy! She opened the door to confront him.

'Hi there, Derrick,' she crooned, applying a hand to his rampant member.

The reader will not be surprised that the darkness of the recess deceived her. For the second time that day, the intruder benefited from being a case of mistaken identity. In his thirty or (strictly speaking) forty years he had acquired quite a knack of exploiting the readiness of people to make such mistakes, a knack he had sometimes been too free with for his own good. But today it seemed that attractive females were being taken in by him with absolutely no volition on his part.

However, in this second case the illusion was only momentary. Miss Muttock's smile clouded into fury, and with her free hand she clutched her gown tightly round her white body, while with the other one she pulled him out by his cock into the sunlight of her study.

'Who the fuck are you?' she screamed.

'Calm down, madam,' he replied. 'I think we ought to have a little chat.'

She dropped into the armchair. Truculently, she indicated that he should take the chair facing her, which he did after tucking his prick, now limp again from the shock, back into his leathers. The baleful glass eyes of a leopard-skin rug glared up at her from the stained carpet.

'Miss Muttock,' be began, 'who I am is no business of yours.

10

They usually call me the Captain. I am a reasonably law-abiding citizen. Reasonably, yes, but not obsessively so. You take my meaning?'

'No.'

'I'm always ready for a bit of fun myself, and I don't see why others shouldn't take their pleasures where they find them. But there are limits, as the most easy-going jury would probably agree, especially if they were professional men with daughters to educate.'

'Jury? Why – what are you after, you jumped-up yob?'

He explained, improvising brilliantly, that he felt no scruples about appealing to her conscience as well as to her more generous instincts, the case being one of obvious gravity. The students were at risk of quitting her care as damaged goods, corrupted in mind if not in body.

'Not true!' she retorted. 'Their minds are allowed to flower naturally. Nearly all of them are already sexualised when they come here. If you doubt that, you don't know what sort of a world we're living in. And as for their bodies, you can ask Miss MacDonald. She's in charge of English and Physical Development and part of her job's to keep an eye on their maiden integrity.'

The Captain replied that he found her answer contradictory. Clearly, she was both a thoroughly unsuitable person to run an academy for young ladies, and in breach of the law. She was in danger not only of imprisonment but also of professional disgrace. And yet . . .

And yet his own stance, he declared, was a liberal one. He was a believer in the benefits practical guidance could furnish in the sexual education of the young. They needed to be socialised and sometimes this could best be achieved by first acknowledging their innate lustful proclivities, giving these proclivities their head and then gradually accommodating them to the outward forms of respectability. He was prepared, he said, to overlook the scandalous episode he had witnessed – on certain conditions which she should not find it too hard to accept.

'What conditions?'

'Well, for starters, I'm going to give you a dose of your own medicine. Over my knees!'

11

For a moment she looked at him, hesitating, before gathering her gown together at one side to expose her venereal mound, flank and backside, and laying herself face down across his lap. She was conscious that her bum was white and beautiful, with a tuft of lush brown fur sprouting up between the cheeks at the point where their curves terminated at the thigh-tops.

Gently tweaking this tuft with the fingers of one hand while he stroked the soft white flesh with the palm of the other one, he continued to lay down his terms.

'My main problem, though now it's your problem, is that I need a fairly well-paid job, no questions asked and cash in hand.'

'What kind of job? We only take female staff here.'

Instead of pressing this one and insisting on the kind of academic sinecure so many articulate, mature males considered themselves well qualified for, he offered himself as a casual groundsman and odd-job man, and with a little persuasive manipulation of her perineum got himself accepted. She promised to hand over a set of keys to the outbuildings the next day, and to fill him in on any information needed to enable him to pass for a legitimate employee. To be sure, she explained, such a position was already occupied but, as the incumbent was so negligent of his duties, she thought there would be plenty for the Captain to turn his hand to if he wished. If, on the other hand, he had no burning inclination to do so, a firm of outside contractors had been retained to attend to such basics as cutting the grass. Inquiries about his previous employment and requests for references he brushed aside with a finger that deftly parted the lips of her pussy, and with a vague mention of 'freelancing'.

'I must warn you,' she sighed, 'that opportunities for "free-lancing" on these premises are less abundant than you might think. There are spies among the girls. We must be constantly on our watch. The Governors are just itching for an excuse to get rid of me and introduce a stricter, leaner, market-led regime.'

'Come on,' he urged, probing with an eager fingertip. 'A place like this is full of dark holes and corners where nature could take its course undetected.'

'It's precisely there that the danger lies. Those holes and corners are where our spies are most likely to find you. Why, they lurk there themselves. No, if you really want this job I must

12

insist that you keep right out of the main college building. The only exception will be if you need to see me in this study.'

He accepted these terms. To clinch the bargain, he kept his digit in its moist lodgment and brought his other hand down resoundingly, first on one buttock, then on the other, and finally, with fingers spread, on both together. With each blow she felt the flush on that fair skin growing brighter and heard herself gasping more loudly as she made the grip of her vaginal muscles tighten on his finger.

But it was not only on Mary Muttock's anatomy that these activities were having an effect. Indeed, they would have put lead in the pencil of a paralysed eunuch. Crushed beneath her panting weight and confined within tight leather, his member was unable to rear its head, but she felt its struggles as it tried to press into her belly. He ordered her to get up and bend over her desk in the gothic-traceried bay window. Out of the corner of her eye she caught a glimpse of him hurrying the garment which encased his lower limbs down to his ankles. She flinched a little as he applied both thumbs to pulling open the capacious cunt she now flaunted in all its sopping glory. Once the tip of his glans was lodged between the lips, he twanged the black elastic of her suspenders against the upper thighs, gripped her firmly by the hips and lunged deep into the receptacle of joy.

At this instant, a stubbly face crowned with spiky black hair appeared at the window and began to apply a wet cloth to the panes.

'It's fucking Derrick!' exclaimed Miss Muttock as her partner withdrew. 'He came after all.'

'And so did I,' the Captain added, spraying the carpet with uncontainable sperm. Then, pausing only to adjust his clothing and retrieve from its hiding place his crash helmet and the large manila envelope, he fled from the scene, leaving Miss Mary Muttock, M.A., to face the startled window-cleaner.

Eighteen, slim and indeed cock-stiffeningly pretty (as attested by the strenuous tightening in the front of the Captain's jeans), the girl who had accosted him earlier and led him into that unexpected adventure not long before stood there before him once more. She held the camera in front of her left eye, her right eye closed as she peered through the viewfinder. Her left hand steadied the top of the camera and her right hand the bottom, so that her left elbow was raised almost to shoulder height while her right one was down against her side. Her head was tilted very slightly to her right, and a thick yellow plait fell forward over her right shoulder. She wore nothing but a cool, slightly loose white top of the utmost simplicity. It was just a rectangle of white cotton which wrapped round the chest and buttoned down the front, supported by two shoulder straps. The right strap had fallen to hang loosely down her upper arm. Only the top two buttons were fastened, and below them the front hung open, so that the whole of her belly, creamy-pale and gleaming against the dazzling white of the suntop, was bare. Her weight was supported on her lean left leg, while the right one was flexed slightly outwards and backwards. Because of her natural slimness and this elegant posture as she stood there between a derelict sports pavilion to the right and a high, crumbling brick wall to the left, a hint of living muscle was evident on her thighs, especially the right one, braced back as it was. These contours were echoed by the suggestion of abdominal muscles tensed under the gleaming skin of her belly, so that the small hipbones and central tract from the opening of her garment down over the navel towards the cunt were highlighted by the afternoon sun. Paler than the creamy-pale of the surrounding skin, the negative image of absent knickers or a bikini bottom could be detected below the level of her hips. Not much of this white image was to be seen, though, for it had clearly been a diminutive garment, and the main part of that triangular region was tufted with a light, gingery-blonde bush, close examination of which showed that it terminated in a little peak hanging down between the thighs. The tuft masked the inward curve of the buttocks, but just visible was the beginning of this curve at the top of the right thigh, darkly shaded by overhanging fuzz.

Although his loins were infused with lust at this sight, the Captain's erection could hardly be compared with Derrick's, and began to wilt as the youth's proud tool caught his eye.

It needs to be explained to the reader that after returning to his dingy digs in the village, the Captain had climbed out of his leathers and toasted himself with a tumbler of Teacher's,

14

convinced he was on to a good thing. He had torn open the package that charming girl had pressed on him, and there she stood, depicted in all her beguiling beauty.

Derrick was the subject of the photo facing hers in the right-hand half of the plastic folding frame. He, too, toted a camera. Since he, like her, was posed between the wall and the pavilion, but facing the other way, it could be inferred that they were immodestly photographing each other. Derrick displayed himself shamelessly in black leather motorcycling tunic and boots. Between boots and tunic, to the Captain's mind quite spoiling the effect, a pair of short, stubby thighs, paper-white but scribbled all over with ink-black hairs, supported a dense black thicket. Below this thicket hung a bare, bulging scrotum, while out of it sprouted that monstrous prick, upright and red. In front of the wall waited a mean black Yamaha. He had laid his leather trousers and shiny black helmet beside him on the ground with an unnecessary tidiness, and clearly had no inkling of how ridiculous he looked with his sawn-off legs, stubbly jowls and spiky black hair. The Captain asked himself how he himself could possibly have been mistaken, even in his road gear, for this jerk. And yet, when he had first ripped open the envelope and gazed at these pictures, with the enclosed scrap of paper inscribed 'Derrick, see you by Palace of Sweethearts, 7.30 Wed. as agreed, Love Melanie' – how the Captain had envied the short-arsed youth!

So her name was Melanie, and she was evidently no innocent. He emptied the tumbler and wondered how he might be able to exploit his new circumstances in the light of this note. What and where, he asked himself, was the Palace of Sweethearts?

15

TWO

SPYING OUT THE LAND

For the Captain, the next day brought some promising expectations as well as both frustration and qualified relief. He devoted the morning to a thorough exploration of the grounds, as well as a more cursory and furtive one of the college buildings, and in doing so came across several stimulating scenes which convinced him he had done well to take on his new responsibilities.

Arriving just before ten on this delightful June morning, he stowed his leathers in one of the panniers of the Suzuki and slipped into the overalls he extracted from the other pannier. Equipped for the sake of appearances with a small toolbox, he turned his back on the main building and ambled along the gravel-surfaced avenue of horse chestnuts that evidently led through the grounds and down towards an enticing glimpse of water.

The sun was becoming warmer, so he deposited his toolbox under a tree. There were no signs of human activity, presumably because everyone was engaged in classes, so it could surely be left there safely. In any case, reflected the Captain, whose feminism was pretty superficial, it was unlikely that the young ladies of Cunlip College, let alone their teachers, would have any use for this kind of masculine equipment. His experience so far indicated a preference for tools of a more organic nature.

The course of the avenue, slightly swerving, ran for nearly a quarter of a mile between a field of tall grass on the left and a succession of shrubberies and small copses on the right. He inhaled the smell of summer, fresh but sweet. It was clear that people had made frequent inroads into the long grass, and he guessed that later exploration at a time when the girls were out and about might uncover some agreeable scenes.

Through the undergrowth on his left he caught glimpses of an old brick wall, and struck through the bushes to examine it. Although the brickwork was crumbling and in urgent need of

16

repointing, the wall was a substantial one, some ten feet high. He found no obvious or easy place of ingress until he came to a low door, but this was secured with a heavy padlock. Perhaps, he mused, a dreamlike secret garden lay beyond the door, an ideal private location for fine-weather fucks. Among the tools he no longer carried he had the means of dealing with the padlock, but there was no hurry and hadn't the Principal promised to give him a full set of keys? He returned to the avenue, which now sloped more steeply down to a stream. Beyond this, the college grounds appeared to continue on the other side of the valley, where a path led up through a field of new-mown hay to a small house half-hidden among trees.

Suddenly, as he drew near the water, he was alerted by the sound of girlish voices. Stepping off the gravel footway, he dodged into the bushes on his left to slink closer to his quarry. A few yards brought them into sight. Shaded by overarching foliage, the stream widened out at this point into a shallow pool, in the middle of which two girls of sixteen or seventeen were wading up to their thighs. Both wore the regulation short-sleeved dress of pale blue, buttoned up to the neck. One of them also sported a fetching straw boater, and her companion's arms and shoulders were covered with a navy cardigan. The fact that they were fully dressed heightened the contrasting perfection of their well-formed, pale legs, arousing the Captain's baser appetites. The girl in the cardigan had tucked the bottom of her dress into the elastic of her knickers, and her friend held hers up round her waist, well above the navy-blue pants. Peering through a bush and feeling himself through a pocket in his overalls, their unseen admirer had to acknowledge that to be vouchsafed such mouth-watering glimpses in this context of total innocence could be as arousing as many a hotter display.

Somewhere away to the left, a cheer went up. The girl in the boater laid a hand on the other one's shoulder and giggled. 'They're at it again,' she remarked. 'Whenever it's French, they go down to the Palace of Sweethearts and muck about like that. One day MacDonald's going to catch them frigging each other.'

The Captain's curiosity was fired, and he tore himself away from the present idyll, weaving a track through the bushes and undergrowth towards where the noise had come from. As he proceeded, another noise became audible: the thumping bass of the kind of popular music that caused headaches in those of his generation. Soon he reached the edge of this wilderness, and stopped just short of the sunlit open ground, taking stock of the scene ahead of him.

To his left, the high brick wall reached out, forming the upper boundary of a playing field which at its lower extent shelved down to the stream. Close to the wall, and about a hundred yards from where he stood, he recognised the derelict, shuttered sports pavilion featured in those memorable pictures he had drooled over the night before. This, then, was surely the Palace of Sweethearts.

Along the two sides visible to him, the roof projected over a broad wooden veranda, evidently the source of that loud cheer. Stretched on its sun-touched boards at the corner nearest the brick wall, some half a dozen young misses were taking their ease in varied attitudes of abandon. The air around them throbbed to the beat of a ghetto blaster, loud enough, to be sure, even though it was probably turned down to what the girls considered a low volume to avoid detection.

All of them had pulled their dresses or skirts well up to expose their pretty thighs. Some of them, as far as could be discerned at this range and angle, were exposing rather more than that: several bare tummies gleamed whitely and one girl, lying face down, had worked her navy knickers halfway down her thighs to let the sun play on her rounded bottom. But what had provoked their applause?

Being situated near the corner of the building, he realised, they could see round it into a space concealed from his line of vision. He swore, but unnecessarily, for the scene of the action now shifted sufficiently for him to enjoy the rest of the spectacle fully. Round the corner, a girl with long, dark hair came dancing to the frantic rhythm of the music. Her hips were draped with her blue cardigan; she had removed her skirt and was twirling it round her head.

Casting the skirt aside, she next gave her waist a wriggle and let the cardigan drop to the ground. Instead of the regulation knickers, her slender loins were caressed by a pair of the scantiest black lace panties, high at the sides and setting off a splendid length of thigh which ran smoothly down from her hips to the long white socks. She shimmied and, facing the other girls so that her back was turned to the Captain, appeared to be unfastening the buttons of her shirt. It slipped down over her shoulders, and the narrow black straps now revealed were surely those of a bra to match the panties. As she spun round, he saw that this was indeed the case.

And now, thankfully, her position was such that her most interesting attributes were equally visible to him and to her companions, although they had a great advantage in being so much closer to her. She turned her back on them, bent forward, and peeled the panties down over a shining white bum. The girls cheered. She pulled them up again, and faced them, prancing about and entertaining them with lascivious gestures. Her thumbs were hooked in the hips of the skimpy garment, and she eased it down, first on one side and then on the other, until it became no more than a black string round the middle at crotch level. The top half of her dense black pubic hair formed the base of an inverted triangle of which the apex was black lace. As the Captain watched in fascination and the girls yelled encouragement, she swayed her hips, thrust them forward and slipped a hand into the front of the panties.

Everyone froze. The music had stopped, and all eyes were turned towards the Captain. He felt sure he was well hidden by the greenery before him, but one of them must have noticed a movement in the bushes. He stood there, tense.

After a short while, though, the atmosphere became more relaxed. The girls were murmuring quite audibly, and some were giggling. 'What do you expect?' he heard one of them say. 'They're always on the lookout for an eyeful of pussy. If it's not Derrick it'll be Joker.'

They huddled together, whispering, and then, to his amazement, stood up in a row, the young striptease dancer assuming a central position. With one accord, they all raised any skirts they were wearing and lowered their knickers to their knees. A line of pubes, no two identical in the colouring and configuration of their covering fur or in the plumpness or slimness of the thighs between which they nestled, was thrust in the Captain's direction. Because their knees were constricted by their dropped drawers,

19

they could not perform anything like a high-kicking cancan. Nevertheless, taking their time from the ringleader, who further established her primacy by whipping off the black bra, they gyrated their hips, forming a very acceptable chorus line there on the veranda of the Palace of Sweethearts. Each girl, one after the other from left to right, then licked her index finger, held it up as if for inspection, and inserted it into her undulating cunt.

This lewd performance was interrupted by the sound of a distant handbell. Instantly, these charming young ladies removed their titillating fingers, adjusted their clothing, gathered up their books and other odds and ends, and hurried off round the corner of the pavilion. They seemed to be taking a route back to the college which would lead them in an anticlockwise direction round the Secret Garden, as the Captain was already privately calling it.

As he was about to turn and retrace his steps through the bushes and undergrowth, his attention was drawn to a loud rustling and snapping of twigs not many yards to his left. Into the open sunlight burst the figure of a rough-looking, denim-clad youth with yellowish curls falling in a tangled mass to his shoulders. This figure was hurrying in the direction the girls had taken, as if following them. He fumbled with the zip of his jeans as he went. Perhaps their provocative display had not been for the Captain's benefit after all. The bell was still ringing, and he had no further encounters as he made his way back to the main building to undertake a bit of an interior survey.

Being located high on the top floor, the girls' dormitories were too remote for safe access. It was important at this stage, he considered, to heed the Principal's warning and avoid any behaviour so blatant that, in spite of the overalls he wore and the toolbox he had retrieved, he would be marked down by the inmates as a kind of resident voyeur. So he confined this preliminary inspection to skulking about in the passages of the ground floor. To the raised eyebrows he encountered from both staff and students he responded with polite enquiries concerning the whereabouts of the Principal's study, before sidling off in the direction indicated.

Unexpectedly, he came across a small band of rosy-limbed girls in navy-blue knickers and white singlets. They were carrying towels, and appeared to have just completed some form of organised physical activity. He followed them at a distance.

At the far end of one of the corridors, they vanished around a corner. Negotiating it himself, the Captain walked into the moist embrace of a cloud of steam. This issued from an open doorway, and the muffled, echoing sounds of girlish shouting and laughter suggested that he had stumbled upon a large communal bathroom. As he approached the door, flashes of white towelling and pink flesh became foggily visible through the vapour. Discovery would have been prejudicial to the Captain's long-term aims, so with great reluctance he withdrew. There had to be some safe way of viewing whatever was going on in there.

He hurried purposefully along the corridors, jostling startled stragglers in his haste to gain the open air. Dashing down the steps of the main entrance, he then traced the perimeter of the building looking for steamed-up windows until, at the far end, he found something even more promising: a door bearing the painted sign 'BATHHOUSE'. But the door was closed and unyielding to his circumspect shove. The only windows were small and high up in the ivy-covered walls of this single-storey wing.

Could he scramble up the ivy to reach one of these windows? The creeper hardly looked strong enough to sustain his weight. But beyond a corner, he came across an iron ladder running up the wall. It passed within a few feet of a window. With more agility than he remembered possessing, he set down his toolbox, launched himself up the rusty rungs and climbed to the right level. But however far he leaned, he was unable to get close enough to the window to see more than the odd flash of pink flesh gleaming through clouds of steam. The angle from which he was viewing meant that his line of sight through the window was restricted to a narrow gap.

What about the roof? Another three feet up the ladder brought him to the brick parapet, over which he swung his body with rather less agility than he had mustered for the climb. Stamina was what he lacked, it seemed, the stamina of lusty youth.

He found himself standing over a low-pitched glass roof, its ridge waist high, running forward from where he stood to the other end of the bathhouse. Although the walls of the main building towered above this wing, the Victorian institutional architect had taken care that no windows were so placed as to overlook it. A flat gutter some eighteen inches wide extended on either side between the edge of this roof and the parapet. The glass itself, he noticed immediately, was completely steamed up. But at six-foot intervals along its length were large, hinged panels slightly lifted for ventilation. On hands and knees to make himself invisible from the ground, the Captain crawled to the first of these glass panels. The angle at which it was propped open, no doubt through the application of a long pole from below, was too acute to allow him to peer down through the opening, from which issued clouds of steam. Only a little force, however, was needed to raise the lower edge a good two feet clear of its seating and thus secure a reasonable if partial view of the proceedings below.

Seen from directly above, the girls flitting about in the vapour presented a slightly disappointing spectacle, foreshortened and dominated by the tops of their heads. As they moved about, of course, wet boobs, wet bums and sodden bushes flashed in and out of vision. Even so, there was almost as much towelling as girl-flesh. The Captain was disheartened.

On raising the next panel, however, it seemed possible that, within the limits of this unfortunate foreshortening, his persistence was about to be rewarded. He found himself peering down into one of a row of shower cubicles, and it was occupied by a young lady soaping a pair of breasts so prominent that even from up above he had a clear view of them. In the adjoining cubicle a slender blonde was slowly swaying her hips while the water coursed down over her body. Her hands were clutching her cunt, and judging from a sudden acceleration of her undulations, orgasm was imminent.

But instead of finishing herself off, the blonde stepped out of her cubicle, leaving the water running, and entered the one directly below the Captain to join the girl with the big tits. They clung together in a close embrace, the mere thought of which thrilled him and triggered the stiffening of his cock. And yet, from high above, there was really very little to be seen. Every now and then they would lean apart, revealing two pairs of boobs, one pair plump and the other pert, while they ground their cuntmounds together, before the boobs were again squashed together out of sight. And the frenzied movements of their hands over each other's bums certainly afforded a modicum of titillation. But otherwise, what could be seen left far too much to the imagination. The Captain's imagination was fertile, but could deliver the goods in the seclusion of his lodgings. Today he had the chance of enjoying the real thing.

He was on the point, then, of abandoning this scene and crawling along to the next panel when the busty girl sank to her knees and buried her face between the thighs of her partner. The blonde reacted by throwing her own head back in ecstasy. Her eyes were shut. But if she were to open them the first thing she would see, he realised, would be his own face leering down at her.

He withdrew at once and scuttled along the gutter to a point where the ivy clinging to the outer wall had climbed up and over the parapet in some profusion. From his pocket he drew a sharp pen knife and severed a length of the creeper. This he wrapped around his brows, making sure that several fronds fell over his face. More confident now behind this bacchanalian camouflage, he hurried back to his station above the scene of lesbian cunnilingus.

The cubicle, alas, was now empty. But, as the row of showers had already proved to be quite long, there appeared to be a fair chance that the next panel would open above yet another one. And indeed it did. More to the point, this cubicle too was occupied and, again, the spectacle it presented was of an embracing couple. The two heads, one adorned with short, brown hair and the other with fair tresses down to her shoulders, were pressed side by side. He could see the shoulders of both, and every now and then, as they swayed in passion, the upper curves of a buttock. In itself this show hardly seemed worth watching when there might be stronger action to be seen further along the line, but it was always possible that they would do something that offered a more revealing view. The Captain waited.

After a short time he was recompensed with an astonishing sight. The brown-haired miss backed away from her chum and dropped to her knees, leaning forward to lick a crimson-tipped penis that jutted forward from between a pair of hairy thighs. The man or youth, as he was now revealed to be, the one the Captain had so recently observed enjoying the show put on for him down at the Palace of Sweethearts, stood with hands on hips, his pelvis thrust forward with its succulent offering. His partner took it into her mouth, clamping both hands on his buttocks. Was she going to swallow the load he was about to shoot? Would she spit it out? Or would she disengage from his bursting cock at the moment of crisis and let the seed spurt out freely?

These questions turned out to be misconceived. Before the onset of ejaculation, the cock was withdrawn. Its owner stooped to hook his hands under the girl's armpits and hauled her up on her feet. He then turned her round so that her back was towards him. Feet well apart, she bent forward to rest her hands on her knees. For a moment, the Captain was able to feast his eyes on a pair of gleaming, plump white buttocks. But then they were lost to sight as her lover closed with her and the length of his rampant member was taken up – whether into her arsehole or her cunt was impossible to make out from above.

The lad must have spent in the very act of insertion; he shuddered violently and they collapsed into the white shower tray. Still coupled together, the pair squirmed and rolled over. The young lady now sprawled on his belly and between his thighs, displaying her enticing charms to the Captain's gaze like a tickled bitch. Luckily her eyes were closed as she writhed there, lustily manualised by her beau, who had one hand clamped on a breast and the other rummaging through her hairy pubis to find the clitoris. And now the angle was such that the coupling point could be clearly identified as the vagina. Even the slimy wetness of the restiffening prick could be made out as it slid in and out of its well-lubricated receptacle.

So intense was the girl's delight that she came in an explosive paroxysm that threw her pelvis upward. The cock flew out of its sheath and pointed straight up at the Captain. Responding to the lesser orgasmic waves that followed the first great upheaval, the girl sank back on the boy, his glistening erection now standing proudly between her thighs, its root pressed up against her vulva. She felt it, and squeezed her thighs together. Jets of sperm fountained from the swollen head, falling in a row of puddles down her belly. This second emission, its projective force now spent, ended in a steady and copious but gentle flow of the slippery fluid down the boy's wilting cock to irrigate the chestnut thatch of his partner's cunthair.

Almost at once they got to their feet. Grabbing a couple of towels that hung over the cubicle partition, the lad covered his head and torso to disguise his sex, and slunk off. The girl turned on the shower to sluice away the seminal juices which polluted the front of her body. Soon she was lost to sight in clouds of steam.

When he raised the next skylight, the Captain found himself peering into not another shower cubicle but a large, white-tiled communal bath. Here too the steam was an impediment to vision, although the openness of the bath compared with the shower permitted the vapour to disperse more quickly. Through its swirling wreaths tantalising glimpses of girl-flesh and girl-hair, some of it pubic, could be seen; bodies languidly afloat or playfully thrashing about and promiscuously intertwining with the limbs of their neighbours. How much more beguiling than his schoolboy memories of being humiliated by horrid, rough boys, loud from the rugby field, in a cement-lined trough of tepid, muddy water! If only, he thought, one could hide submerged in this more fragrant liquid, making one's inflamed presence felt only when the bath was full of unsuspecting but lasciviously disposed femininity! His cock stood up.

So did some half a dozen young ladies, giggling and reaching for towels. Their attention seemed to have been caught by something happening out of the bath, beyond his field of view, so he scurried round to the other side of the roof and raised the corresponding panel beyond the central ridge. There, to be sure, stood the dripping girls, grouped in a ring round an amorous scene being enacted on towels spread on the floor. He opened the front of his overalls as he knelt by the skylight, and released his questing penis.

A lovely auburn-haired teenager lay stretched on her back. Unlike the others, she was still wearing her games kit: white T-shirt and short grey skirt, with white socks reaching to just below her knees, and trainers. The regulation navy-blue pants

25

y on the towel beside her. Her thighs were wide open, and she
ad allowed the skirt to ride right up to her hips. One hand
elved busily in the invisible folds of flesh beneath her perfectly
isible auburn bush, while the other, pushed up under her
-shirt, was occupied with a breast.

Between her legs stood another girl, stark naked like the
pectators of the action. Her black hair was tied back with a red
and, giving the Captain a fairly clear view of her shining white
houlders, pink-tipped tits and a slightly rounded belly beneath
which a jet-black tuft could just be discerned. The girl was
randishing an object some nine or ten inches long and about
s thick as her own wrist. It appeared to be some kind of salami.

Moving forward a step so that she stood directly above her
artner's genitals, and placing her feet further apart between the
vide-open thighs, she bent her knees slightly and thrust her pubis
orward. The Captain guessed she was about to fuck herself with
he salami, but instead of inserting it she just seemed to be wiping
ts length backwards and forwards between her labia. The
urpose of this exercise was, he conjectured, to lubricate the
liant piece of delicatessen with her own juices. She flaunted it,
vetly gleaming, above her companion, who was probably too
ar gone in her own raptures to take it in.

But take it in, in a more literal sense, was what her friend now
orced her to do. She dropped to her knees between the open
highs, dragged the masturbating hand from the clitoris it had
een gratifying and jammed the salami without ceremony into
he juicy cunt as far as it would go: about half its length. The
ecipient shuddered, turned on her right side, and raised her left
high.

As if this was a familiar routine, the black-haired girl got down
n the towels, her head to the auburn one's feet. She stretched
ut supine just behind the leg extended on the floor, and the
ork of her own legs engaged with that of her partner's, whose
ack was caressed by the inside of her right thigh and her belly
y the inside of her left one.

The exposed end of the slippery salami projected forwards
and downwards from its receptacle, its blunt tip an inch or so
from the black-fringed vulva edging towards it. Being tough but
slightly pliable, it was quite easily brought into contact with this

approaching cunt by the dark-haired girl's fingers. By wriggling forward rather awkwardly and raising her buttocks from the floor, she contrived to cram every inch of the fat cock-substitute into her love canal. Cunt now meshed with cunt, with no outward sign that they were both so tightly gorged. The spectators cheered.

In this position it was hardly possible to indulge in the movements of copulation. After stroking and licking each other's left feet and ankles for a while, the girls executed a deft manoeuvre which could have been perfected only through previous practice. The auburn one extended her left, upper leg in front of her, straightened it and pulled it back towards her face with the litheness of a ballerina. Her partner did the same, raising her own left leg and pulling it back. She then slightly twisted her hips to the right, pivoting on the doubly encunted salami. Both girls released their legs, which brought them into a newly symmetrical posture. They lay on their right sides facing in opposite directions, bum to bum, their knees drawn up, for all the world like innocently sleeping infants, one dressed except for her knickers, the other one stark naked.

Sleep, however, was far from their thoughts. This time is was the turn of the dark girl to use the unseen device as a pivot, lifting both her thighs as she rolled round first on her back and then on to her left side. Bottoms lewdly conjoined, they immediately heaved themselves up on their knees, letting their heads hang down so that their faces rested on the towels. One of the spectators considerately made sure that the auburn-haired girl's skirt was thrown right up over back. She now presented a truly delicious spectacle from above, her unblemished skin contrasting with this elevated skirt, the T-shirt and the white socks and trainers. She held together her thighs, knees, calves and feet; her legs were thus enclosed within her friend's knees, which were slightly open. And now, to the great delight of their audience, both those surrounding them below and the masturbating Captain leering down on them, the real coition began.

Their arse-to-arse position facilitated the vigorous execution of an exercise which the Captain recalled seeing described in an old translation of Rabelais as the 'game of brangle-bums'. With a synchronised rhythm, again indicative of long practice, the girls

27

bucked backwards and forwards. On each forward stroke, four or five inches of well-lubricated salami came into view, linking the engorged and distended labia stretched to accommodate it at either end, and disappearing completely once more as the pale behinds were shoved together. The Captain could not help admiring the skill of their timing, and tried to follow it in the pumping movements of his own hand. For a dozen strokes or so they would move really slowly, languidly groping their clitorises with one hand as they did so. These slow strokes would be succeeded by a dozen rapid, energetic ones that set their buttocks quivering before the leisurely movements were resumed.

Not many of these cycles had been gone through when the fascinated Captain felt he was almost on the point of no return and found himself in two minds as to whether to release the mounting pressure or hold it back for later. Even as he pondered this dilemma, both girls went into overdrive, battering their bottoms together furiously as they approached their simultaneous crisis. It came, and to a renewed cheer from the naked bystanders, most of whom were clearly frigging themselves as they watched, they rolled over on their backs, their knees up and their heels tucked up to their buttocks. They were exhausted but still attached to each other by a tie more substantial than the bonds of affection.

At this instant the first jet of spunk raced up the narrow channel running through the Captain's stiff and swollen rod. It leapt out of the dilated aperture of the glans and spat through the opening of the skylight. The succession of hot dollops that followed it had already beslimed the woodwork and masonry in front of him before that first magnificent shot hit its mark, but when it did the effect was both spectacular and alarming. A scream rose from below. The auburn-haired darling opened her eyes and stared straight up in horror, at the same time frantically trying to wipe the semen from the pretty mouth it had defiled. The other girls too, some of them still with fingers up their cunts, all gazed up in astonishment at the dark, masculine features peering down at them.

But only for a moment. Cramming his limp, wet member back into his overalls as he did so, the Captain scurried round the gutter, bundled himself over the parapet and more or less slid down the iron ladder to the ground. He must get right away from the building, he told himself, before any of the girls had time to make herself sufficiently presentable — supposing such considerations to weigh with these hussies — to emerge into the open air. Round the corner to the bathhouse he hurried, and stopped short in his tracks.

Advancing at a leisurely but steady pace to greet him came the begowned and upright figure of Miss Muttock. 'Good morning, Captain,' she said in a tone of evident puzzlement. 'The Green Man?'

This seemed an unlikely invitation so early in the day. She saw he was at a loss, and prompted him further. 'A devotee of Bacchus, are we?'

'Never touch a drop before sundown, Principal,' he managed to stammer out. 'Hardly ever. On — on principle.' He was aware, after his exertions, of a hot flush on his face and a tremor in his hands.

'I believe that followers of the divinity were wont to adorn their temples with wreaths of ivy.'

Normally the Captain was able to steer a straight furrow through the potentially treacherous waters of classical allusion, but momentarily he floundered, seeing an absurd picture of himself hanging green garlands on a Palladian folly in these picturesque grounds, or even on the Palace of Sweethearts.

'Your head, Captain, your head. Like Hedda Gabler, I can almost say you have vine leaves in your hair, except that they appear to be ivy.'

The penny dropped and he removed his forgotten camouflage with some embarrassment, reflecting that if any indignant girls emerged from the door marked 'BATHHOUSE', his denials would be marginally more credible now that he had discarded the incriminating headdress.

'I was trimming it off the wall over there,' he explained resourcefully. 'Clings to everything and crumbles the brickwork. Finds every nook and cranny and penetrates like . . .'

The Principal completed his sentence for him. 'Like the ill-disciplined organ I see before me.'

A glance down confirmed that his partially reanimated cock had indeed flopped out of the overalls he had had no time to

29

fasten in his flight from the roof. Briefly he contemplated throwing himself upon her mercy, or simply throwing himself upon her, but the circumstances seemed unpropitious and he adjusted his clothing, mumbling something about a defective zip fastener as he did so. But Miss Muttock had already taken her leave and swept on majestically round the corner. He headed in haste for a nearby shrubbery, and gasped in relief. Relaxing, he set down his toolbox and unclenched the fingers of his left hand. The sun glinted on a set of keys among which, no doubt, were those granting admittance to the Secret Garden and the Palace of Sweethearts. The Principal must have pressed them on him without his being aware in his nervousness. Well, he would put them to good use. But first, he decided, prompted by a gale of girlish laughter that seemed to emanate from a first-floor classroom, he would follow the example of Derrick yesterday afternoon and find a ladder he could use to give some attention to the windows.

THREE

WORK AND PLAY

Mary Muttock sat in her study the next morning, peering into a hand mirror and taking sips from a tumbler of vodka. Her spectacles had been discarded, and lay on the desk. She was engaged in a largely unsuccessful search for blemishes on the remarkably youthful skin of her face. Yes, she admitted to herself, there could be no denying that behind the front of pedagogical severity she cultivated there lurked a dangerously beautiful woman. Now that a new man had appeared on the scene, it was good to be reminded of the fact. She had already entrapped him, and was ready, very ready, to take advantage of his surrender or to let him take advantage of hers. As if seeking confirmation of this readiness, she parted her legs, pulled her long skirt up to her waist and tugged aside the gusset of her black silk drawers. Holding the mirror in one hand, she parted the labia of her luscious cunt with the other and gazed with satisfaction at what she saw.

Since puberty, and indeed since an even earlier age, but above all during her American phase, hundreds – no, thousands – of stiff and swollen cocks had rudely forced their way into that tender flower of her womanhood. They had stretched it almost to destruction and flooded it with the most noxious discharges. Yet the fresh, girlish pinkness of the reflection pouting moistly in the mirror retained all its virginal allure. Think away the dense brown curls in which it was now so prettily embowered, and the present sight was hardly different from that which had overcome the scruples, all those years ago, of Chief Inspector Hardbuckle, investigating a case of teenage extortion. She could appreciate now that she had got off lightly, but at the time the indignities visited on her by that shag-bellied brute had seemed a high price to pay for escaping the juvenile court. In fact, her resentment had lasted about a week. It was converted into gratitude for his having torn down the barrier to pleasure when she then found a willing prick more proportionate to the needs of such a small lass – that of her younger brother. For the next few years they had grown together in perfect amity. As his engorged prick thickened and lengthened to ever more manly dimensions, the elastic wall of her vagina enlarged to accommodate it like an oily kid glove. And the cunt muscles which embraced that maturing member so tightly and so frequently moulded its firm contours into a phallus to delight and thrill any woman. Fate, alas, had drawn them apart, but even now she throbbed to the memory of their early incestuous romps whenever a particularly fat-headed cock was being wedged between the succulent pink lips she now stroked with relish.

Just as her thumb alighted on her clitoris, someone knocked on the study door. She was almost too far gone to control herself and after a loud, involuntary gasp remained silent, but the door opened all the same. Her hands, one of which clasped the mirror, were still arranging the front of her skirt, the hem of which had got caught in one of her suspenders. Before her, grinning randily in his shabby overalls, stood the Captain.

'Sorry, ma'am,' he said. 'I thought I heard you calling out for help, or I would never have barged in like this.'

'I'm quite sure,' she replied, 'that you're the complete gentleman. Your attentiveness is most welcome. But first, let me ask what I can do for you?'

'Well, mainly, I'd like an advance on my wages. Fifty quid should do the trick, if you've got it in petty cash.'

The Principal's expression changed. 'You can just piss off if you think you can burst in here every day with demands like that,' she snapped.

'Don't be getting me wrong,' he replied, in what were meant to be emollient tones but struck her, the erstwhile practitioner of teenage extortion, as quite threatening. 'I'm sure we can reach an understanding. I sympathise with you, believe me, I really do, with all your worries.'

'Oh yes? What worries would those be?'

'Well there's things going on here, wouldn't you say? Dodgy things, know what I mean? Remember our little chat the other day? Like, there's plenty of little peccadilloes a man of the world like me can take in his stride. Plenty of little ones, and even some great big fat ones. But what I always say is, the innocent have got to be protected. Yes, it's the innocent lambs I'm concerned about. And I should think their parents would be too, if they got to hear about it. See what I'm driving at?'

Miss Muttock saw all too clearly. 'Tell me what you've seen,' she said.

The Captain explained how, after their encounter the previous morning, he had conceived the idea of extending his ivy-trimming activities. In a shed to which the keys she had given him allowed access he had found a long ladder, and armed with a pair of secateurs he had set this up against a heavily overgrown first-floor window. According to his version of events, of which the Principal was disposed to doubt the details but credit the broad outlines, he had been working away at the mass of creeper for some time, carefully parting it from the gothic tracery, before peering discreetly through the fronds. From the rows of young girls perched on high stools at long benches equipped with sinks and Bunsen burners, not to mention the shapely, dark-haired teacher clad in a white coat, he judged that this was a science lab. And from the explicit anatomical drawings chalked on the blackboard under the heading 'PHYSICAL DEVELOPMENT', he guessed that the teacher must be Miss MacDonald.

Miss Muttock interrupted. 'She's very good at her subject.'

'Oh yes,' agreed the Captain, 'a real professional.' He went on to describe in outline the course of the lesson, of which he had enjoyed a clear and unobserved view although he could hear nothing except occasional bursts of laughter and gasps of astonishment from girls at the back.

Out of this class of, most likely, sixteen-year-olds, Miss MacDonald had selected one who was smaller, weedier and visibly less mature than the others and summoned her to the front. Although she chose to keep the fact to herself, the Principal knew exactly who was meant. This girl, called Helen Lascelles, was one of her many favourites-in-reserve; she had not yet got round to an intimate *tête-à-tête* with her in her study, but was intending to do so soon. In spite of her bony knees and elbows, the short, straight hair which always looked a bit greasy, and the dark rings under her eyes, there was something perversely pretty and arousing about her. More than that, those dark eyes and long thin lips suggested to Mary Muttock's trained awareness a hint of something that went beyond residual childish naughtiness. Something more like a taste for sin. She was a case, surely, for the most rigorous chastisement.

The Captain continued his narrative, perching on the edge of the desk and insolently helping himself to his employer's vodka. He told how Helen, turning her back on the class, had stripped off skirt, shirt and knickers, everything save shoes and socks, before climbing up on the front bench and displaying her undeveloped body to all present. Using a long wooden pointer, Miss MacDonald had singled out for comment her flat chest, small nipples, narrow hips and a pubic mound hardly darkened by a slight shading of silvery-yellow fluff which did nothing to conceal the delicate vertical slit. The other girls appeared to be writing notes and sketching the features under discussion.

After some time the teacher had gone to the door of the room and brought in an older girl who had been waiting outside. 'It was that Cathy I saw you punishing the other day,' he remarked. 'She had a white lab coat on, but MacDonald made her stand on the bench next to the other girl and take it off. A good way of showing how girls can grow up into women. The comparative method.'

'The MacDonald ought to be ashamed. She could have used her own blowsy charms to point up the contrast. But I suppose she wanted to avoid giving the impression that the process of maturation is one of tragic decline. Cathy's certainly a lovely girl. Just ripe, and not an ounce of spare flesh.'

As far as the Captain could judge, these observations were prompted by jealousy. Appetising though he found the unembarrassed Cathy, Miss MacDonald, who was a slim woman in her early thirties, had seemed no less attractive, unless her clothing concealed some off-putting flaw. But he kept these thoughts to himself, and went on with his account of the proceedings.

Cathy, too, had had her salient features, which were so interestingly different from those of the younger girl, prodded with the long pointer. To make things even clearer, the teacher had applied bare hands to the full but well-shaped breasts, demonstrating their yielding but resilient firmness and letting them bounce up and down. Concentrating then on the left nipple, she had worked it between her thumb and forefinger, teasing and tweaking it into purple prominence.

The Captain regretted that his crude eloquence could scarcely endow the events he described in such detail with their full erotic charge. In a bid to remedy the situation, he rose and advanced on Miss Muttock. She got out of her easy chair and he took her place, drawing her down on to his lap. He then unbuttoned her blouse, released a plump, rounded breast from the black bra which cradled it, and fondled the nipple in the manner he had been explaining.

'She went over to the blackboard and drew diagrams of tits,' he said. 'Three of them. Once was meant to be the young girl's, just a small nipple on an almost flat surface. The other two were Cathy's. On one of them the nipple was soft and flat, on the other erect. She got the girls to copy them in their notebooks, and I could see that some of them had stuck their hands in the front of their shirts and were trying it on themselves.'

He shifted his hand and, hoisting the hem of the Principal's long skirt right up to her belly, delved into her knickers in support of the next part. Miss MacDonald had positioned herself in front of the two girls as they stood side by side, making them lay their arms on each other's shoulders and open their legs a little so that their private parts were more or less level with her face. She had her back to the class, which was so enthralled that she could afford to do so without risk of injury from flying chalk or other missiles. First she drew attention to the tuft of dark hair which adorned the older girl's exposed armpit, and contrasted it with the shiny smoothness of the more backward one's. Then, after running the fingers of one hand through Cathy's bush to display and part the fleshy lips, she had raised her other hand and applied it to Helen's cunt. In sight of everyone in the room (and of the Captain outside the window), she had used her long middle fingers to tickle the two clitorises and demonstrate equal sensitivity in both of them. The girls writhed, blushed and clung to each other on their elevated perch, but were not allowed to reach a climax, as far as the Captain could judge. Instead, Miss MacDonald left Cathy quivering and for a moment devoted her full attention to the other girl. First fondling and pinching the naked vulva, she licked a finger and stuck it up between the folds of moist pink flesh.

Helen winced and the finger was withdrawn. The teacher had turned and held it up to show the class how far she had been able to insert it before encountering the painful obstacle to complete intromission; it had penetrated as far as the first joint. Everyone laughed as she licked it clean and repeated the experiment on Cathy. This time, of course, the channel was unobstructed and two digits were thrust into it for their full length. Cathy's quivering grew more violent. The flush spread from her cheeks, racing right down the front of her body, and she crushed Helen to her bosom as the pent-up forces exploded inside her. Miss MacDonald had then marched straight to the blackboard and inscribed in large capital letters: 'ORGASM! POW!' The class applauded.

Brushing the chalk dust from her hands, she had whipped open the door of the lab and led in a tall, red-headed youth, whose white coat suggested that he too was to be used as an anatomical specimen. Up on the bench beside the two girls he climbed, and off came the coat. His nudity was shockingly mitigated, or rather emphasised, by a profusion of rusty fur all over his limbs, chest and belly. The focal point of this blazing display was a thicket between his thighs so dense that only the foreskin-covered tip of a shrunken dick had peeped out from its hirsute protection. As a specimen, would this wilting hunk do justice to the potential of his sex?

Miss Muttock interrupted the Captain's amused droolings, pulled his fist out of her panties and rose to her feet. 'You can save your breath,' she said. 'You've got me really interested now, and I think there's a treat due for both of us.'

To his surprise, she stepped over to the TV set and switched it on. When the picture appeared, she fiddled with the controls. The sound took on a fuzzy, reverberating quality, and the image changed to monochrome. Initially the Captain supposed he was looking at some kind of antique educational documentary: girls sat in regimented desks while a mistress, book in hand, marched up and down. But as the Principal flicked from channel to channel, it dawned on him that the whole college was bugged with concealed surveillance cameras. The picture hopped from room to room, from corridor to corridor. She pressed another switch and it was replaced with a hissing snowstorm.

And now she was occupied with a kind of sophisticated video recorder equipped with a whole battery or tapes. She was whizzing through these, searching, surely, for the scene the Captain had been describing to her. Soon she found it, and there, black and white on the screen, the two naked girls stood above Miss MacDonald, their cunts cupped in her hands.

The camera must have been located somewhere to the side of the room, about halfway between the front and the back. For this reason the view it gave was not ideal, but (except for the absence of colour) much better than the one he had enjoyed from outside the ivy-festooned window. Miss Muttock activated a button which made the tape hurry forward, causing the teacher to frig and finger-fuck her young demonstrators at a frantic speed sending the older one crashing into the body of the younger one while she herself in one sweeping movement scrawled on the blackboard opened the door dragged in the youth and jumped him up on to the bench off with his coat and . . .

Normal playback speed was resumed, taking up the story where the Captain had left off. Once more, the Principal relaxed on his lap.

'This is Heini,' she explained. 'He's a German lad staying with relatives over here. A big hit as Romeo in our college play. An unsubtle performance but loud, which can be more important. Miss MacDonald says Heini is one of those Germans who think of Shakespeare's text as a rather poor translation from the version of Tieck and Schlegel – I defer to her feeling for these matters. Cathy was his Juliet, but I didn't know the relationship was going to be followed up under laboratory conditions. Let's hope for a less tragic outcome this time.'

Subdued but unremitting murmurs and giggles and the scraping of stools on the floor provided the foreground of an unsatisfactory soundtrack. Behind this racket Miss MacDonald's voice could just be made out:

'Down on your knees, Helen. Squeeze his balls ever so gently while you suck his penis. You know what his penis is, don't you?'

Judging from the alacrity with which she knelt to carry out her instructions, there could be no room for doubt that the girl

37

did know. At first she had to keep backing away, laughing — each time she took that apology for a cock between her lips her face was tickled intolerably by the wiry bush in which it nestled. Soon, however, it began to grow, so that its dark, shining head burst forth from the foreskin that had hooded it. It projected further and further forward. At last its dimensions were so imposing that although it was now clearly rammed right down the young lady's throat as far as she could take it without gagging, a rod of hard gristle two inches thick and a clear four inches long separated her distended lips from the flaming bush and the testicles she was fondling. The sight was impressive, and Mary Muttock was aware, between her thighs, of the Captain's own member struggling to emulate its proportions. He must have unzipped his trousers, she reckoned, while she had been fiddling with the video.

The figures on the screen seemed to be gripped with a sense of urgency. Helen, disappointment written on her vicious but pretty features, was pulled away from the throbbing phallus, and Heini jumped down on the floor. Miss MacDonald made Cathy lie on her back at the end of the bench nearest the camera, her shapely legs hanging down over the edge. When Heini stood between her thighs, her cunt gaped against his hairy belly, almost as high as his navel, so a wooden box was placed on the floor for him to stand on. This new elevation was ideal. All the classroom noises died away, and a general gasp could be heard as that huge erection first plugged and stretched the moist orifice and was then plunged laboriously and deeply into its innermost recesses. Cathy was obviously no virgin, and this time the nexus was complete. Their pubic hair intermingled, and the fat prick was visible only momentarily on the outward strokes as they engaged in violently athletic coition. Somewhat more sluggishly, the Captain's, feeling almost as fat to Mary Muttock, slipped up into her vagina. She heaved herself up and down on it luxuriously.

A truly inspiring exponent of popular science, the MacDonald reached with sensitive fingers between the boy's thighs, explaining that she hoped to detect, from a thickening at the base of the penis, when the moment of crisis was imminent. In her free hand she clasped an empty glass beaker. No sooner had she delved below the bulging scrotum than she yelled out, 'Back off!' The command needed to be supported by action. Out came her probing hand. She flung it round the panting youth's waist and forced his buttocks backwards against her own white-coated front. His cock, now glistening with his partner's streaming love-juices, reared up even thicker and longer than before its insertion. Just in time, she held the beaker inverted over its bulbous head as load after load of creamy fluid gushed, flowed, oozed and finally trickled from the opening. During this process, which seemed to last about half a minute, the magnificent organ gradually surrendered most but not all of its volume and rigidity, and the beaker had to be lowered with it as it declined into a dripping downward curve.

'Come on, dear,' she called to the neglected Helen, who had been sitting on the bench sulking in her nakedness, 'it's your turn. You know what you usually do now, don't you?'

The girl slid to the floor and with reviving interest used thumb and forefinger to grasp the piece of meat she had sucked with such devotion before being so cruelly deprived of participation in the ecstatic scene. Gently pulling and squeezing its slippery length while the teacher held the steaming beaker just below it, she milked out the last thick drops.

Miss MacDonald moved briskly to a pair of balances and placed the beaker on one pan. 'You will remember we had already weighed the empty beaker before today's experiments began,' she said. 'Now all I have to do is add weights until they balance the beaker with sperm in it to find out how much the sperm weighs.' Accordingly she added little brass weights to the other pan. Then, triumphantly, she moved to the blackboard and wrote: 'EIGHTY-FIVE (85) GRAMS!' 'He's broken his own record,' she cried. 'That's not far short of a quarter of a pound!' The whole class cheered as the Captain's semen fountained up into Mary Muttock's convulsing vagina, the pressure of succeeding spurts forcing the initial discharge out of her tight-stretched cuntlips, to flow down the tops of her thighs into the hairs on his bollocks.

'Come, Captain,' she exclaimed. 'Don't you know we have a hosepipe ban in these parts?'

'They seem well enough irrigated to me,' the Captain quipped back. 'Everything blooming – positively overflowing with milk and honey. Would you say we're beginning to understand each other?'

'Yes, came the reply, 'I'd say we had the beginnings of an understanding. I'll let you have a chitty you can take to Grote for an advance on your wages.'

That afternoon the Captain got round to trying out some of the keys he had acquired. First he tried the outside door of the bathhouse, which opened easily. Nobody was about, and he took the opportunity to find a place of concealment that might, on future occasions, give him a better view than he had enjoyed from the roof. This was not easy. Up above he had been able to move about and peer down into any part of the large room, the only drawback being that the angle of vision was unsuitable for viewing standing bodies. There was, however, an old wooden cupboard or locker which a small key on his ring fitted. It was possible, he found, to stand concealed in this narrow locker, peering out through a round hole at eye level. The hole was situated directly opposite the row of shower cubicles, and these, as he knew already, had no doors.

Emerging into the open air, he retraced the way he had taken down the avenue of horse chestnuts. Everyone seemed to be occupied with classes today, and the richly fragrant grounds were deserted. When he came to the low door in the crumbling brick wall, the padlock proved to be so rusty that it was hard to tell if any of his keys belonged to it. He had anticipated such a problem. In the top pocket of his overalls he carried a small can of oil. A few drops made a surprising difference, and the lock yielded.

The height of the grass and tangled state of the undergrowth convinced him that this walled garden was indeed unfrequented and totally neglected. Most of it seemed to be impenetrable jungle, but he found a stick and beat a way through nettles to a small clearing to which he might well return some time. The Secret Garden was secret enough for his purposes.

Next the pavilion, the Palace of Sweethearts. He tried the door, but it was locked. In spite of the building's neglected and dilapidated condition, however, the lock, being sheltered from rain by the overhang of the roof which sloped out over the veranda, offered no resistance to one of his keys.

Inspection of the gloomy, litter-stewn interior convinced him that other people enjoyed access to this shuttered den. Its facilities comprised one large changing room furnished with lockers and pegs for clothes, and a smaller side room which seemed to have once accommodated a shower and a toilet, but was now quite empty. As well as the empty cigarette packets lying about among a scattering of dusty cushions in the main room, he found in a broken locker a little cache of unopened ones. Enough sunlight filtered through the shutters to reveal, in another locker, a stack of 'adult' magazines and a small library of erotic fiction. On top of the pile his eye was caught by the delightful cover of a volume entitled *Adventures of a Naked Girl*, which he slipped into his pocket.

From a lower shelf in the locker he took a large, opened envelope. This contained about a dozen photographs. Not all of them were remarkable for the quality of their lensmanship, but even the technically poorest sent the blood hurrying to the Captain's loins. Crudely illuminated by flashbulb in this shuttered room or blinking against the sun out on the boardwalk of the veranda, they portrayed, singly and in couples and groups, Cunlip students posed lasciviously in various states of dress and undress. Their attire ranged from skirts raised and knickers pulled down saucily to total, shameless nudity. He replaced these pictures reluctantly and left the Palace of Sweethearts to explore further.

His wanderings brought him back to the top of the hill, not far from the redbrick gothic pile of the college. From here he scanned the wide prospect before him. Beyond a clump of low trees and bushes to his right, his attention was drawn to movements where a high wooden fence marked part of the perimeter of the grounds about half a mile from where he stood.

He strained his eyes in the bright sunlight. Three boys had just dropped to the ground from the top of this fence, and a fourth was still scaling it. His companions, impatient, helped him down, and all four ran to a nearby patch of long grass. Out into the open they dragged a girl who must have been sunbathing

41

there; she wore only a vest and regulation knickers. In a flash, the knickers were dragged down to her knees.

Fired with the spirit of chivalry, his nostrils flaring, the Captain dashed down the slope. He flung himself into the thicket separating him from the scene of this damsel's violation, and in no time became lost in a maze of paths, most of which were dead ends choked with nettles and brambles. At least no screams of protest offended his ears, so perhaps the encounter he sought was not a fearsome gangbang but a pleasurable group grope. Either way, he was still keen to view the sport. At length be broke out into the open, but in a place quite different from the one he had been looking for.

And now he did hear cries of protest. These, though, sounded like male cries, and they were accompanied by the silvery laughter of girls. He dodged back into the thicket and was able to keep hidden while following its edge round for a hundred yards. Establishing himself in a capacious bush, he peered out at what was indeed a kind of multiple rape, but not the kind he had expected.

Two hefty girls in tracksuits, assisted by a more delicate one in her blue summer dress, were wrestling with an uncouth-looking, long-haired lout the Captain recognised from the day before: the one who had been entertained by the strippers outside the Palace of Sweethearts and had then fucked the girl in the shower.

One of the big girls, sitting aside his chest while her assistants grappled with his arms and legs, yelled at him gleefully: 'You've had this coming to you, Joker! Think we're just here for your sport, do you? Well, now it's our turn to have a bit of fun, isn't it, girls?'

The others screamed their assent. 'He may fuck Josie,' said the other big one, 'but that doesn't mean he can go jerking off whenever one of us drops her drawers to get a bit of sun on her bum.'

The unfortunate Joker struggled furiously, but the two track-suited amazons were powerful enough to subdue him between them. The one on his chest now had control of his wrists, which she held forced against the ground above his head. Her busty mate sat on his knees. At this point the smaller girl in the blue dress, who had been tying his socks round his ankles, stood up. The Captain recognised her as the Helen who had made such a plucky guinea pig in Miss MacDonald's Physical Development class. 'Bags I do it to him!' she cried.

Reluctant to miss her performance, the first captor swung herself off Joker's chest and deposited her ample weight on his immobilised hands. He now had one girl at each end. His protests and heaves of resistance had died down, and he seemed to anticipate his fate with interest, as did the Captain.

Helen crouched beside him and unbuckled his belt. Then she unzipped his jeans and pulled open the front. She rummaged in his underpants and tugged out a long but sluggish penis. All three girls laughed unkindly.

Helen's next move was to get up and stand over him, her legs astride his chest. When she lifted the skirt of her dress and wrapped it round her little waist, everyone present was surprised to see she was knickerless. She swayed about above Joker, flaunting her silvery mound and the pink secrets below it. Dropping to her knees, she presented it lewdly to the youth's face and parted the lips. From his hiding place, the Captain clearly saw the lazy prick reach up towards the sun. Joker tried to strain his head forward, but the proffered cunt was immediately withdrawn a couple of inches to frustrate the endeavours of his questing tongue. To tantalise him still further, she inserted a finger, stirred it about in the juicy entrance to her vagina, pulled it out and held it under his nose. The cock doubled its length.

For the next ten minutes this lithe youngster masturbated wantonly just above the captive's tormented face, writhing in orgasm after orgasm. Most of the time she sat with her buttocks just below his collarbones, but every now and then she stretched up on her knees so that the inviting cunt hovered directly over his eyes.

'Go on, Mags,' shouted the first girl. 'Pump him out!'

Busty Mags grabbed the swaying cock in her fist and worked it fiercely. At once, white jets were thrown into the air and rained down all over Joker's denim jacket. The first girl whispered in Helen's ear, and she edged her bare bottom back to slide it backwards and forwards and from side to side in the creamy

43

pools even as they soaked into the cloth. It was not altogether clear whether this action would ruin the garment or actually improve its weatherbeaten appearance, but such considerations were not relevant; the little rogue's purpose, executed with dramatic effect, was to resume her forward position and smear her spunk-dripping bum all over her victim's face. To judge from her expression as she did so, he was in need of a shave.

At this stage, the Captain was having difficulty assessing whether these proceedings were perceived by Joker more as a punishment or as a treat. Nor was the motivation of the girls entirely clear, although what was certain was that all three of them, but especially young Helen, were enjoying themselves immensely. After the face-smearing operation she didn't linger with her private parts so near his mouth, but pulled back to tease the youth again before he could get his tongue up her. Mags went on pumping and pumping, and after three more orgasms he was so exhausted that she was able to move aside and allow her mate to take over. Still the teasing continued, and still there was no easing up on the remorseless pumping. The cock, now limp and thin, was stretched out grotesquely, and visibly sore. Joker's eyes were shut – even he had had enough of the glorious sight offered so profligately to them. To terminate the sport, Helen suddenly raised herself on her knees, parted the lips of her cunt even wider, and discharged a stream of hot, golden piss over his face. The girls ran off laughing, and the Captain withdrew into the thicket, heading back for the college buildings.

After he emerged into the sunlight, he found himself skirting a beech hedge which, as he could see from the tall goalposts at each end, enclosed a netball court. By this time the reader will not be surprised that the Captain, who was what a distinguished contemporary playwright has called a 'betwixt-twigs peeper', paused to study the foliage and what was being transacted beyond it.

Miss MacDonald was conducting the proceedings, attired in the bottom part of a claret-coloured tracksuit and a tight-fitting T-shirt. But it was the costume of the fourteen players that caused the jaw to drop. Although he knew nothing about netball, he had seen enough in the pursuit of sport and beauty to have noticed that the rules or conventions of this game required the players to wear, front and back, a kind of bib displaying large letters – GS, GD, WA etc. – presumably designating their position or function in the game. In the present case, he observed, one team wore these letters, red on a yellow background, in the usual way, with the difference that, apart from their white socks and trainers, they wore nothing else. Their opponents played bare-breasted, the lettered bibs, yellow on red, being secured round their waists and hanging down fore and aft over bums and pussies.

Such an unexpected scene thrilled the Captain and his prick jumped to attention. A true connoisseur, he delighted in the contrast between the uniformity of – well, of uniforms, if they could be called that, and the variety of breastage and cuntage. The exertions of the game, punctuated by blasts from Miss MacDonald's whistle and her cries of 'Come on, let's see some action, Topless!' and 'Put it in there, Bottomless!', set tits of all sizes and shapes a-jiggle, and opened thighs between which seven young cunts of striking individuality flexed and sweated. To heighten the effect, the bibs of the bottomless girls gaped outwards to reveal the profiles of their breasts each time they bent forward, while the pussies and bottoms of the topless team were also exposed in teasing glimpses whenever they leapt to intercept the ball or stooped to pick it up.

With so much activity and such a range of beauty to relish, the enraptured Captain hardly knew where to look. Sometimes he tried to take in the whole scene, with its overpowering, impressionistic whirl of flashing thighs, laughing faces, jostling shoulders, shining bellies, bouncing boobs, bumping buttocks and forward-thrusting pussies. Then he would focus on one particular player, but if he had selected a bottomless one he would soon feel a hankering for a topless one and vice versa. Eventually, however, while still keeping one eye on the general flow of the game, he found the other settling more and more on one girl. She was a loverly, auburn-haired bottomless WD, positioned at his own end of the court only a few feet away. He recognised her as the one who had been salami-fucked in the bathhouse.

As he watched, she fumbled with the ball, provoking an

irritated comment from Miss MacDonald. 'Wake up, Gina!' she yelled. 'That was supposed to be a push pass. You'll never make the grade if you just stand there and scratch your snatch!'

The Captain felt an urge to shout back in Gina's defence. While he stroked his cock, he realised he had fallen in love with this freckled darling. At this moment the final whistle shrilled. The girls withdrew to the side of the court and pulled on the garments they had discarded there. As they trailed off through a gate at the far corner, Miss MacDonald marched straight towards him. He froze. She halted six feet short of the hedge, rested her hands on her hips, and winked. Then she, too, left the court.

FOUR

FUN AND GAMES

The following afternoon found the Captain once more patrolling the grounds. Again, everyone seemed to be in classes or doing exams. It was very hot, and he soon decided to abandon his prowling in favour of sunbathing. With this in mind, he left the avenue of horse chestnuts, and plunged into the thigh-high grass. Not many yards in from the pathway, just beyond the shade cast by the trees, he stopped short. There, immediately ahead of him, was a small circular area of flattened grass. This was certainly no mysterious crop circle but a sign of recent human presence. To one side of the circle lay a pair of regulation knickers. He resisted the urge to step forward and examine this garment, realising that if he left the scene undisturbed he would stand a better chance of scoring.

The scene of what? No other traces of activity were visible to indicate whether the waving grass had concealed a solitary sunbather, a passionate embrace, or the easing of a non-sexual bodily need. It was a long shot, but as the sun was so warm anyway, he resolved to lie in wait on the off chance that the young lady would return to collect the discarded pants.

Caution would be needed to avoid arousing the suspicions of the hypothetical young lady. Taking care not to disturb the seeded stems more than was necessary, he lowered himself to the ground. He kept himself as narrow as possible by pressing his elbows against his body and dragging his legs behind him as he crawled forward by wriggling his shoulders. This, he remembered from the distant past, was called the leopard crawl. Inch by painful inch he advanced until, on reaching the flattened circle, he withdrew a couple of feet and closed the abundant grass not only in front of him but also, as far as was possible above him. Now, fortunate not to be a hay-fever sufferer, he was lying concealed in a green tunnel. He was fortunate, too, not to be a loud snorer, for almost at once he fell asleep.

He awoke to the subdued sound of voices close by; so close

that they could only be in the arena he had come to spy on. Two voices, it seemed. And one of them, contrasting with the ladylike, giggling tones of the other speaker, was that of a rough-sounding male.

Much as he would have liked to edge forward and part the stems before him, the Captain judged it would be safer to lie doggo and wait for things to develop so far (if they developed at all) that the couple had eyes only for each other. So he pretended he was as small as possible and also that he was an innocent sleeper who just happened to have stretched out in that particular place. He listened.

'These them?' asked the male. 'Can I keep 'em?'

'What on earth for?'

'To take to bed wiv me an', well, make love to, like.'

The girl's voice grew indignant. 'You mean you're going to wank off over them? And what will you do with them then?'

'Get you to wear 'em while they're still damp an' stink like fuckin' fish,' came the ungracious reply.

This exchange was followed by the sounds of the couple getting down on the flattened grass and trying to settle themselves. Grunts, groans and intermittent squeals of protest occupied the next few minutes; the Captain was tempted to edge forward and risk exposure. Then the girl spoke.

'Look, Joker,' she said, 'you can be good fun and I like you a lot. But you've been getting much too fresh lately. I'm not that kind of a girl.'

At first the seemingly ubiquitous Joker was at a loss for words, but after a series of spluttering gasps indicative of surprised protest, he found his tongue. Where it had been before he found it was a matter for lewd conjecture on the Captain's part.

'Not that kind of a girl? That's the fuckin' point. That's why I got the 'ots for you, innit? I ain't never screwed a virgin – not a proper friggin' virgin.'

'Listen to me,' she retorted. 'This is ridiculous. You're just getting carried away. I'm not a virgin, so you can forget it.'

'What you mean, not a virgin? You said – you fuckin' swore to me – you never been laid.'

'I might have said I hadn't had intercourse with the opposite sex. But we girls, well, we get up to all sorts of tricks with each other. That's how my virginity went.' She paused. 'Months ago.' Dumbfounded, Joker remained silent, and his partner continued. 'You've been setting me up on a pedestal. I want us to go on being good friends, but no more than that. I'm just not your kind of thing, Joker.'

Joker erupted in a torrent of eloquence. 'Know what you are? You're a fuckin' cocktease. What you really mean: I ain't good enough for you. Jus' 'cos your ol' man can send you to a dump like this. Not a virgin, eh? You fuckin' cheated me! Let me suck your tits an' lick your bum all right, don't you? An' you let me sniff your friggin' cunt an' stroke all round it, like. But every time I get me leg over it's the same story, innit? "Oh no, I'm not ready for it yet! Oh no, don't be putting that horrid thing inside me, we got to *work on our relationship!*" What fuckin' relationship? That's what I want to know, you little cow. Not a virgin? In that case it won't 'urt so much. Get that skirt up.'

'Look,' she said, 'cool off, will you? OK – you can just lift it up at the back and touch my bottom. But no funny business, mind.'

After some moments of rustling, grunting and heavy breathing, Joker resumed his diatribe in somewhat softer tones, as if his mind was more on what he was doing than on what he was saying. 'That's it, though, innit?' he mumbled. 'It's all the same wiv you little tarts. I know your lot. *Daughters of professional men.* Well, you can stuff that. Got a nice little bum in a way, but I can get the same down the disco on a Saturday for a fiver.'

'Don't be silly,' his partner replied. 'And stop pinching me like that. You can just tickle my arsehole if you like, but don't go inside it. No, Joker, you must get it into your head that I'm not into that.'

'Oh no? You was yellin' out for more last time I done it.'

'I'm not talking about arseholes, Joker. I'm talking about this stupid business of you not being good enough. That's just not true. This idea of "daughters of professional men", for instance. It's just a sham. All that matters here is your parents being good for five K a year in fees. You don't have to be professional – they take any riffraff. Emily's dad's an estate agent. On Open Days we get bank managers, garage owners and middle-aged pop stars swanning round. Take that little slag Helen's mother, Mrs Lascelles. She's a single parent, and has to write dirty books to make ends meet. And look at Melanie. Why, her father's just some sort of professor, not even an Oxbridge one. I suppose they let her in because he's a Governor. It'll be the odd job man's daughter next!'

The Captain (and honorary odd-job man) squirmed at the denigratory implications of this remark. In any case, who did this little madam think she was? Just because her dad could afford an annual 'five K', as she had put it, using the jargon of the very yuppies she affected to despise! He resolved to humble her and bend her to his will before he surrendered his new post of general dogsbody. He had no children as far as he knew, and if he had he would hardly aspire to submit them to Miss Muttock's tender attentions. But nothing was too good for him, and nothing would be too good for them. He prided himself on getting what he wanted from life. And what he wanted here and now was to get a decent peep at the action. Cautiously, he parted the long stems in front of him.

Yes! He held his breath for fear that the girl would feel its heat on the thigh and buttock immediately before him. Her grey skirt was hitched up over the small of her back to expose the delicious curve, and the side of the buttock was slightly concave as she clenched her bum on the probing finger. Joker's long curls fell across the backs of her knees as he peered up between her thighs. She had finished her egalitarian disquisition, and no wonder – all pretensions to refinement had been flung aside, and she had sunk panting to the level of common humanity.

The finger was moving in and out, and on each inward stroke her hips rose to meet it. Inside his overalls, the Captain's manhood bored down into the warm ground.

'Oh – oh!' murmured the girl, twitching and gasping. 'Oh, this is good. More – more. Faster! Go on – give it to me!'

Losing all control, she hurled her arse violently upwards so that the whole length of Joker's finger entered it, causing her to scream out in agony or rapture. The hairy youth uncorked his finger and stroked her bottom to calm her down.

'Joker,' she whispered breathlessly, 'I don't mind if you just lick me down there between my legs.'

50

Still lying on her stomach, her face way up beyond the Captain's field of vision, she opened her thighs and Joker dipped his head between them. Stirred by the slopping sounds, the Captain's cock swelled almost to bursting point. But it soon became clear that the sound held fewer charms for the girl whose abundant juices were being relished.

'I bet you make noises just like that when you're eating, you peasant,' she snapped. 'Look, I've told you. I only want us to be good friends. Nothing intimate. Well, OK then; you can fondle my breasts.'

Joker's nose was withdrawn from her arse and his tongue from her vagina, and his red face emerged gasping from between her shapely thighs. She rolled over on her back, and wriggled round to get more comfortable. This movement brought her feet to within a few inches of the Captain's face, but she then drew up her knees and let them sag apart so that her auburn-fringed vulva was aimed directly at him, while the uncouth youth fumbled with the buttons of her shirt.

Joker was the sort of lad who would have complained that his girlfriend thought the sun shone out of her arsehole. Right now, the Captain was revelling in the fact that it was shining directly into her cunt. A slight breeze rippled the pretty curls adorning the wet, pink leaves, which had fattened up and parted invitingly under Joker's tonguework. Joker's hands, meanwhile, had evidently found their way to her nipples and were well on the way to inducing another climax. Her hips began to heave rhythmically, lifting her buttocks from the ground. Her thighs opened even wider, and the Captain gazed, lost in lustful admiration, as the dark entrance to her tunnel of love opened itself and his nostrils caught the scent of the syrups that flowed out and down, over her bottom and on to the ground. The heaves became faster, and more of the heady juice was released. He felt intoxicated by the sight and smell. Quite carried away, he plucked a long, stiff stem of grass and reached forward to tickle the pulsating pussy.

At the moment of contact, the girl threw her knees together and her labia closed around the stem. Then the thighs fell open again, wider still, flat on the ground. The lips, now a burning scarlet, disclosed themselves once more as they were forced apart by a gush of love juice. At the top of the slit the flesh drew back to reveal an enlarged, throbbing clitoris.

The Captain withdrew his grass-stem from the syrupy cunt, but the viscous fluids had rendered it too limp for what he had in mind. His own manly member was not at all limp, and would have been highly suitable for the job, but discretion was of the essence. He plucked another stiff stalk, and touched its tip against the straining clit.

Pandemonium broke loose. The girl's bottom bucked up into the air as if electrified, and stayed up there, quivering, the cheeks clenched together. She was supported by her feet, head and elbows. With her fists she pummelled the ground on either side of her. Joker had been hurled aside, and looking up past her bunched-up skirt the Captain glimpsed the hard, red tip of a white breast.

'Oh!' she groaned. 'Oh, oh, oh! My God! Oh no, you've made me come. You big, yobbish brute, how could you? Look at that huge cock – don't you dare splash that stuff all over me. Here, stick it – stick it in my mouth!'

Suddenly she sat up and altered her position so that she lay on her stomach with her head lifted to the level of the kneeling Joker's erection. For the first time, the Captain saw and recognised her face. His heart sank. This abandoned creature was none other than the copper-haired darling he had fallen in love with on the netball court the day before. She was Gina, the salami-fancier.

At least, he reflected ruefully, there was a chance that, if he persisted with patience, his might still be the first real penis to plough into that juicy quim. And at least her association with this lout, Joker, was not a romantic, moony one. She couldn't stand him, could she? It was her nostrils he got up, not her cunt. He supposed she just fancied a bit of rough now and then. Well, he could come on rough himself when it was called for, couldn't he? And romantically tender, too.

Her distended lips slid up and down Joker's cock while Joker leaned forward and stroked her bum. Using one hand to hold the white cheeks apart, he moistened a finger of the other one and began to slide it loosely up and down the rift. But all at once this gentle pleasuring was interrupted. Gina reached out to grab the knickers lying beside her. She pulled her mouth away from the swollen cocktip and squeezed the thick, slippery stem firmly between finger and thumb. As the spunk began to gush, she caught every fluid ounce in the gusset of the navy pants, finally wiping the exhausted prick clean on the dry parts. Then she stood up and stepped into the knickers, pulling them up high to her waist and pressing the saturated gusset into the cleft of her privates. The short grey skirt was smoothed down over her upper thighs, and she looked at her wristwatch as if congratulating herself on her timing.

At that same moment, the handbell rang out from the top of the hill. The Captain tried to shrink, and willed the grass-stems to close above him. But Gina and Joker were too intent on exactly retracing their own way back to the path to notice him lying there. After allowing them plenty of time to get out of sight, he rose to his feet, stuffed his cock back into his overalls, and followed their example in threading his way back without treading down any more of the long grass. He even tried to weave the stalks together at the point where he emerged on to the turf bordering the avenue. Perhaps he would be wanting to return to the scene of the delight he had just witnessed.

His steps took him down to the stream and then along its bank to the field leading up to the Palace of Sweethearts. Today, nobody was to be seen. With his key he let himself into the pavilion. He had brought a gimlet with him, and devoted some time to boring a number of spyholes in the shutters to give clear views from within of the length and breadth of the veranda. As a little indulgence, a reward for having so patiently prepared for possible future pleasures, he opened the locker and took out the envelope of salacious photographs. He spread these out on a wooden bench illuminated by a shaft of sunlight shining through one of the larger holes he had made, and began to masturbate slowly. But he was careful to avoid reaching orgasm. He merely wanted to work up a good head of spunk he could hold in readiness to sluice into whatever vagina was next thrown across his path by fate.

The amateurishness of most of these pictures was somehow more arousing than the technical accomplishment of commercial sleaze. These were no hired models coldly simulating eroticism, but lewd young students getting excited by displaying their hidden charms to the camera (and the photographer) and sticking their fingers up their cunts. The tip of Captain's prick was now wet with the clear, viscid juices oozing from it, and when he removed his hand the swollen phallus showed a definite tendency to jerk up and down spontaneously. He had almost reached the point of no return. Reluctantly, he replaced the pictures. As soon as his upright member had declined into a stiff but flexible downward curve, he bullied it back into his overalls and emerged into the midday sunlight.

Surprisingly, more than half an hour had elapsed since he had entered the Palace of Sweethearts. The grounds were still deserted as he climbed slowly towards the main building, wondering how long he would have to contain himself. Somewhere to his left a whistle shrilled out. He became aware of the swell and fall of girlish shouts, and more whistle blasts. Quick – to the netball court!

He parted the leaves of the beech hedge just as Miss MacDonald blew the final whistle. Standing right in front of him, no more than two feet from the hedge, he once more confronted none other than the lovely Gina, the freckles clearly visible on and around her upturned nose, and her neat little auburn bush flaming between white, rounded thighs. More infatuated than ever, he held his breath. She stooped to retrieve the ball at her feet, and her yellow bib hung forward to reveal the pink tips of smallish breasts. He held his cock. She straightened up and turned – the pretty bottom, too firm to wobble, flexed with youthful suppleness as she ran off to the far corner of the court to get dressed with the other players.

But before anyone could begin to dress, Miss MacDonald blew her whistle. 'Wait, girls,' she called. 'Don't bother to put your clothes on. We're going straight up to the bathhouse for a shower. I'll open the outside door so we don't have to go through the corridors like this.'

The Captain turned and ran. He ran and ran, outstripping the stripped girls and their tracksuited mistress and reaching the bathhouse door just in time to unlock it and enter before the first of them rounded the corner of the shrubbery to cross the last few yards of open ground. As he had hoped, the place was unoccupied. He concealed himself in the wooden locker, one eye pressed eagerly against the hole opposite the shower cubicles.

He was not a moment too soon. Under Miss MacDonald's supervision, the fourteen girls were hurried through a perfunctory routine of showering – even now the distant handbell could be heard summoning them to the delights of an institutional lunch. Only two cubicles were fully exposed to his spyhole, but about half the girls, one at a time, were being processed through them, on this occasion with no opportunity for horseplay. At last he was rewarded with the sight of his beloved Gina, whom he now at last viewed in all her nakedness, luxuriating in the streams of hot water, soaping her pretty breasts and washing from the folds of her cunt the sweat of the recent game as well as the residual secretions from her earlier sport with Joker. But not for long: the MacDonald took hold of an elbow and dragged her out reproachfully, pushing into the cubicle she had occupied a fat pink girl who held no charm for the Captain.

As if to compensate for his disappointment, a tall, slim young lady of distinctive and supercilious appearance stepped into the adjoining shower. He thought he recognised her. It was her short brown hair and hard, dark nipples that served to identify her as one of the girls he had witnessed from above as she took her pleasure in this very cubicle two days earlier. Yes, she was surely the one who had been fucked by that cocksure Joker on the unforgettable occasion when, seeing him in her embraces, he had mistaken him for a girl.

Languidly, the girl raised an arm and let the steaming water course down into the dark hair of her armpit. She bent down and held the cheeks of her bottom open so that it could run between them to irrigate the fleshy purse the Captain could see pouting between her thighs. She stood up again, caressing her narrow white belly and long legs.

Miss MacDonald halted in her rounds directly between this fresh, young beauty and the Captain. 'Oh, by the way, Josie,' she remarked, 'no need for you to hurry. You're to have lunch with me today, in my room. Take your time, dear.'

She moved out of the way, and could be heard jollying the other girls along. Less privileged, they were barely allowed to make themselves wet before being hurried into their clothes and herded out of the room. In the meantime, Josie soaped, rinsed and massaged herself with lazy, voluptuous movements, turning and bending and displaying every part of her slender form to the hidden eyes that watched her.

It was now clear from the welcome silence which replaced the reverberations of the bathhouse that all the others had left. Once again Miss MacDonald interposed herself between Josie and the Captain, but this time she had removed her tracksuit. He gazed on her naked back and buttocks.

'Looks like a real treat, that shower,' she said. 'Mind if I join you, dear?'

Not waiting for a reply, and obviously not expecting a rebuff, she stepped into the cubicle beside the glistening girl. As she gave herself to the steaming torrent she turned to face outwards, showing off the well-cared-for attractions of her lean, athletic body. The breasts were generous but firm, the stomach flat, the thighs hard and shining. A dense brown thatch, similar in colour to the girl's but more extensive, adorned her pubic area and hung in a sodden, dripping tail between her legs. In contrast, Josie's hairs had been parted by the fast-flowing water to reveal lips that projected out in a pink line which bisected the plump triangle at the base of her belly. Both sets of genitals were lost to sight as the older woman threw her arms round Josie's waist and embraced her. They kissed passionately, swaying from side to side and digging their nails into each other's backs.

The MacDonald's bum was now turned towards the Captain, and he saw the girl's hand slide down to fondle it. A finger slipped between the gleaming cheeks, and was pushed into a secret place. This lewd intervention took the sporty woman by surprise.

'What are you doing?' she cried out. 'Who taught you these naughty tricks, Josie? Come on, let's make ourselves more comfortable.'

She broke from the embrace, took her partner by the hand and led her, dripping, out of the shower and out of the Captain's field of vision. Frustrated, he waited a good twenty-five minutes before venturing forth from his hiding place. There was no trace of the besotted couple – they must have withdrawn to their private lunch.

* * *

Mary Muttock sat in her study behind locked doors, asleep. In her dream she was being raped by a leopard. 'At least,' she said to herself, 'in this dream it seems to be a leopard, but in reality I'm sure it's a tiger.' They said a leopard couldn't change its spots, but in the course of long glacial (or did she mean galactic?) ages it could surely evolve into a tiger. Or from one, for that matter. That was it: everything was evolving. In those days, her own hairy pelt having grown outwards from her genitalia to cover the whole of her body except her lips and nipples, she was known to the cave-dwellers as Mary Mammoth. *Muttock* was a transparent derivative of *mammoth*, of course. Even the linguistic medium in which we lived was subject to inexorable evolutionary processes: the Great Vowel Shift, the grim law of Verner, and the venerable law of Grimm (immortalised in the vernacular tales of the Grimm brothers). In those icy caves she queened it over the Neanderthal apes with her proud, jumbo-sized bestiaries – no, her bestial, prodigious mammaries and cavernous nether mouth – but now she had been hunted down and cornered by the king of beasts, not yet overtaken in the Darwinian stakes by the mangy lion. Hounded by a leopard – correction: dogged by a sperm-flecked tiger! Its expression, snarling but amused, was that of the Captain but its short, stubby legs – all four of them – were Derrick's. Her suspicion that it was really a man transformed into a beast was confirmed when it began to mount her, missionary-fashion. Its amber eyes bored into her own, and her nostrils inhaled fiery blasts of vindaloo. This reminded her of the improbably located Rocky Mountains Tandoori House she had occasionally patronised in her ranching days ('Breakfast Served 24 Hours'). Prominent on the menu was 'Goat Vanda-loo'. Now she understood. The insight came to her in a vision of a light-footed mountain goat, an impala impaled on the sabre teeth of a tiger which savaged and vandalised it, ripping open its womb and twisting the sinews of its heart. Fired with goatish lust, she thrust upwards with her hips, trying to force the great animal higher so that the crowds below, outside the window, could catch a glimpse of its genitals. 'I want you to show off to them,' she gasped proudly, or at any rate loudly. Or, she reflected as she felt for the big cat's sex, perhaps her precise words were more like 'I want you to show them off', or even 'I want to show myself off'. But as the brute's suffocating weight descended on her belly, she couldn't feel whether it was male or female. Suddenly she found herself wide awake. Propped up in her easy chair, she held a cheese and pickle sandwich in one hand and her hot, hairy mound in the other. Her vodka and tonic stood on the table beside her.

After flicking through all the channels of her internal TV system, which she had been watching in patient boredom before falling asleep, she settled to monitor the proceedings in the bathhouse. Although two cameras had been concealed in this part of the college, one directed at the shower cubicles and the other at the area containing the communal bath, benches and lockers, the arrangement was not a satisfactory one. Steam kept misting the lenses. Only one of the showers was fully exposed to the probing eye of Camera One. And the sound system was rarely able to cope with the resonant uproar characteristic of bathrooms.

Clouds of vapour swirled across the screen, and the floor was wet, but the place seemed to be deserted. Everyone must have gone for lunch. But what was this? Two figures were embraced in one of the cubicles. Unfortunately it was situated to the side of the picture, so that all she could see was a hand fondling and probing a bum. The amorous couple emerged from the shower, but too quickly to be identified.

The Principal switched to Camera Two in time to catch them as they fled to the far end of the room. On the floor they found wet towels left behind by others, and as they stood up their faces came into view. Well, now: if it wasn't the randy MacDonald and that tomboy Josie Greene! Miss MacDonald screwed her towel into a tight knot and went for Josie's bum and belly mercilessly. For her part, Josie folded her towel just once, and applied it in vicious flicks, lashing out at all parts of the mistress's dripping body but making the buttocks and thighs her favoured targets. They chased each other from end to end of the room, in and out of the camera's range, until the girl was cornered by her more powerful adversary. Inadequate as the sound system was, it brought to the Principal's study a very fair notion of the shouts of excitement, slaps of wet towelling on flesh and squeals of pain. And though the picture lacked the enhancement of colour, the marks inflicted on the tender parts of both the contestants were clearly to be seen. The tiger was vandalising the goat, but the goat was still merrily adding to the tiger's stripes.

Exhausted, laughing and weeping, they called a truce and retrieved their own dry towels. But instead of drying themselves, they carried them to the great, empty communal bathtub and spread them on the white-tiled edge and the bottom of the bath beneath. Josie sat on a towel, her legs dangling over the edge of the bath. Her companion leapt down to kneel between her knees, and proceeded to fondle and kiss her wet way up the girl's right leg from the sole of her foot to the crease of her groin. She took her time. Lots of time – and then repeated the process on the other leg.

As she watched these monochrome images, Mary Muttock was reminded of her early days and nights at the Raunch Ranch. In those pre-electronic times they had a rattling old sixteen-millimetre film projector for the entertainment of clients, especially those in need of prestiffening, and a collection of blue movies, most of which were, in fact, in scratchy black and white. There was the one with the bored housewife who was screwed by the milkman, the postman and the man who came to read the gas meter. And she recalled one with an inadequately clad teenage hitchhiker who got fucked by three rednecks in Texan cowboy hats on the back seat of an old Buick. And one portraying a swinging party which developed into an all-out orgy of lecherous grunts and flying sperm.

As well as such favourites as these, they had a few jerky silent shorts dating, she supposed, from the 1920s. These featured moustachioed villains and suave Valentino lookalikes having balletic congress with flat-chested girls in dark lipstick. Against an unconvincing background of palm trees and camels, a pale-skinned Arab would take the Western beauty into his tent and seduce her with sweetmeats and opium. A pheasant-shooting party of bewhiskered aristocrats out on the moors would encounter and hunt down a flock of chorus girls in black stockings and corsets, and rudely roger them in the heather. A white-faced man with sleek, oiled hair and silk pyjamas sucked on a long cigarette holder while a naked girl in handcuffs fellated him.

But the film she remembered most vividly was called *The*

Wedding Night. It was set in an overfurnished bridal suite. The couple must have come straight from the church or registry office, as the bride, a pretty but timid girl with corkscrew curls, was still arrayed in her long white finery. Her groom sported full evening dress, American fashion. He was much older, and the pencil-line moustache above his thin lips marked him as a man of the world. Beside the bed on to which he pushed her stood a trolley with an ice bucket. From this he took a bottle of champagne, poured two glasses and plied her with more than she could take. He ripped open the front of her wedding dress and dragged out a breast, stopping her screams first with a kiss and then, as he transferred his lips to her nipple, by placing a large, hairy hand over her mouth. His other hand raised her skirt, sliding it up the white silk stockings, over the plump white thigh above the bridal garter, and right up over the waistband of the lace-trimmed drawers. Tearing these from her quivering loins, he tugged at his own buttons to release a huge, straining cock. The camera cut from this to the bride's open cunt, now gaping shamelessly from its furry nest. All signs of fear and indignation had fled from her pretty features, and were replaced with a smile of lustful complicity as he leaned forward to kiss her once more. At this moment, he plunged his cock into her, pumped vigorously, withdrew, rose on his knees and spent all over her face and ringlets.

Miss MacDonald had completed her ministrations to the inside of the girl's legs. She climbed nimbly out of the bath, made Josie stretch her arms back on the tiles behind her head, and knelt above her head, her left knee pressed against the girl's left armpit and her right knee against her right one. With her lover in this position, Josie was able to apply her hands to her bottom and genitals. At the same time, the MacDonald stooped right down to kiss her on the mouth.

Her kisses became both wetter and more fiery. (Miss Muttock wondered if this was a physical paradox.) The older woman's tongue strayed from Josie's lips down to her nipples, letting her own breasts dangle into the girl's mouth. As she browsed her way slowly down to the soft belly, a dangling tit was dragged from Josie's mouth and bounded down to join its mate, already engaging with the flattened bosom below.

The MacDonald's hands were busy at her partner's hips, and then between her bruised thighs. Josie's calves, which were hanging down over the tiled edge of the bath, kicked out as the muscles of her belly and thighs tensed; a probing finger had found its mark. And now the knees were drawn up, the heels planted on the edge, and the thighs allowed to sag open. Down went the mistress's head, concealing the girl's hot cunt from the camera. At the same time, she stretched back her lithe body over her, so that her own pussy descended to seal Josie's lips. As one person, the lovers quivered in rapture, rose, dressed and departed.

By this time Mary Muttock had calmed down, and felt somewhat remote as she activated switches to perform a desultory search, summoning up a series of unexciting images of the rooms and corridors of Cunlip College. But her interest was engaged when one of the cameras picked up the slim form of Melanie Winspur mounting the main staircase. From her own observations, as well as from things she had heard from Derrick, she knew Melanie's reputation was such that her ascent to the dormitories might be worth following.

On reaching her own room, spartanly furnished with four beds, bedside lockers and a large cupboard for clothes, the girl immediately undressed and lay down naked. But instead of entering on the expected masturbatory routine, she then left the bed and knelt on the floor. It was hard to make out what she was doing, but she seemed to be lifting the rug in a corner of the room. Ah, she had found a loose floorboard and was removing something from underneath it. It appeared to be an exercise book.

Melanie returned to lie naked on the bedcovers, propped up on pillows. She took a pen from her bedside locker, opened the book and began to write.

FIVE

PRICKS AND TRICKS

Stretched naked on her bed in the noonday heat, Melanie Winspur opened the yellow exercise book and wrote:

Thurs, May 31

Yesterday evening, 7.30, my latest date with Derrick. Put on weekend clothes – long mauve wraparound skirt, seethrough blouse, floppy-brimmed hat – and slipped out through delivery door so no one saw me. Kept under cover most of the way down to Palace of Sweethearts. Everyone in Hall watching PhysDev movie – MacDonald and Muttock had insisted. That's why I'd chosen Wed. evening for date.

Sat on edge of veranda and read while waiting. *The 120 Days of Sodom* – MacDonald lent it me after last English lesson. Boring and sickmaking – the book I mean, not the lesson. MacD told us all about what she called the Romantic Agony, and the Decadence, or Decadents, or whatever. No, Sade's not my scene, all the shit-eating and amputations and that. Must say, though, I quite liked the bits about teenage weddings. Has given me idea! Startled by rustling in bushes; thought it was Derrick, but wasn't.

Late, as per usual, the lazy prick. Wondered how he liked pix I gave him on Monday. Could have taken trouble to turn up early to thank me for getting them done. Must have been 7.50 when heard motorbike coming along path by stream. Why does he use it when he only has to come from Old Lodge? Can't be quarter of a mile. Just showing off, the creep – unless he comes straight from drinker down in village, which I've often suspected. He parked bike behind Palace and pulled off helmet. Whistled when saw what I had on, and kissed me. Leathers felt good through seethrough.

Sat down in sunny spot on veranda. Asked about pix.
BASTARD DERRICK: What pix?

ME: You with fucking hard-on taking picture of me, and me with fuck-all on taking one of you.

(Well, I had that white top on, but that's not the point.) Made out he'd never seen them. What's the fucker playing at? Maybe he forgot all about them – got worked up wanking in Muttock's cupboard and left them there. Had just thought of that and was going to ask him, but he started French kissing and feeling me through blouse. Frigging hat fell off and we rolled over on it.

Wooden floor hard, so we went down to grass by stream. Nice there. He pulled my skirt open up the side. Licked outside of leg from ankle to top of thigh, then same inside. Slipped hand right up to crotch and found I had no knickers on – that got him excited and he ripped skirt right open so he could kiss my snatch.

Unzipped him and yanked out his thing: quite swollen, but all floppy and wouldn't stand up by itself. Pushed him down on back. Made tent of skirt with D's head in middle, licking me. Bent forward to blow him while he tore blouse open and mauled tits. Got him a bit stiffer and thought might just be able to stuff it in.

Shifted round so tent over his tent-pole, and kissed him with mouth open. Twat open too, but pole went floppy again. Sat up and tried to cram it in with fingers. Limp dick all wet and slippery from him and especially me, but wouldn't go in. Derrick had PROBLEM.

Next I took blouse off and lay back. Made him kneel over me and paint nipples with juicy cocktip. That got my clit good and hard and horny, but no real effect on him, even when I unzipped his top and ran fingers over hairy chest.

Made sort of cunt with armpit and let him frig cock in it. Been letting it get quite furry lately (armpit I mean). All of a sudden he goes stiff and squirts. Armpit can't hold as much as cunt – spunk splashes out back and front, rather thin and runny but lots of it. Glad I'd taken blouse off. D wiped me with hanky, but hairs all gooey and matted so made him lick armpit out.

Asked him what was wrong. 'Going off me, then?' I asked. He said he was a bit tense. Nervous. Had feeling we were being watched. Tried to reassure him, and promised to wait every evening for rest of week at 7.30. He said he would try to make it soon, and would keep hands off prick till then. Zipped himself up and I put blouse on. As we walked back to Palace arm in arm like pair of soppy lovers, thought we heard noise again in bushes. D dived into undergrowth, but fuck all there. Put helmet on and rode off noisily. My hat too far gone to wear again.

What's the matter with him? Used to screw like a fucking stallion. And how could he leave me all hot, horny and dissatisfied like that? If he can't get it up next time, I'm going to be looking out for stronger meat. Big D can stew in his own juice; it's time I got me a REAL MAN!

Sick at heart with frustration at missing the main part of the MacDonald's romp with Josie, his balls weighing a ton, the Captain had slunk away from the bathhouse and made for his Suzuki. In a few minutes he was sitting outside the Green Man, consoling himself with a pint and a pie. Soon he felt more optimistic, and even formed a kind of plan. He returned to the college and marched up to the Principal's study, giving one loud knock and walking straight in.

Miss Muttock, who sat at the desk with her back to the window, hastily closed a yellow notebook and rose to meet him. 'Good afternoon, Captain,' she said. 'To what do we owe this quite unlooked-for pleasure? I had instructed Grote not to let anyone in.'

'To tell the truth,' he replied, 'we owe it to biology. Physical Development. Hormones. Here – have a feel.'

Opening the zip fastener in the front of his overalls, he produced a towering phallus of fearsome dimensions and pressed it into the Principal's hand. 'Don't know about you,' he continued, 'but I'm ready to shoot my load.'

He shot not his load but his tongue into her mouth, bending her backwards over the desk and removing her spectacles. Even as the back of her head was forced against the green leather surface, her hands were busy with the fastening at the side of her skirt. The Captain saw this, and tugged it away from under her bottom, down over her black-stockinged legs. It slid to the floor. The operation was repeated with her loose silk knickers.

The desk being just the right height, all he had to do was to stand close to it, with his hands drawing Mary Muttock's buttocks towards him. And then he simply walked into her, shook her like a rag doll, and voided his bursting reservoirs into the pulsing receptacle.

He pushed her back six inches on the slippery desktop so that his still hard prick was released, wet and gleaming, into the afternoon sunlight. Thick semen oozed from the slack cuntlips. It clogged the cleft of her bum and plugged her pink arsehole on its way to form a spreading puddle on the leather. From here it dripped sluggishly, in slimy ropes, to augment the stains on the carpet below. Miss Muttock lay back panting while the Captain waved his proud tool over her.

In no time at all she had recovered. Suddenly she sat up. Oblivious of the reeking effluent, she slithered her bottom forward over it and dropped to her knees, taking the cock into her mouth without a word. Her ravisher held her head firmly against his crotch to deny her any movement back and forth. Her nostrils were stuffed with his wiry hairs – she was unable to breathe. Her only recourse was to use all the skills of tongue, lips and teeth she had acquired as a ranch girl to bring him off without such movement of her head. In this she succeeded magnificently. In no time at all she was once again breathing through her nose. Spunk dribbled down over her chin, but most of it had slid down her throat like half a dozen oysters.

Still the Captain had not finished with her. He made her bend over the desk and, abandoning his raw briskness, applied himself with real tenderness to the task of licking her bottom clean. He began with the shining white cheeks, slowly working his way inwards until his tongue was performing its cleansing office along the length of the central slit. To facilitate his task, he dropped to his knees between her parted legs and worked repeatedly up and down from clitoris to arsehole and back. Mary Muttock moaned with delight. The tip of his tongue darted so quickly that she was unable to judge which orifice harboured it at the moment of her orgasm.

'You're getting good,' she observed, rearranging herself, 'but I rather suspect you see it as being all in a day's work.'

The Captain's reply was suitably gallant. 'With you, madam,' he said, smiling, 'it's a labour of love, and no hard labour at that. It's the most rewarding aspect of my current employment, though I'm sure there's some hard cash to come. And perks. Yes, I must definitely request a couple of perks.'

'What exactly were you thinking of?' she asked, taken aback. 'Haven't you had enough perks already?'

'It's to do with that what-d'you-call-him, that Derrick,' came the reply. 'Don't really need him now you've got me, do you? Bit of a nuisance, isn't he? Just a thorn in your flesh, so to speak.'

Miss Muttock had lately come to a similar conclusion, namely that Derrick was not her favourite prick. She had already resolved to pay him off and install her new lover in the Old Lodge, which Derrick had been occupying rent free. Accordingly, she planted a friendly kiss on his rival's cheek and told him to be ready to move into the Lodge the following morning.

The Captain left her with new-found enthusiasm for the unfamiliar world of employment, and returned to the village to throw his scant possessions together. These amounted to hardly more than a few well-worn garments, some toiletries, a small travelling library of erotic novels, a camera, a telescope and a pair of powerful binoculars.

Miss Muttock completed her perusal of Melanie's journal, the ink of which, had it been written in the days when young ladies wrote proper journals with proper pen and ink, would have been hardly dry when she removed it from under the loose floorboard. Having checked the surveillance TV to make sure the dormitory was again deserted, the Principal hurried the notebook back to its hiding place.

Her next task, on returning to her study, was to type a note:

Thursday afternoon

Dear Derrick,

In great haste. An emergency meeting of the Board of Governors has just been held at which a complaint from a parent-governor was discussed. It concerned your part in the corruption of one of the girls, and the decision was taken to dismiss you forthwith, giving you the usual notice to vacate the Old Lodge.

In the strictest confidence, however, I must advise you to clear out of it immediately, making sure that every trace of illegal substances is removed, and to take yourself off to some remote corner of this kingdom. As you know, one of the Governors is Mr Hardbuckle, the Deputy Chief Constable, who is an old and valued friend of mine. He warned me that in view of the disclosures laid before the Board a swift and discreet raid on your quarters has been scheduled for this evening. Leave the place immaculate, Derrick, and I do not suppose they will bother to pursue a small fish like you.

As you have never been officially employed by the college, I herewith terminate all agreements entered into and enclose a cheque to see you through the coming weeks until you find another indulgent patron. Be sure to destroy this letter.

Yours, M. Muttock.

There was, of course, no truth in what she had written about impending measures to be taken against him – only in the substance of the pretended allegations.

The first girl who knocked on the Principal's study door was spared her expected chastisement and entrusted with the task of seeking out the discarded lover and delivering this letter into his hands.

Twenty-four hours after these events, the afternoon sun fell on the dusty carpet in the Captain's new accommodation. The Old Lodge was a neglected hovel thrown up by the Victorian architect behind a pretentious crenellated façade. The architect had intended it, as the Captain had learned from a garrulous old party at the pub, to serve as the main gatehouse; at that time a railway station was due to be opened nearby, served by a new road running along this side of the valley.

It was only in recent decades that the misogynistic philanthropist Sir Julius Cunlip's establishment had been turned over to educational purposes. Sir Julius had grown fat on the profits accruing from his Little Miracle Prophylactic Suppositories, which made their astonished users heartily thankful that medical science had stopped short of a full-sized miracle. He had devoted his declining years to good works, of which Cunlip Court, as it was then called, was one. Originally, the sombre buildings had been designed for the reception and detention of hysterical women and unmarried mothers of the lower social orders, or 'moral degenerates' as they were officially designated. A new railway station in the vicinity, Sir Julius thought, would accelerate the ever-increasing one-way traffic to his grim portals. But saner counsels had prevailed, the station at Upchester, some five miles distant, being deemed by the authorities to be quite sufficient for the needs of this rural area. The new road was never built, a blind perimeter wall rose across the front of the redundant lodge, and instead of the grandiose bridge of sighs that would have carried visitors over the stream on their way up to the main building, the rotten old planks which had always been there were simply replaced with new ones.

Since that time, the Old Lodge had been inhabited sporadically by violent and deranged inmates, vagrants, menial servants of the establishment, a horse and, in recent years, by one or two eccentric and unpopular teachers. Derrick had been the last occupant, and it was clear to the Captain that he had set little store by his creature comforts. A woman's hand would be needed here.

Reaching for his binoculars, the Captain dragged a chair across to the window and took up his station. It allowed a comprehensive view of the valley. Everything he could see through the open window belonged to Cunlip College. Its dull brick buildings commanded the ridge opposite, less than half a mile away, and the line of dormitory windows flashed in the sunlight. Not all the grounds were visible, of course. It was already high summer, and the valley, though not densely wooded, was adorned with stately horse chestnuts and inviting groves.

Open to his inspection: the field of soon-to-be-mown hay, now grown waist high on the facing slope, the pathway leading down the slope from the college buildings, a more gently shelving playing field above it to the left and another below it to the right (and therefore within closer range of his binoculars from his viewpoint in the Lodge). At one end of this field stood that rickety old pavilion, the Palace of Sweethearts. He could also make out two or three stretches of the stream in the valley bottom. Most of it flowed unseen through woods, but a wider pool was partly visible bordering the hayfield. Rising from the stream to the Lodge spread an expanse of freshly mown hay which had already been gathered into heaps, or stooks, as they were probably called.

Green, blue and white were the colours of this enticing scene. Green predominated, with all the rich and varied shades of summer. A few white clouds drifted across the blue of the sky. And, sprinkled over the hillside facing the Captain, flecks of blue, some moving, some stationary, indicated the presence of students, now released from their afternoon classes.

Blue was the college colour. Idly traversing the prospect with his binoculars, he picked out and drew into sharp focus some of these blue flecks, most of them disposed in pairs or little groups of three or four. Many of them wore the pale blue summer dress, demure with short sleeves and reaching to the knees, with white socks below. These dresses fastened as high as the neck and buttoned down the front. Others sported crisp, white shirts, usually without ties, the sleeves rolled up to the elbows, and short grey skirts. In many cases the girls had removed their skirts to reveal standard issue navy knickers, which to the Captain's mind looked best on those who had let their shirt hang outside; it was easy then to imagine that the knickers too had been removed. A few wore not shirts but white vests or sports singlets above their knickers.

The girls were of all ages the college admitted, namely from sixteen to eighteen, but most of those who had already skipped and gambolled their way to the bottom of the valley must have been sixteen-year-olds, bursting with the energy of late adolescence. Those in one group were climbing an ancient horse chestnut. The Captain homed in on the tallest of this group, a girl with long, dark hair, who was deftly unfastening the buttons of her dress. She peeled it off, and at first he thought she was wearing nothing under it but her regulation pants. But no: she

69

proudly flaunted a little white bra. Having disencumbered herself thus far, she swung herself up into the tree and was lost to his sight.

A pair in white singlets and navy-blue knickers came romping hand in hand down the slope of waist-high hay. Every now and again one or the other stumbled and was tugged to her feet by her impatient companion. They seemed to be heading for the cool waters of the stream − but no, they halted ten yards or so above it, in a position which just avoided being masked from view by a sturdy oak tree. The Captain felt he recognised the smaller girl: wasn't she that pretty Nikki whose behaviour with the Principal had so shocked him on the day of his arrival? With trembling fingers he adjusted the focus of his binoculars as the girls circled round like cats preparing a nesting place, before dropping to their knees. Damnation! Because the grass had grown so tall, they were completely hidden, except that their heads kept bobbing up and down, in and out of sight.

Whatever they were doing, they were very active. Nikki rose, so that he could see her from the waist up. She stripped off her top and tossed it aside. As she was facing the Captain he could easily make out her gleaming, boyish chest. She was a late developer, not yet boasting much growth in those parts. Would her partner follow her example? It seemed not, but Nikki, surely, was now wrestling with her. Up and down bobbed the two tousled heads, and, if he was not mistaken, the object of contention was the second girl's singlet. Now − yes! − they were on their feet, swaying as they struggled in a tight embrace. Bare-topped Nikki had seized her friend from behind, and swung her round so that she faced in the Captain's direction. Faintly he heard screams of laughter. Nikki leaned back. Her friend was forced to wave her legs in the air before finding her feet again and reaching behind her, trying vainly to tip the bare-topped girl forward over her head. They struggled, seemingly dead-locked, but Nikki's hands were now for a moment free. She used them to grab the hem of the other girl's singlet and jerk it up to her neck. And there, exposed to the observer's delighted scrutiny, two plump little pink-tipped breastlets rose above the white tummy.

But only for a moment. Her hands came forward and she

snatched the vest down. This proved a fatal tactical error: even as she tugged at the vest, her saucy friend used a free hand to grab the front of her navy knickers and drag them down to her knees. At this range the young pubis, thrust forward and squirming as if for the Captain's benefit, could just be seen, or perhaps imagined, to be lightly furred with fair down. (His penis strained angrily and he unzipped to release it, but he decided to go easy, as its full forces would be needed, he hoped, that evening.) The next moment, locked together, the girls fell to the ground and were hidden. He waited and watched, for five, then ten minutes. Occasionally the long grass stirred, but not even their heads came into sight.

The Captain reclined back in his chair, his feet on the window ledge, scanning the grounds dreamily for further interesting activity. He was following the example of others he had encountered in this strange place, he told himself, and becoming a regular voyeur. At the same time, he reasoned, he was not attempting to touch those hot little cunts but only to view from a safe distance the wanton pranks which nature and the promptings of this sexy environment suggested to them. All the time his binoculars kept coming back to that cat-patch above the stream, as this surely had to be the scene of the afternoon's hottest action. Even the girls swinging in the branches of the old horse chestnut were unlikely to distract him from his pursuit of Nikki and Pretty-puss, but to the Captain at least they were showing no signs of life, whatever they might be showing each other.

After a while he grew impatient. He adjusted his clothing and taking up the first book that came to hand, which happened to be *Adventures of a Naked Girl*, he went downstairs and stepped out into the brightness and heat of the afternoon. Down to the stream he hurried, and across the plank bridge. Then, turning left, he proceeded warily along the bank until he reached the sturdy oak, and sat down under it on the side facing the stream.

As he pretended to read his book there in the dappled shade, he heard giggling and murmuring. So the two girls were still there in the grass. What would be his best approach? Should he get to his feet and walk straight towards them, his nose buried in his book? Or what about creeping up on them

71

through the long grass, as he had done when he spied on Joker and Gina?

Still pondering the choice, he realised from the sound of their subdued voices that they were on the move, and seemed to be moving in his direction. Their voices might be subdued, but the Captain's impression was that just one of the girls was doing her best to subdue the voice of her companion, who was protesting and perhaps struggling. And now their words became distinct.

'Come on, now, Susie,' urged the voice that must have belonged to Nikki. 'It's only a lark. In any case, there's nothing wrong in it – it's a really hot day.'

The half-stifled protests continued and the Captain, adept at interpreting such dialogue, was aware of a hardening in his loins. He held the erotic paperback close to his face, his fingers spread over the appealing picture on the cover, and peered over the top of it, waiting for the girls to enter the corner of his field of vision.

But that was not quite what occurred. Instead, they suddenly appeared right in front of him, having passed on either side of the tree. They joined hands and stood there, their backs to him, on the bank of the stream. Nikki wore only her navy knickers, and her friend Pretty-puss, whose name was evidently Susie, only her white vest. Susie's yellow pigtails were secured with neat blue ribbons, but Nikki's straight brown hair was cut short, well above her white shoulders. As he watched, Nikki let go of her friend's hand and laid the palm on her bare bottom. She slapped the cheeks playfully, and thrust her hand between Susie's legs from behind. But this was too much for the knickerless girl, who seized Nikki's wrist and dragged the hand out, with a great deal of giggling on both sides. Now, thought the Captain, they would surely step into the stream and forget their inhibitions in the laving current.

Once again, however, their actions were not what he had predicted. Nikki, taking the dominant role as usual, whispered something in her companion's ear. There was more giggling. Then, placing their arms round each other's shoulders, they turned to confront the Captain, and advanced until they were standing right over him. Nikki grinned and Susie blushed.

'What are you reading, mister?' asked Nikki.

'Oh, it's just a book I found lying about.'

'I've seen that one before,' she continued. 'Melanie's got it. Miss MacDonald gave it to her. Pretty steamy, but I'm not sure if the girl ever gets properly fucked. Still, I only got to read about half of it. How far have you got, mister?'

'Well, now,' he replied, 'I'm just starting the chapter called "The Bellywedding". I'm not sure it's suitable reading for young ladies of your age.'

'We're both sixteen, you know. I'm nearly sixteen and a half. People think Susie here looks older than me, even with her pigtails, but she's really younger. They let her in early because the Principal knows her dad – she only had her birthday last month.'

'Well,' remarked the Captain conversationally, 'she's got a very nice birthday suit, as far as I can see.' While they had been chatting, his eyes had been flitting back and forth between Nikki's cheeky face and boyish chest on the one hand and Susie's light dusting of yellow pubic fur, which did little to conceal the attractive slit running down between her thighs. 'Do you think I could see the rest of it?'

Susie's blush became more pronounced, and she brought her free hand round to cover her pussy.

'Just a peep, if you give us that book,' said Nikki. She stood behind her friend and, for the briefest moment, lifted the girl's white vest up to reveal the plump little pink-tipped protuberances. Then, just covering them again, she rolled the bottom of the vest tightly so that it fitted snugly below the breastlets. These she squeezed through the cotton, making the nipples stand out hard and well defined in the sunlight.

'She's all yours to look at for a moment, mister,' this amazing girl went on, 'but she's very shy and doesn't want to be fucked – not until she's married. I'm her special protector. You can look at me, too, if you give us the book.'

Without waiting for the Captain's reaction, she dragged up the sides of her knickers as high as they would go. The navy fabric was stretched taut and pulled into her crotch, so that the fat labia bulged on either side of the division. Maintaining the tightness, she rolled down the sides round her narrow hips until the garment was reduced to the proportions of a G-string. She

73

advanced, stood right over the Captain, turned round and bared her bottom completely, thrusting it back towards his face. Then she restored the makeshift G-string to its position between her cheeks, snatched the paperback from him, grasped the coy Susie by the hand and ran off with her into the long grass.

That night, quite unaware that Miss Muttock had discovered its hiding place, Melanie retrieved her diary. While the three girls with whom she shared the room slept, she sat by the window and tried to write in the moonlight. As the moon was only in its first quarter, this proved impossible, so she took a small flashlight from her bedside drawer and scribbled eagerly.

Fri, June 1

Went down to Palace yesterday evening and waited. And waited. Didn't really expect Derrick to turn up, not after Wednesday's fiasco. Went again tonight – thought maybe he'd had time to stiffen up. Same clothes on: wraparound cheesecloth skirt with see-through blouse, but no hat of course. Sat by stream reading *Sodom*.

Nearly eight when heard sound of bike. Roared right past me along bank, then up slope and stopped. Heard him running at me from behind. His leather gloves – gauntlets, he calls them – shot up under my arms and grabbed tits. Dragged me up on my feet, hauling and mauling. A bit more like the old D: strong and silent. Turned me to face uphill and made me bend over, resting hands on bank. He pulled skirt up over bare bum, and slapped bum about a bit with gauntlets. Felt leather shoved in between legs and pressed against belly. But he took it out again, pulled off gauntlet and put hand back, bare and bony. Lovely feeling when he stroked tummy and scratched around in cunthairs. Other hand, still in leather, mauling and slapping bum, but not hard.

He slid thumb and forefinger of bare hand into creases at thigh-tops so he held twat between them. Squeezed gently and rhythmically (spelling?), then a bit harder. Rather like squeezing lemon – could feel juice starting to run. One of his lovely leather legs rubbed against one of mine.

Felt tip of thumb running up and down slit, opening it. Then thumb stabbed into me, while he laid length of forefinger along slit with tip on clit. Gorgeous feeling when he pinched thumb and forefinger together. 'Fuck me, Derrick,' I moaned.

He pulled hand away. Sound of zip. Then both leather legs against backs of my thighs and huge cockhead nudging into open cunt. In it went, inch by inch. He gripped me tight by the hips, one hand gloved and one bare, and dragged me right back to him. I just hung there all limp, as if hanging from stiff rod stuck up me. Then pumping started – in, out, in, out. Pump well primed – shot his spunk into me almost at once and backed off.

Saw him standing there in all his gear. Hadn't even taken helmet off! Zip down, of course, and cock poking out, still semi-stiff and all wet. He stood there like statue of slightly drooping macho prowess or something, pointing towards Palace. I looked up in that direction and he nodded, so I ran up slope with him following. Hadn't got my key with me, but D had one and let us in. Seemed very dark after evening sun outside. He unfastened my skirt and put those old cushions on floor. Made me lie on tummy. Took off helmet at last, and other gauntlet, but still kept rest of gear on. Felt him kissing bottom. He stuck two or three fingers into my twat and dredged out some of the goo, his and mine mixed, to massage into my bum.

Then he turned me on my side, with my knee lifted up. He got into position so he could lick me while I took his cock in my mouth. Just *loved* having my face buried in all that shiny black leather with this stiff, white, red-headed thing sticking out of it. Not as long as usual, I thought, but much harder, especially compared with how it was on Wednesday. 'Fucking hell, Derrick,' I said, 'you're inspired tonight.'

So good with his tongue that I came extra quick. D's knob swollen and throbbing, all salty. Seemed to be just about to flood my mouth when he pulled out and stood up behind my back. Heard lots of zips unzipping and leathers falling on floor. Then felt his bare skin. Really strong and silent tonight, I kept thinking – hadn't said a word to me yet. Nothing but action, and when I say action I mean action. What a difference!

Fronts of his legs pressing against backs of mine. His chest and belly against my back, a hand on one of my tits and his dick between my thighs with my lips closing round its length. I reached my hand down and pressed the knob against my clit. But like I said, he was nearly exploding. Couldn't take this. We both shifted so he went straight up into me. Bliss! Cupped my hand round his balls and gave little squeeze. That drove him wild. He pinched my nipple really hard just as I felt the hot spunk jetting up my insides, wad after wad. Twisted my head round and tried to bend forward to kiss him.

Fucking hell! It wasn't Derrick at all, but some old guy I'd never seen before, lying there with his piece of meat going limp in my sopping cunt. What's a girl supposed to do in a situation like this? Me, I screamed. Not loud, in case anyone heard. A sort of whispering scream or screaming whisper.

ME: What do you think you're doing screwing me like this? And who are you, anyway?

STRANGER (*rolling my nipple between thumb and forefinger*): My friends call me the Captain.

ME: And other people?

STRANGER: How should I know? I keep myself to myself. Try to maintain a low profile.

ME: Yes, I noticed you had your head down a lot of the time. What are you doing in these parts, Captain, when you're not fucking the natives?

STRANGER: New odd-job man, that's me. Just taken over from that prat Derrick. It was – well, it was understood I was to get all the perks that go with the job.

ME: Don't you call me a perk, you jerk.

Well, we both started laughing then, and got really friendly, comparing notes about this crazy place like a couple of conspirators. He got big again without slipping out of me, and screwed me like the clappers. Told him it was an ace fuck, and promised to visit him tomorrow evening – he's been given Derrick's hovel. Still, I felt a bit duped. Must watch out in future for differences between Yamaha and Suzuki.

Melanie closed the yellow notebook and replaced it under the loose floorboard, where it remained untampered with until she retrieved it the following night to continue her narrative.

SIX

ROMEO AND JULIET

Sat, June 2

Dear Diary – Lots to report tonight, but pretty bushed, so must make do with briefest notes. Really thorough shower after dinner, and sprayed 'Seduction' on nipples, armpits, bellybutton, cunthair and small of back. Then put on little white cotton knickers (ones I call scantpants) and my tight white shorts. Cut into crotch a bit, but wasn't reckoning on keeping them on for long! They make me look incredibly leggy. Button of waistband left undone, and zip only two-thirds up. Borrowed Josie's sky-blue boob tube, which leaves most of tummy bare. To finish off, tied hair back with black ribbon and put on sunglasses, white ankle socks and white sandals. Looked like sixties teenager! Even made my own mouth water – hoped other lips would stay dry until shorts came off.

Had dorm to myself as other three away for weekend, so no problem with video. Unplugged it, disconnected it from TV and managed to get it into canvas holdall. Also took zapper so he could have slow motion or freeze frame without getting up – he probably wouldn't want to be getting up. Nearly forgot cassette. Most girls who hadn't gone home doing serious revision for exams, so didn't meet anyone as I lugged bag down to stream and over plank bridge. Door of Lodge open, so walked straight in. Shocking mess downstairs, just like with Derrick. Probably still D's mess. Caught glimpse of kitchen. Yuk-makingly disgusting.

Captain came downstairs grinning and kissed me – couldn't help my knees shaking. He's BIG, the Captain. Rather like Rochester in *Jane Eyre*, but much less hypocritical (spelling?). Barechested, with white boxer shorts on. Felt his thing getting hard and pressing into my tummy when he held me, and when I pulled away it looked pretty 'outstanding'. Took bag from me, and I followed him up to room he uses, same as D, as bedsit. A bit less messy, but only because he hasn't got much gear. A few books lying around, and I noticed pair of binoculars on cupboard by window. Terrific view over valley – what he gets to see down there doesn't bear thinking of.

Made him set up video – explained he couldn't keep it because really Emily's. Quite difficult to get it working with TV. Two white stripes he had to get in focus. Luckily he'd done it before.

Asked me what we were going to watch, and didn't seem too enamoured when I told him video of college production of *Romeo and Juliet*. Explained this wasn't MacDonald's full-length movie of her ace production, but our own private go at just one scene, with Emily and me as camera-persons.

Some boring nature documentary on BBC2. Lots of mating, but not the sort of thing to give you the horn. Toads turn me off, definitely. We sat side by side on dusty old settee, and I noticed wet stain soaking through his shorts at highest point of bulge. Made me cross my thigh over his, and reached hand round my back to squeeze nipple through boob tube. He pressed PLAY button on zapper and started to play between my legs as movie began.

Too tired to give details. We had lovely time, truly romantic. Said he had hots for me and wanted us to be *close* friends. I promised to keep him in touch with all the Cunlip action, would try to meet him every day to compare notes. Screwed three or four times – can't remember exactly. He helped me carry video back up hill. Must get to bed now or will look like mutton dressed as lamb tomorrow.

The Captain's spirits had fallen, though not his prick, at the idea of having to endure a couple of hours of worthy amateur dramatics. It was some relief to learn that they were to watch just a single scene and not the whole play. At least he would have this delectable girl to fondle and grope while watching it, and he could tell from the way she was dressed as well as from her past form that Melanie would want to go all the way.

He activated the PLAY button of the electronic remote control unit, and settled back to palpate his companion's right breast through the elasticated garment containing it. The underside of her left thigh rested warmly on top of his right one. The tip of his erection pressed into the outer side of it while the inner side was caressed by the fingertips of his left hand. On the screen a blown-up image of pullulating toadspawn was replaced by the titles modern technology had enabled these schoolgirls to super-impose on the underlying picture.

CUNLIP CULTURAL ENTERPRISES
present

he read. Desultory guitar chords accompanying random scales, and quavering trills on a recorder, were probably intended to suggest Renaissance music. The sequence of titles continued:

ROMEO AND JULIET
(Act III Scene 5)
by
William Shakespeare

The next frame introduced the players:

Starring
HEINRICH HINTENBURGER
&
CATHERINE CONDON

As these names loomed up on the screen in towering red letters, the Captain could have sworn that they altered very slightly after their first, almost subliminal appearance. He took his right hand from Melanie's breast and used the remote control to wind the tape back until he froze it at the appropriate point. Just one character in each name was different: **HEINRICH HINTEN-BUGGER & CATHERINE CONDOM**, he read, without much surprise. He let the tape run on.

Miss Condon's Wardrobe: Bumfrees of Upchester
Lighting & Camera: Cockup & Handheld
Additional Dialogue: Lord Bacon
Best Boy: Joker Dickstrap

Grip: Tightars Winsperm
Gaffer: Derrick Dipwick

Directed (*in absentia*) by
'BIG MAC' DONALD

The letters of these titles had been displayed over closed curtains hanging from a proscenium arch. It seemed that the camera had been positioned somewhere near the back of the auditorium, which Melanie identified as the college hall. The chairs were empty, except for a few people huddled in the middle of the front two rows.

As the last titles scrolled up off the screen, the house lights were dimmed, the camera zoomed in and the curtains swung open halfway. They stuck, were shaken from behind by an unseen hand, and opened completely to reveal a set which undoubtedly represented the heroine's bedchamber. This room was lit by dim lamps. Archways gave access to the inevitable balcony, and beyond the parapet a painted backdrop suggested the foliage of an orchard, silhouetted blackly against a midnight blue, star-spangled sky. In the manner favoured by modern stage designers, the floor was steeply raked towards the auditorium. This had the advantage of displaying the sheets of the four-poster bed very clearly to the spectactors, whose eyes would otherwise have been below the level of any actions transacted on it. Its obvious disadvantage was that the couple between the sheets needed to take repeated compensatory measures to stop themselves sliding to the floor. At least their heads were pointed upstage and their feet towards the audience; if they had been lying sideways they would surely have rolled over the edge.

The lovers were, in any case, securely tucked in at this preliminary stage of the action, their two heads facing each other and only a few inches apart on the pillows. Cathy/Juliet's medium-length brown hair shone on the white sheet, contrasting with the flaming carrot-coloured mane of Heini/Romeo. At this point, the auditorium-based camera was replaced by one that must have been set up on the stage itself, giving a much closer view of the bed.

As the strains of the improvised music faded down, a burst of amplified birdsong shattered the silence. Heini sat up suddenly. He shook Cathy by the shoulders, and she slowly wriggled up into a sitting position beside him, clutching the sheet modestly to her bosom. Again the birdsong reverberated round the almost empty auditorium. Heini rubbed his eyes, yawned, and pointed at a pile of clothes heaped on a chair. He kissed his Juliet rather primly and stretched a ginger-fuzzed leg down to the floor.

Without relinquishing her hold on the edge of the sheet, Cathy nuzzled up to the well-built youth and threw a restraining arm around his neck.

Cathy: Wilt thou be gone? It is not yet near day;
It was the nightingale, and not the lark,
That pierced the fearful hollow of thine ear.
Nightly she sings on yon pomegranate tree.
Believe me, love, it was the nightingale.

She pushed Heini back on the pillows, folded the sheet down to uncover the fiery mat of hair on his chest, and laid her cheek against it. The ungracious lad's response was to push her aside and sit up again.

Heini: It vos ze lark, ze heralt of ze morn;
No nightingale.

He pointed demonstratively at the sky, in which the stars were fading as pink rays crept up its expanse like rosy fingers.

Look, love, vot envious shtreaks
Do lace ze severink clouts in yonder East.
Night's kendles are burnt out, ent yocunt day
Shtents tiptoe on ze misty mountain-tops.
I lonk to plunch my lusty prick vunce more
Betveen ze clingink folts of zy sveet cunt,
But no – my cotpiece shell contain my lust;
I must be gone ent live, or shtay ent die.

Cathy: Yon light is not daylight; I know it, I.

It is some meteor that the sun exhales
To be to thee this night a torch-bearer
And light thee on thy way to Mantua.
There is yet time to fuck thy Juliet full,
Letting thy spouting seed gush into me
And firing me to transports of delight;
Therefore stay yet; thou needst not to be gone.

As she uttered these words, the lovely Cathy lifted herself over her Teutonic Romeo so that her well-formed breasts with their small, dark tips dangled above his face to tempt him like pears. In the course of his next speech, the delivery of which was less than fluent, her hand wandered down over the white cover to clutch a remarkable erection which had reared itself beneath the sheet. It might, of course, be no more than a simulated piece of stagecraft, the Captain told himself, especially as it looked considerably more massive than might have been expected under the stresses of a public performance.

Heini: Let me be – vot vos it now? – let me be ta'en, let me be put to dess,
I am content, so zou vilt hef it so.
I'll say yon grey is not ze mornink's eye,
'Tis but ze pale reflex of – *wie sagt man das?* – Cyntia's brow;
Nor zet is not ze lark whose notes do beat
– Do beat ze – ze heaven . . .

His rendition was here interrupted by the girlish treble of the prompter: 'The vaulty heaven.'

. . . ze faulty heaven so high above our hets.
My burstink balls grow heavy viz desire,
Zy cunt alone ken kvell my cockhet's fire;
Zet cunt exhales such scent, such honey drips
In shticky droplets from zose coral lips,
I hef more care to shtay zen vill to go.
Komm, Dess, ent vilcome! Yulia – nein, Yuliet – vills it so.
How ist mein soul? Let's talk; it is not day.

But Heini's idea of talking was to pull the sheet right down to his girlfriend's thighs and to start mumbling into the dark bush he had uncovered at the base of her belly. His own parts now stood proudly and nakedly revealed — these were, after all, no mere stage props. The monstrous blue-veined phallus, still clasped in Cathy's dainty hand, pointed stiffly out from a blazing scarlet thicket as he knelt over her, his balls swinging above her face. The pink light that had suffused the whole sky was now fading into a pale blue. Sunlight fell on the bed, and a crackling dawn chorus began to vie with the words of the dialogue. Juliet was now insisting, rather unnecessarily, that the day was indeed arriving.

Cathy: It is, it is! Hie hence, be gone, away!

She released the noble cock and withdrew her loins from the lips of the ardent youth before continuing:

> It is the lark that sings so out of tune,
> Straining harsh discords and unpleasing sharps.
> Some say the lark makes sweet division;
> This doth not so, for she divideth us:
> Some say the lark and loathèd toad change eyes;
> O, now I would they had changed voices too,
> Since arm from arm that voice doth us affray,
> Hunting thee hence with hunt's-up to the day.
> Would I were yet thy quarry in the hunt
> In which thy prick played havoc in my cunt.
> O, now be gone! More light and light it grows.

Heini: More light ent light — more dark ent dark our voes.

At this point the Nurse entered from the wings. Just for this video, Melanie explained, they had departed from the regular casting in which the part was played by old Grote, the Bursar. She told the Captain that her friend and dorm-mate Emily had been dressed up in defiance of theatrical tradition in a diminutive and revealing nurse's uniform obtained by mail order.

Blonde and cuddly, the pretty nurse hurried over to the bed.

The sexy wiggling of her bottom was exaggerated by the difficulty of crossing the sloping stage on high heels. She shook her head in mock horror at the sight of Heini's erection, which seemed to swell tighter every minute. Then, throwing herself on the bed between the lovers, she laid a hand on Cathy's hairy mound and leaned forward to deliver a loud stage whisper:

Emily: Madam!

Cathy: Nurse?

Emily: Your lady mother is coming to your chamber.
I have but time to slip my finger up
And dabble it in Romeo's pearly seed
Commingled with the juices of your cunt,
The while I press one last brief amorous kiss
On these hard rubies, your engorgèd teats.
The day is broke; be wary, look about.

Cathy: Then, window, let day in, and let life out.

Emily rose from the bed panting, her scanty uniform bursting open at several points to reveal a fine breast, a well-rounded belly, a pair of inviting buttocks and a tuft of straw-coloured hair between shapely thighs.

Even now it was proving hard to get rid of the tumid and slow-moving Heini, whose acted fear of the Capulets was a weaker motivation than the actual hunger of his penis. The camera swooped right in over the bed as he eased himself off the end of it and, standing between Cathy's legs, seized them, dragging her down the slope until her buttocks were poised on the edge and her thighs rested on his hips. In zoomed the lens, focusing on the glistening pink lips that now sagged open as that enormous cockhead nudged into them. Inch by inch it forced its way in, encouraged by the amplified gasps of the audience.

Heini thrust away valiantly, but without due regard for the laws of mechanics. The steeply sloping angle of floor and bed caused his Juliet to slide forward stroke by stroke until, drawing back for the tenth time, he drew her with him as he collapsed.

She tumbled clumsily on top of him, and they rolled over until he was above her. Wet and throbbing, his member was forced out of its sheath by all this turmoil, and discharged the accumulated reserves that had been welling up within its base. The sticky flood drenched her body from throat to pussy, and the Captain guessed that Heini had once again broken his record – this looked like considerably more than eighty-five grammes!

Cathy stood up and pulled her lover to his feet. They resumed their places on the bed and she splayed her thighs in invitation, but Heini remained crestfallen and abashed. Some wit in the audience cried out, 'Wherefore art thou Romeo?' The disappointment on Juliet's face was too convincing to be merely the product of her histrionic talents. She took him by the ears and forced his head down into her sodden thatch, a piece of improvisation which formed an appropriate bridge to her next memorised speech.

Cathy: Full many a virgin bride, who ne'er received
Man's flesh, with fingers hath her itch relieved.
Such wanton pranks, my Romeo, I disdain;
Hear this example, which the poets feign:
That scapegrace Cupid, ere his parts waxed big,
Showed his dam, Venus, he could suck and frig.
E'en Venus blushed: her senses were more struck
By Cupid's spittle than stout Mars his fuck.
Though now thy lance hangs vanquished and unsung,
Stoop down, sweet youth, to pierce me with thy
   tongue;
Upon these fields of pleasure feast thine eyes,
And feel thy weapon with my passion rise.
That blazing bush hath kindled my desire,
And soon thy burning brand shall quench the fire.

And indeed, even as these words were uttered, the virility of the youth kneeling beside her was restored. The flaccid member that curved down over the testicles lengthened, the foreskin withdrew, the glans swelled and shone, the stem grew longer yet and slowly reared itself up, uncurling and stretching until it pressed up against the red-haired belly. The camera lingered lovingly on this process before turning its attention first to his partner's upturned eyes and the rapturous expression illuminating her features, and then to the action of his tongue in and around her vagina and clitoris.

By the end of her speech, Cathy's clear tones had become somewhat muffled and feverish. She was casting her limbs about wildly, tossing her head from side to side and thrusting her hips up from the bed. Abandoning herself to her lustful urgings she rolled over on her stomach and reared herself up on her knees, keeping her face down in the pillows. Her thighs were parted, and the Captain could scarcely contain his own carnal desires as the screen displayed in close-up those smooth, rounded buttocks with the dark rift running down between them to the bulging split fruit of her sex. So close was the view this shot afforded that he could almost smell the bittersweet tang of the juices trickling from the swollen lips.

For a moment his eyes wandered to the girl sitting beside him, whose nipple had grown hard and proud between the thumb and forefinger which had worked their way down inside the snug top she wore. No, he had not imagined that familiar but ever-arousing odour: Melanie had completely opened the front of her white shorts, which had already been partly unzipped, and was playing with herself through her tiny, soaking panties.

On screen, Heini's stiff cock was bludgeoning away at Cathy's bum. It seemed to have penetrated some way up her arse before she reached one hand back between the two of them to pull it out. Immediately she guided it to the yawning vulva her other hand held open to receive it. The purple head was swallowed, followed by inch after inch of the thick, dark-veined shaft. Finally it was lost to sight as the romantic couple closed together in perfect union, thigh to thigh, belly to bum.

Heini, the Captain had decided, was a stud of some staying power. But having so recently discharged a copious freight of semen, the rusty-haired lad made a leisurely meal of the present engagement. His balls could be seen swinging backwards and forwards and from side to side. The camera moved round to give a better view. Almost the whole length of his manly stiffness, glib and sticky, came into sight each time he drew back from his darling, hovered panting over her and slowly plunged it in once more until his bush was flattened by her buttocks. The bodies of both the lovers were oily with sweat, and Cathy appeared to be in a state of recurrent minor orgasm. Slow, voluptuous waves of pleasure coincided with each inward thrust, and since Heini's hands were employed in fondling her pendent breasts, the only thing that prevented her from collapsing spreadeagled on the mattress was the steel-stiff cock that stretched her quivering cunt.

At this juncture, part of the Captain's attention began to stray from the lewd but slow-moving spectacle to the accelerating movements of the slender girl cradled in the crook of his own right arm. Melanie had worked herself up to the point of no return. She placed her right hand over her companion's and pressed it firmly into the breast it had been caressing. Taking her other hand from the damp crotch of her panties, she took the Captain's free one and moved it to the tight white cotton. Through the knickers he applied firm pressure into the cleft of her sex, then ran the tip of a finger upwards until it came to rest on the hard, protruding clitoris.

The girl exploded at the touch, kicking out her legs and bending her head right back as she shrieked out to proclaim her ecstasy. Gradually her convulsions subsided. She relaxed in his arms, sobbing. 'Fuck me, please,' she whimpered, and tugged on the waistband of his shorts to release the erection imprisoned within. 'Please fuck me. I want you right up inside me – now!'

The Captain stood up and shuffled off the unwanted item of clothing, then took an upright chair from the table and placed it sideways-on to the screen on which Romeo was still slowly screwing Juliet, dog fashion. He sat on the chair and made Melanie stand between his knees, facing him. He ran his fingertips up the back of her thighs before cupping his palms over the small buttocks still neatly cased in crisp white shorts. He kissed her belly. His tongue left a trail of saliva as it slithered up to the bottom edge of the boob tube. With the tip of his tongue he hooked back the elastic and grasped it between his teeth. A brisk movement of his head brought the whole garment up and over the pert, conical breasts.

Next, having pulled her shorts down over her buttocks and

thighs, he eased the back of the panties down just far enough to fondle her bottom. Melanie responded by pressing a breast against his mouth. He looked down. Above the top of the cotton panties, which his activities behind had pulled down slightly in front, a cluster of ginger-blonde curls peeped out charmingly. He stooped his head, ran the tip of his tongue through the curls, and applied both tongue and teeth to the elastic of the panties in the same way that he had done to the boob tube, but pulling down instead of up. Once over the slight outswelling of her thighs, they dropped and joined her shorts around her ankles. She stepped out of both garments and kicked them aside. She stood before him, naked except for the blue boob tube rolled up under her armpits, and the white socks and sandals.

On the screen, Heini was alternating a dozen faster thrusts with a dozen slow ones. Determination was written on his features, while Cathy's spoke of delirium. Sweat dripped from the hair of both of them and ran down over their faces.

The bold Captain placed his hand, palm upwards, between Melanie's thighs. He pressed the thumb and little finger into the creases between upper thigh and vulva, using them to squeeze the plump purse of her sex. His three remaining digits he then hooked upwards into a vagina still flowing with the juices released while she had sat beside him. After some wriggling and stretching he withdrew the fingers, sniffed their wetness and smeared it thoroughly into her left breast. The breast was taken avidly into his mouth and licked clean.

Heini had now abandoned his slow thrusts altogether, and was bonking at a rate that threatened to send the bed sliding backwards down the stage; Cathy cried out each time his balls slammed up against her thighs.

Making Melanie step back a couple of paces, the Captain closed his knees so that she could straddle his thighs. He placed his hands firmly on her bottom and drew her towards him. She held her slack lips open with one hand, and lowered herself carefully on to the red-tipped spear that reared up from his lap. Down and down she sank, the fat cock plugging her more tightly with each inch of her progress, until she was sitting snugly on his thighs and his face nuzzled her breasts.

In this position, of course, it was the girl who made the

running, but the Captain's hands, now resting on her hips, were able to second her movements. He felt the pressure mounting unbearably at the root of his penis. Had he been in control he would have held back, but it was Melanie's turn now to call the shots, and she rode him headlong to a mutual crisis. Like a solid rod the hot cream distended his urethra, racing up the tube and bursting from the glans to stretch the elastic girl-flesh that gripped it. Yet even as the cunt stretched to receive the uninterrupted torrent, the girl's muscles tightened in violent, conclusive orgasm. He felt the thick fluid squeezed out all round the base of his prick and running down over his testicles.

At the very moment of their double climax, the eyes of both participants witnessed the culmination, on the screen, of Cathy's and Heini's deferred delight. The lovers collapsing panting on the bed, and Heini withdrew his instrument, still long but now down-curving and dripping stickily. He climbed off the bed and made for the balcony, where he paused and turned to utter the next line of his scene: 'Farevell, farevell! Vun kis, ent I'll descent.' Hurrying back to his beloved, who now lay languidly on her back with her thighs distended, he planted a series of burning kisses among the spillage that issued from her lovelips. Then he raised his head and brought his mouth, foaming with the spermatic emulsion he had sucked from her, smartly into contact with his Julia's face. The osculation that ensued could hardly be called chaste, and the combined effect of this lubricious spectacle and the plashy sounds accompanying it was to cause the Captain's prick, still sheathed in Melanie's vagina, to swell up once again.

But everything must end. Heini finally withdrew to the balcony, and lifting a leg over the parapet with rather less than his usual athleticism, lowered himself until only his head could be seen through the railings.

Cathy: Art thou gone so? Love, lord, ay husband, friend?
        I must hear from thee every day in the hour,
        For in a minute there are many days.
        O, by this count I shall be much in years
        Ere I again behold my Romeo
        And grip his prick between my trembling thighs!

Heini: I vill omit no opportunity
           Zet may convey my greetinks, love, to zee;
           Each hour zet shtrikes I'll curse ze creepink clock
           Ent muse on Yuliet vile I skveeze my cock.

Cathy: O, think'st thou we shall ever meet again?
           Methinks I see thee, now thou art so low,
           As one dead in the bottom of a tomb.
           Either my eyesight fails, or thou look'st pale.

Heini: Ent trust me, love, in my eye so do you.
           Dry sorrow drinks our blut. Adieu, adieu!

The lad's red hair dipped out of sight and the curtains swept across the proscenium arch to muted applause and bawdy catcalls. When, with some difficulty, they were again drawn open, the lovers were standing, hand in hand, at the edge of the stage to take their bow. Rosy-skinned from their exertions, they put the Captain in mind of Adam and Eve after their transgression but before they had covered their nakedness. To the side of them, Emily stood awkwardly in her disarranged nurse's uniform. Melanie (for she it was who had really provided the salacious additional material) had contributed a short but spirited epilogue, which all three now recited in unison:

> Condemned by Shakespeare's pen to death's dark
>   jaws,
> We stand again, revived by your applause.
> The tragic muse consigned us to the tomb,
> But Romeo's cock still yearns for Juliet's womb;
> Lo! see it rise, once more in pride to stand,
> Revived by your applause and Juliet's hand.
> Yours is the triumph, friends and critics true,
> And for your patience recompense is due.
> With all our love we'll balance the account;
> Mount first this stage, each man a maiden mount
> (Or, if no maidenheads are to be had,
> Cunts ready broached await each lusty lad);
> Let pricks high-mettled in those cunts be stuck,
> And intermingling pairs promiscuous fuck.

Come, friends, and cast your flimsy weeds aside;
Let each hot girl be every fellow's bride;
And critics, if your censure must be hard,
Come fuck the players, but reprieve the Bard.
We've served the tragic muse enough this day,
So shed not tears, but seed, in amorous play!

Stimulated by the expectations this speech aroused, the Captain spent a second time into the girl still impaled on his lap. She climbed off him, and they both resumed their places on the settee. Their hands wandered lazily to each other's genitals as they glued their eyes on the screen.

The camera had drawn back. Three shadowy figures got up from the front row and mounted the stage. The first was Melanie herself, closely followed by the objectionable Derrick and that yobbo Joker. How, and in what erotic combinations, would they respond to the actors' lewd invitation?

Another dozen spectators climbed up and, laying hands on Emily, hurried her upstage, away from the others. The Captain made out three of the girls he had seen in the bathhouse and three younger ones, including Helen and Nikki. The males appeared to be denim-clad youths from the village. Some frenzied stripping left the members of this self-contained group naked, half naked and, in a couple of cases, simply with penis or breasts exposed. Emily's uniform was peeled right off and it looked as if she was taking one cock in her mouth, another in her cunt and a third one up her arse.

When her assailants had finished with her, they pulled out and encouraged her to participate in the next stage of their pleasuring. This was the promiscuous copulation incited by the epilogue: 'each hot girl' became 'every fellow's bride', sometimes serially and sometimes simultaneously, furnishing a soft-focus backdrop of generalised lechery against which the camera, pulling back, concentrated on the main action downstage.

Meanwhile, Derrick and Joker were undressing. Melanie, who wore her see-through blouse and wraparound skirt, stepped up between Cathy and Heini. Congratulating them on their arousing performance, she took them each by the hand and led them up the slope of the stage to the bed. The couple lay down on it once more, but head to foot and with Melanie kneeling between them.

'I had to do it this way,' Melanie explained to the Captain, 'because Cathy and Heini are going steady and shouldn't be fucking other people, in spite of what I got them to say in the epilogue. With that Joker around I was going to have to be really careful.'

The Captain, whose member was already growing stiff yet again in her warm hand, merely nodded as the video continued. He soon realised that when Melanie ruled out fucking as an improper activity for the lovers on this occasion, she meant fucking in the narrowest sense of the word. On the screen she was applying practised masturbatory techniques to both of them, while Derrick and Joker, standing on either side of the bed with their tools ready in their hands, looked on wide-eyed.

'Come on, you two lazy buggers,' said Melanie. 'You could at least be kissing us girls.'

Joker curled up on the bed next to Cathy in such a way that his rampant dick was nudging one of her nipples. He laid a hand on the other breast, and clamped his lips over her mouth. Derrick climbed up on the other side and reached across Heini to give Melanie's skirt a sharp tug at the waistband. It fell away, exposing on the screen the pretty ginger tuft the real counterpart of which was at this moment being probed by the Captain's finger. While she continued to frig him in real life and Heini in the video, her electronic manifestation was subjected to the wet kisses of Derrick as he ripped open the front of her blouse.

After a few minutes of these lewd games, Melanie drew back her lips to address Derrick. 'You can jerk off over Cathy now,' she said. 'I need my mouth for something else.'

Stooping, she proceeded to fellate the ecstatic Heini, who displayed every sign of being close to orgasm. She now had two hands available; with one she continued to masturbate Cathy while the other one was applied with vigour to her own cunt. Derrick, meanwhile, positioned himself so that an arm encircled Melanie's body, allowing him to fondle her breasts, while his other hand toyed with his erect penis, poised menacingly above the upper parts of Cathy's body.

This situation, the Captain could see, was an inherently

unstable one. The five bodies constituted a multiple time bomb on the point of detonation. And here in his untidy room another bomb, a double one, was also primed. Melanie – the electronic Melanie and her flesh and blood original – was a component of both bombs, and it suddenly seemed vitally important that the two explosions should happen simultaneously.

Pushing the real Melanie down on the floor, he made her kneel facing the screen, her head down and her bum in the air, and plunged into her without ceremony. He shagged her furiously and as he did so Joker, up there on the screen, saw Derrick's threatening cock enter his field of vision. At once, he stopped kissing and caressing Cathy and moved round behind the video version of Melanie, whose kneeling form he penetrated from behind, so that she was now being fucked twice over: in the picture and here in this room while watching herself on TV.

The Captain's sense of fair play was gratified when he saw that Cathy's clitoris was still being frigged by Melanie, who might have been thought too preoccupied to give a toss. And now it did indeed happen, and happened in glorious simultaneity: seven shuddering orgasms with their concomitant groans, gasps and yells. Derrick's semen splashed over the lovely Cathy's face and breasts. Cathy's loins bucked repeatedly in response to Melanie's frigging. Melanie's head jerked back with a mouth full of the quivering Heini's sperm, which was running out of the corners of her lips. Joker, his eyeballs bulging, discharged shamelessly into Melanie's cunt, while Melanie herself, spurred on by the action of her own fingers on her clitoris as well as by the stretching of her vagina by Joker's cock and the effect of the boiling infusion he had jetted into her, hurled herself backwards with a feral cry of triumph. At the same time, their eyes fixed on this lascivious display, the Captain and the real Melanie enjoyed their lingering moment of melting bliss.

She collapsed limply on the floor, the expiring Captain on top of her. 'We must get together again tomorrow,' she gasped.

SEVEN

SPORTS AND PASTIMES

On Monday afternoon, while Melanie was engaged on business with her new friend the Captain, Miss Muttock slipped into her dormitory and out again with the yellow exercise book concealed under her gown. Behind the locked door of her study she made herself comfortable with a drink, and began to caress her privates as she turned to the latest entry.

Sun, June 3

What an old dear he is, the Captain! Went down to Lodge this afternoon – found him sunbathing on front porch in tatty straw hat and girl-sized black bikini trunks. Myself, I had on my short white tennis dress, the one that buttons down front. It hugs tight down to waist, then flares out at hips. Nothing under it, but left him guessing about that at first. He was drooling over those photos of me and Derrick. Had hand on balls and must have been getting in mood to jerk off over photos. Change in shape of front of trunks showed how glad he was to see me. I went indoors and brewed up in grotty, mould-sprouting kitchen. When I came out with tea he got up and took me upstairs. Put cushions on two hard chairs side by side in front of open window, and let me look through his binoculars.

Wow! Some magnification! Turned them on dorm windows and actually saw Emily, back after night on tiles, taking off bra, though not near enough to get worked up about it. Lots of girls lazing about on Upper Field, some by themselves, some in couples and some in a big circle with their books. Half-hearted revision for exams. Guessed Captain was dying to have binoculars back! Even without them you could tell girls were getting sun on parts they usually kept to themselves and their best friends. Told him this. He laughed, went over to chest of drawers and came back with long telescope. Said

95

he'd picked it up at an auction. Even more powerful than binoculars, but tripod missing, so hard to hold still for any time. Sat on chair beside me, put foot up on window ledge and rested telescope on knee. I told him to focus on group sitting and lying in circle, so we could compare notes.

CAPTAIN: Do I know any of these fresh young beauties? Who's the dark-haired one in the red bikini?

ME: Oh, that's Alexandra – you must have noticed her doing her audience participation thing in the video yesterday. One of the 'hot girls'. Mind you, she was already 'everybody's bride' before that performance. But she's got lovely legs, hasn't she?

CAPTAIN (*stroking my thighs with free hand*): So have you, sweetheart. But yes, they seem to be good slim ones from this distance. Look, she's just rolled over on her tummy. She's taken her top off. Oh, and now she's rolled the bottom down over her bum. What d'you mean, 'everybody's bride'?

ME: Her mum keeps a so-called boarding house in East Wittering – really a residential brothel. Before she came here, Alexandra used to service those wittering geriatrics. They'd come queueing after they'd drawn their pensions – she had to squeeze the dribble out of their dried-up dicks and let it drip all over her tits. Definitely goes for the younger man now – not surprising, eh? Looked like a bit of jail bait I saw her with the other morning. She's the only eighteen-year-old I know with a gang of toy boys in tow.

(This was a load of old bollocks. Alexandra's the biggest tease at Cunlip. Everyone thinks she's a virgin, but she told me she's faithful to her brother and only fucks in the hols.)

CAPTAIN: What about you, Melanie. Do you like youngsters?

ME: I like watching them at it. But I prefer the mature, man-of-the-world type – to have up me, I mean. What did *you* do in the war, daddy?

Without thinking, he said he used to play doctors and nurses and mess about with girls' fannies down the air-raid shelters. Said he rewarded them with bits of shrapnel he picked up still hot after the all clear, for them to give to the big boys they really fancied, who collected it. How old does that make him? He got all confused when I tried to pin him down. Said it was the Korean war, but when I asked her later the MacDonald didn't think there was much gunfire over Home Counties in those days.

Anyway, he wanted lowdown on all the girls, or at least their names. Couldn't always make out who they were at first glance. They were sprawling about on ground and mostly not wearing usual clothes, though some of them had weekday Cunlip clobber on. Some had stripped down to vests and navy drawers. But most in Sunday glad rags, or bikinis, or sexy undies. Well, I pointed out a few of them he was specially interested in, pretending not to notice he'd eased up hem of dress and sat with free hand resting on my snatch.

CAPTAIN: Look, over on the left. See that couple side by side, the blonde one on her back and the other one face down? They've both got long red skirts pulled right up to their waists. Can't make out if they're wearing anything under them, but they seem to be fondling each other.

ME: They would be. That's Lucy Wagstaff on her tummy with the long dark hair, and the other one's Sarah Cummings. The MacDonald calls them the heavenly twins – always got their hands on each other's arses.

CAPTAIN: Seen them before. Just happened to come across them the other day in the showers. Lucy's got big bouncy ones, right? Ah, what's up over there on the far side? See that one with the shoulder-length black hair and long white socks – the one in the black lingerie? Saw her doing a striptease down by the Palace of Sweethearts. Oh yes, she seems to be getting up now – just you get an eyeful of this!

It was gorgeous new dorm-mate Prissy Gibbs. She stood up in the middle of circle and started bumping and grinding. Could see they had Sonys with them – could even hear, just. Prissy ought to be a belly dancer. She really *writhes*. What a teaser! Slipped bra strap off one shoulder and fetched out tit. Nursed it in one hand, stroking it with other – danced round circle showing it off, pushing it right into girls' faces. Then went all prim and covered it up again. Bared bum, stuck that in faces, covered it up. Same with quim. Really brazen the way she stuck it out. Knickers down round knees, knees apart as far as knickers allowed, hips shoved forward, head down, both hands pulling herself open. Looked as if she was letting some of girls lick, but always backing off and yanking knickers up again.

Captain stuck a finger into me. He wanted to know who girl with short spiky hair was who kept grabbing at her and suddenly got her down on ground. It was that horrid, stuck-up punk, the Lady Honoria Redmayne, in gold leotard. Wrestled with Prissy and dragged knickers down to ankles. Prissy ripped front of leotard down over tits – could hear cheer from where we were watching. Redmayne got mad and stormed off with towel round her. Prissy kicked knickers right off and did victory dance.

CAPTAIN: See that lovely auburn-haired one who's still got her white shirt and grey skirt on? She's called Gina, isn't she?

ME: Fancy that snobby madam, do you? Already spoken for, I'm afraid. Belongs to a guy called Joker Jennings who works the pumps at a garage out on the Upchester Road.

Could see something was happening down at Palace of Sweethearts – told Captain to point telescope that way. Six girls on veranda. Recognised them quite easily, thanks to binoculars. Named them to Captain: Anne Amory, Carla Merryweather, Nikki Culpepper, Helen Lascelles, Celia Prout and Mags Campbell. All sixteen-year-olds, for heaven's sake, apart from Mountainous Mags (a busty eighteen) and Celia (seventeen, and gang-banged only the other day they say, Wednesday I think). Mags, sweating in white vest and navy knickers, sat on steps with what looked like cash box. Others standing, trying to look sexy for benefit of group of boys watching them from down on grass, where they were lined up as if queueing.

Captain pulled finger out and used free hand to unbutton front of dress so he could fondle one of my boobs. Said he had seen Anne and Carla paddling, his first day here – they'd seemed really demure, he thought. Well, I suppose you could say they were playing demure now, to get blokes interested. Little Anne quite cute in straw boater. Apart from that, all she had on was white shirt, Cunlip tie and long white socks.

Shirt just reached to twat level. When she turned round you could see bottom curve of bum cheeks. But mostly just stood facing them with legs crossed, thumb in mouth and other hand pretending to hide cunt. Carla sort of opposite effect to her – socks and grey college skirt, but topless. Well, she was wearing tie. Had hands on tits, her own I mean, not that she's got any. They moved close together, and Carla leaned head on Anne's shoulder.

Nikki, with her short, straight brown hair, up to usual tricks. I've seen her reading *Adventures of a Naked Girl*, which would explain why she had on pale green T-shirt, like Applepeel character. Only came down to her belly button. Stood there with feet apart and hands on hips, flaunting her sex. OK, so she's a sexy kid and there's no use denying it. But I wished she'd brought her friend Susie with her. Susie's such a little prude – says she's saving herself up for Mister Right, but if ever a girl needed fucking it's that one. Going to see if I can't get her fixed up. Will arrange for Nikki to put her on finger exercises next week.

Helen always a bit shagged out when you see her close up, though very pretty with it. From up in Captain's window she looked really appetising in white baby-doll nightie, holding her big teddy. Kept turning round and lifting nightie behind to show bum, then pulling it up in front and pretending to scratch tummy. She dropped teddy bear and started cuddling Celia, who was wearing black hot pants and a boob tube like my one, but red. Helen stood behind her and stuck one hand up inside top and other one down front of hot pants.

Guys seemed to be getting restless. Couldn't recognise any of them – all looked the same to me with their hair gel, jeans and T-shirts. Expect I've had a few of them, but can't have been too impressed. First one went up to Mags and gave her money. Waited for change (what's she charging, 50p?) and stood there choosing. Actually, not sure if he chose or thought he had to take first one from display, taxi-rank style – went straight for little Anne. She came down off veranda and took him round corner to space between pavilion and brick wall where we could see but that lot couldn't. He made her put hands on knees and kissed her bum. Unzipped and let jeans down to ankles. Could make out hard-on, but binoculars not really strong enough for close-up detail. He shoved it into her, but we couldn't tell which entrance. Seemed to go in quite easy, and she didn't seem to mind, so most likely her cunt.

Captain got me to put one hand in his tight little trunks so I only had one hand to hold binoculars. Hard to hold them still enough -- everything wobbly, but tried to steady them by resting elbow on his shoulder. First couple came back and others cheered. Then next guy went up and chose Nikki. Soon as they were round corner he pushed her down quite roughly on ground, pulled out cock and just threw himself on her. All over inside a minute -- wham, bang, etc! Talent like that Nikki's wasted on him.

Next boy more adventurous. Didn't get any change for what looked like fiver, but took Helen *and* Celia. Captain's cock really big by now, so I dragged it out of trunks and let it bob up and down in fresh air. This next guy took jeans right off. Got down on his back and made Celia kneel between his legs and suck him, with her boobs hanging out of the red top, while Helen squatted on his face, still hugging teddy.

Captain thinking same as me. Now that one guy had taken two girls the others wouldn't want to be outdone -- we'd be getting two boys with one girl, two with two and maybe a general free-for-all (though not *quite* free if Mags had anything to do with it). So we put our toys away, both the optical aids and the parts of our bodies we'd uncovered, and hurried down the stairs and outside. Wanted a much closer view. Well, we crossed plank bridge -- sound of laughing and splashing upstream, so not wanting to be seen we trotted up avenue to level of what he calls Secret Garden. Then through undergrowth and along wall, snagging dress on brambles and trying to avoid nettles, till we reached place where wall comes out into open quite near Palace of Sweethearts. Fuck! They'd packed up and gone away. Must still have been some full bollocks and empty quims among that lot.

Captain keen to see what was happening down at pool with all that noise -- thought our whores might have gone to cool off. Instead of approaching along bank of stream we crept through bushes, keeping under cover.

But they weren't gang from Palace after all. No, it was girls we'd seen lying around in circle up in Upper Field, Alexandra and that lot. Told Captain to keep head down and watch the fun while I stripped off and joined them in water. Had lovely time with girls, but when I came out about half an hour later he'd gone.

Miss Muttock felt that Melanie had done less than justice to the 'lovely time' mentioned in this closing paragraph, of which she herself had been a witness. To be sure, by the time she reached the scene of those aquatic delights, her sexual equipment had been brought into a state of red alert by an exciting encounter on her way to the pool.

On this hot Sunday afternoon she had abandoned her monitor screens, all of which showed empty rooms, and sallied forth into the grounds. A diaphanous turquoise sundress only partly concealed her skimpy black undies, and the effect was crowned by round, turquoise-framed sunglasses and a black, floppy-brimmed hat.

As she swept down the avenue of horse chestnuts, her attention was caught by a party of girls over to her right on the Upper Field. They were sprawled, sunbathing, in a ring. As soon as they noticed her, they hastily covered up the expanses of nakedness they had exposed to the sun, got to their feet and hurried off down the hill, laughing nervously. Instead of trying to keep up with them, Mary Muttock veered away to the left, skirting the walled garden in a clockwise direction until she had descended to the corner just above the old pavilion.

Agitated voices of mixed gender could be heard, so the Principal moved very warily round the angle of the brick wall and into the sunlit space between the wall and the pavilion. She had not realised, however, that the voices were so close at hand, and her caution was insufficient to prevent her from almost stepping on the flagrant foursome she found herself glaring down upon.

Carla Merryweather lay on her back, knees apart, a bare-bummed youth ramming away between them. The effect of her partial nudity was heightened by the fact that she still wore long white socks, a grey skirt hitched up round her waist, and the college tie. Although her hips rested squarely on the ground, her shoulders were twisted round to her left. Her left arm supported the head of a second village lad, who lay beside her kissing her and playing with her undeveloped breasts. This boy's T-shirt was rolled up to his armpits, and his jeans were down round his ankles. While he and Carla clung together at chest level, their loins were angled somewhat away from each other so that a second girl had room to straddle him. It took Miss Muttock no time at all to recognise this second girl from her narrow white back and short, greasy hair – actually yellow but in its usual unwashed condition more of a dull brown. It was her long-desired Helen Lascelles. A flimsy white garment which seemed to be a nightdress designed for glamorous appeal rather than utility hung round Helen's neck and shoulders. Repeatedly she rose on her knees, bringing the gleaming shaft of the boy's cock into view between her lean thighs before sliding down and impaling herself on it again. Even as the scandalised Principal watched, Helen reached down with her right hand to toy with the testicles of the lad rogering Carla and to insert her thumb, as she did so, into his anus. He twisted his head to the right in response, and Helen stooped to shoot her tongue into his mouth.

At this moment the other youth, the one being kissed by Carla and fucked by Helen, caught sight of the imperious turquoise-clad figure standing over them. His panic communicated itself instantaneously to the other three. They leapt to their feet, cocks disengaging from cunts somewhere between the horizontal and vertical dispositions of their owners, and ran off round the corner of the pavilion. The boys lagged behind as they tried to drag their jeans up over their thighs.

'Helen and Carla – my study!' shouted the Principal. 'First thing tomorrow morning, both of you!'

Instead of inhibiting future displays by following them round to the front of the ramshackle building, where the presence of more young people was indicated by an alarmed hubbub, she wandered down the slope to the water and turned right along the bank to investigate another hubbub coming from the direction of the shaded pool downstream. With her customary discretion she approached the pool under the cover of dense

102

foliage. Parting the leaves of a laurel bush, she found herself gazing on the same party she had disturbed on the Upper Field.

They had fled from the afternoon heat to the refreshing delights of this watery retreat, of which her present hiding place gave her a good view. Puddles of lime-coloured sunlight were reflected, quavering, on the undersides of the broad leaves embowering the pool, a kidney-shaped basin about forty feet long and half that in width. For most of its length it was overarched by trees, but at the far end these opened out into a little clearing on the opposite bank. Here bright sunshine was able to fall on the surface of the water, over which a pair of mating dragonflies danced, and on a small, sloping lawn, starred with daisies.

Three of the girls were already splashing about hysterically in the dark water – Alexandra Fellowes in a little red bikini bottom, Priscilla Gibbs in nothing but her long black hair, and Sarah Cummings, whose pert breasts were confined by a white bra and whose loins were hidden under the surface of the pool. At the water's edge stood Lucy Wagstaff in a frilly white blouse, fiddling with the fastening of a long red skirt, the waistband of which had already slipped down at the back over a pair of glossy buttocks. Beside her sat the aloof, auburn-haired beauty Gina Wootton, modestly attired in weekday white shirt and grey skirt. Gina dangled her legs in the cool water.

Mary Muttock's roving eye now came to rest on the striking though diminutive figure of the Lady Honoria Redmayne. From the lawn at the sunny end of the pool a small wooden jetty ran out into the water, and Honoria stood poised on the end of this, encased in gleaming gold. A pity about that ridiculous spiky hairdo, thought the Principal. In due course she would have to be punished for flouting Cunlip traditions and regulations so blatantly.

As Mary Muttock reflected along these lines, the naked Priscilla climbed up on the jetty and shook herself like a dog, showering droplets all over Honoria. The golden aristocrat kept her cool, ignoring the intruder who now usurped her place as centre of attraction. Priscilla stepped on to the sunlit lawn and entered an impressive dance routine which included cartwheels and hand-stands as well as the lewdly undulating stock in trade of traditional

103

striptease performers. In Priscilla's case, of course, there could be no further stripping off and, in this non-commercial context, no ripping off either. Her lithe body glistened with the thousands of water drops still adhering to it, and water streamed from a love tuft which had parted to show the pink line of the central rift. After a few minutes of her energetic demonstration, she stood on the bank, ran her hands up the insides of her thighs, thrust her pelvis forward and pulled open her labia, to the applause of all present except Honoria, who remained motionless, staring out over the pool. The metallic green dragonflies interrupted their ritual of courtship to hover in front of Priscilla. She inserted a finger into her vagina, drew it out and held it up before licking it. Then she turned to present her bum to the audience, and with a neat backward flip effected her re-entry into the water.

As Miss Muttock peeped through the leaves, she saw Honoria ease the resplendent but now no longer dry garment down off one shoulder, and then off the other. Her arms were drawn up through the shoulder straps, releasing a pair of milky white breasts tipped with small, dark nipples. Instinctively looking round before proceeding, the girl peeled the leotard down over the convexity of her white belly, then tugged it over her bottom and the outcurving of her thighs. A small black triangle of pubic hair was revealed. The leotard dropped to the girl's ankles and she stepped out of it, picked it up and tossed it back to the shore.

The Lady Honoria stood there on the jetty, gracing the pool like a piece of polished statuary, uncertain whether to take the plunge. At this instant the bushes on the opposite side were parted, and the white-clad figure of Melanie Winspur emerged into the sunlight. Greeting the other girls with a laugh, she unbuttoned her short tennis dress from top to bottom. It hung open for a moment, and its dazzling whiteness contrasted beautifully with a pale honey-coloured tan which was interrupted at the levels of chest and crotch with bands of lighter flesh. The lower of these bands was adorned with the little flamelike growth of gingery curls which so endeared Melanie to her admirers. Off came the dress, and then the tennis shoes and socks. The naked newcomer stepped carefully into the pool, splashed water on the upper part of her body and lowered herself into it up to her neck.

Honoria Redmayne stretched her arms out horizontally in

front of her, the thumbs touching. She inhaled, rose on her toes and *dove*, as Mary Muttock had mentally conjugated the verb since the days of her transatlantic apprenticeship – *Guess the word just kinda snuck into my vocabulairy*, she would tell herself. The girl entered the water cleanly, but those already in there were unavoidably ruffled and made for her with one accord.

By now, Lucy Wagstaff, on the bank, had completely disencumbered herself of her long skirt and white blouse, and stood fiddling with the fastening at the back of her white lace bra. She knelt and persuaded Gina to help her with this. A pair of well-grown but shapely breasts flowed out of the cups as the tension was eased. Some of the girls in the pool flicked water at her provocatively. Lucy retaliated by getting up and launching herself towards them with deliberate clumsiness, swamping them and causing an uproar of spluttering screams.

Six young ladies, three of them naked and the others nearly so, were now ducking, laughing and lunging at each other with all the noisy, uninhibited energy of youth. Only the taciturn Gina remained on the grassy bank, loosening her skirt and undoing the buttons of her shirt but going no further. Lucy was in hot pursuit of her blonde friend Sarah. With a great onslaught of splashes she chased her away from the others into the part of the pool just below Miss Muttock's concealed station. Her head disappeared beneath the surface, and Sarah, still tantalisingly adorned with her little white bra, screamed out in shocked delight. Lucy re-emerged, her dark hair streaming. She made a grab for her friend's bra, but Sarah eluded her by twisting round. Now Lucy made a lunge with both hands beneath the water, clearly aiming for the submerged crotch. Assisted by the buoyancy, she heaved upwards, bringing the streaming loins, now seen to be unclad, above the surface as the startled Sarah was tipped backwards. Lucy threw herself on top of her, and when the pair finally resumed an upright posture, gasping for breath, they were clinging in a tight embrace. Playful preliminaries completed, they fell silent, engaged beneath the water in intimacies the Principal could imagine but not see.

Her attention was distracted from this charming scene by a disturbance on the far side of the pool. Crashing through the undergrowth like a bull elephant came a male figure, lured

105

thither no doubt by the shrieks of girlish laughter. The figure paused, panting, on the water's edge; it was Joker Jennings.

A bull elephant – Mary Muttock was reminded of her recent dream. Yes, she must have been misled in her interpretation by all that nonsense about leopards. The leopard was a blind. It had stood, symbolically and prophetically, for the shining *leotard* discarded by Honoria Redmayne, sleekest of the big cats even though her mane was reduced to phallic spikes. Surely, this girl was destined to possess the Principal's body and sip her juices. And the uncouth Joker, known to her as a frequent trespasser on Cunlip property, must be the bull elephant foreordained to mate with the mammoth in token of genetic continuity. He it was who would tear his way through the flimsy barrier of her modesty.

To ease his ramping passage, she slipped off her lacy black knickers and hung them on a handy branch of the laurel bush that concealed her. Being wet and heavily stained, she reasoned, their pheromonal scent would entice the rogue elephant to his prey, and those questing tusks would split her asunder.

Joker stood surveying the scene. The girls in the water were now silent, watching him in fascination as he towered above them with a marked bulge in the front of his jeans. He whipped off his T-shirt and trainers, and took an untidy header into the pool. Mary Muttock held her breath as his ragged but powerful crawl carried him towards her.

But what was he thinking of? Perhaps the water had put him off the scent of her knickers, rank though that was. His course was not aimed at her at all, but at Gina, who still sat primly with her feet in the water. Reaching the shore, he grabbed those feet and pulled. Gina was quite taken by surprise. As her bottom was dragged over the grassy rim, her loosened shirt rode up over her hips to become lodged, twisted, round her waist. No undergarment concealed the auburn-fringed cunt, momentarily visible before its immersion. The poor girl splashed and struggled with her adversary, and the front of her unbuttoned shirt parted over her stiffened nipples.

By now the other girls were cheering, urging Joker on to greater efforts and advising his recalcitrant sweetheart to let herself go. Her reluctance to do so was, however, confirmed not only by her furious shrieks, but by the red lines her nails had scored down his chest. Far from relaxing, she was hurling her rigid body this way and that in desperate attempts to free herself from his embrace.

It was Honoria who first realised that the spectacle of this wet rape might not be the best sport the occasion could furnish. 'Come *on*, girls,' she yelled. 'Get him!'

Sarah and Lucy were too tied up with each other to respond to this call, but everyone else, swimming and wading, made straight for Joker and pulled him away from Gina, who lay back in relief and let herself float, rocking up and down in the waves. Alexandra and Melanie seized him by the arms and Priscilla grabbed his hips, while Honoria reached for the buckle of his broad leather belt. Having unfastened it, she drew the belt from its loops and waved it round her head in triumph. Priscilla now undid the button and pulled down the zip. Alexandra managed to bring both his feet to the surface, and held them there so that Priscilla was able with some difficulty to drag the sodden jeans and underpants down to his ankles. But the masterstroke was administered by Honoria, who used the belt she was flourishing to secure both the garments and the ankles they encumbered.

Under the inspired direction of Lady Honoria, Joker was towed across to a shallow place at the far side of the pool and forced to sit on the bottom with the water just reaching up to his neck. The lovebirds Lucy and Sarah were then summoned over to render assistance. Their not disagreeable task was to stand in a close embrace, Lucy with her feet planted on either side of the delinquent's hips and Sarah's immediately behind the lad's buttocks. Joker had to lean back slightly to facilitate this arrangement, supporting his water-lessened weight on his hands, and his head had to be tilted back, the primary effect of which was to bring his nose and mouth tightly up against the cleft that ran from arse to arse as the saturated cuntmounds ground together.

Not surprisingly, the operation also had the secondary effect of bringing his penis to a hard stand, monitored by Honoria as she knelt beside him. 'Come and feel this, girls,' she laughed. 'It's nearly big enough to poke up out of the water.'

One by one her companions accepted the invitation, and Miss

Muttock guessed from the excited upwards thrusts of the youth's face into the crotches actively engaged above him that they were not just feeling but pumping. First it was the turn of the long-legged Alexandra, who bit her lower lip in determination as she worked away for her allocated moment with both hands. When she stood up again, it was evident that only one of those hands had been employed on Joker: the other one was still stuck down the front of her scarlet bikini bottom.

Alexandra was followed by Melanie, who reached her free hand round behind Sarah's legs and placed it beneath Joker's backward-arching neck. In this way she was able to force his nose and mouth even more firmly into the oozing double crotch as she frigged his prick in the cool waters. Only when his spluttering and struggling showed his need for oxygen to be imperative did she desist. 'Your turn now, Prissy,' she said.

Priscilla Gibbs lowered her nakedness into the shallow water. She took a hank of her long black hair, slick and streaming from its immersion, and bent her head forward so that she could use the hair for a purpose Mary Muttock could only conjecture. Her conjectures were confirmed, though, when the tormented youth complained in damply muffled tones that the girl had wound it too tightly round his penis. Afraid that ejaculation was imminent, she withdrew the lock that had now taken the form of a loose-hanging corkscrew, and after briefly squeezing his balls gave way to Honoria, in spite of the fact that the latter had already had her turn.

Honoria flexed her wrist and got down to work. As Miss Muttock watched, leaning forwards agog with her hands supported on her knees, she was not aware that her gauzy dress had been lifted up over her back. But by now her emotional state was such that she evinced no alarm or repugnance when she felt two large, calloused palms alighting on her naked hips, the wiry coarseness of pubic hair rammed against her bottom, and the length of something stout, rigid and hornlike pressing up along the cleft between her sexlips. This, then, was *it*; she ought to have worked it out for herself. No elephant, however roguish, could have savaged her with its tusks – not with both at the same time, not even if it had tried to fork into vagina and rectum simultaneously, as these were too close together in creatures on

108

her rung of the evolutionary ladder. Her feral ravisher had to be a beast with a centrally located weapon: a princely prancing unicorn, an armour-plated rhinoceros with Spanish flies swarming around its piggy eyes, wallowing down to slake its lust at this lecherous watering hole, or even a phallic-snouted wild boar, snuffling and rooting for truffles in the succulent, gamey folds of her flesh.

'*Tusk* me! she sighed.

'At your service, my dear madam,' came the Captain's reply as the swollen tip of his member nudged its way into her moist sheath. His hands slid round from her hips to her belly; he scratched gently among the cunthairs and searched out the growing velvet horn of her clitoris. In he bored, an inch at a time, delving maddeningly. After each firm thrust he withdrew half an inch, gradually but insistently laying waste the whole length of her vagina and stretching it as he swelled even thicker within her tight clutch. The Principal moaned lasciviously but kept her eye on the proceedings of her young charges.

Honoria was tugging at Joker's penis, trying to drag him out from under the girls' genitals just as they quaked in mutual orgasm and collapsed into the water.

'Ouch!' he wailed. 'You're rippin' me friggin' cock off.'

'Push up with your hands,' Honoria told him, 'and let your bum kind of float up. Then, when I pull, I can tow you through the water.'

Joker, in no position to argue, did as he was instructed. This mode of transportation, however, proved rather cumbersome, so Priscilla and Melanie grabbed him by the feet and drew him along behind them at high speed, leaving a wake of sparkling foam. His erection stood up proudly like the superstructure of a battleship, or, when he was towed into the unshaded part of the pool, like the gnomon of a sundial.

All seven girls now cooperated in lifting him, his ankles still secured in his jeans and belt, up over the edge of the bank. Shaking with laughter, they climbed out after him into the sunlight. Sarah and Lucy rolled him on to his stomach and held his shoulders down while Honoria removed the belt and belaboured his buttocks into a network of purple welts. When he was rolled over once more he tried to rear his bum off the ground. His prick, inflated into even angrier tumescence by the belting he had just received, put a lewd idea into Melanie's head, which she communicated to the others. Miss Muttock, her cunt crammed full of the Captain's manhood, guessed what was about to happen.

Put briefly, the idea was that the girls should take it in turns to sit on Joker's rampant cock while the others held him still. First came Prissy Gibbs, who bobbed up and down just twice before giving way to Melanie. The latter administered three such bounces. Alexandra varied the routine slightly by pulling aside the red bikini bottom she still had on, exposing her vulva and letting the elastic snap shut on the victim's organ at the top of each of her four upward heaves. Honoria gave him her fivefold fuck in cool disdain. Lucy Wagstaff made a point of dangling the points of her bouncy boobs above his face six times as she plunged down, skewering herself. Not to be outdone, her bosom chum Sarah inflamed him to even greater heights by unfastening her white bra and inviting Lucy to pinch her nipples into erection as she bucked up and down a full seven times.

The pattern was broken, however, when it came to the pretty Gina's turn. She straddled his loins like the others, but just let the well-oiled gland touch her gaping lips before dismounting. 'You're *never* to stick that thing in me, you downmarket jerk,' she taunted. 'I've heard what you did with that Josie Greene in the showers!' Poor Joker was made to stand facing her as she knelt holding his cock some six inches from her open mouth. Once more Honoria took up the broad leather belt and brought it down resoundingly on his sore behind. As it bit into the flesh, his semen spurted in thick jets straight into the waiting mouth. Immediately, Gina rose from her knees, threw her arms around him and pressed her open lips to his mouth.

But Mary Muttock hardly noticed this final refinement of their passion. As the spunk flew from the youth's cockhead into his sweetheart's mouth, she had felt her own innermost recesses suddenly flooded as the Captain's hot emission gushed into her in a succession of powerful waves which died down only when the viscous fluid was already draining out down her thighs.

'Oh, Tiger!' she gasped, as her whole being shuddered in orgasm. 'That eruption's blown my polar icecaps. Now the

Golden Age can begin in earnest. The leopard shall lie down with the goat, and the Vale of Upchester shall resound to the pipes of Pan. Lead me home, my Captain, and I shall repay the sweet debt of Nature.'

The Captain expressed a hope that this could be a cash transaction. As he withdrew his overspent appendage, the dragonflies successfully consummated their union and the young ladies who had ruffled the surface of the pool prepared for their return to the world of revision and exams.

EIGHT

A RIDE AND A BRIDE

Tuesday morning found the Captain lying on a blanket in front of the Old Lodge. Melanie had slipped inside to make tea, a business he knew to be irksome; the Lodge was not equipped with an electric kettle, and any approach to the cooker and kitchen sink was made noxious by the clutter of unsavoury detritus left there by his predecessor. Rummaging casually through the small canvas bag she had brought with her, he came across an open exercise book which had been thrust into it. He knew what it was, having first investigated its pages the day before, when he had been entertained by the account of their distant view of whoring over at the Palace of Sweethearts. Without removing the diary from the bag, he was able to scan the exposed pages and turn them over to read the continuation before Melanie returned. What he read revived some thrilling recent memories.

Mon, June 4

Even hotter this morning. Put on second-best bikini, one with pink and turquoise diagonal stripes that ties with bows at sides. Cunlip skirt and shirt over that, so looked quite respectable. Pinned hair up on top of head. Put a few books in bag, including diary, and wandered down to Old Lodge.

Captain sunbathing outside again – sent me indoors to make tea. While water was heating on ridiculously slow hotplate I popped upstairs and peeped down through window to see what dirty devil was up to. As I thought! He'd pulled cock out of trunks and had nose in my bag reading diary – probably yesterday's goings-on as I'd left it folded open at that page.

At this point the Captain stopped reading and glanced up at the window. The curtains were drawn. Was Melanie concealed behind them even now, peering down at the victim she had snared in this sly way? He padded across the grass to the open door and was relieved to catch a glimpse of her pottering about in the kitchen. Returning to his place in the sun, he was careful to position himself between the bag and the Lodge before he continued with his reading of the latest entry.

When I took tea out to him [*the diary went on*] he was sitting there all innocent except he hadn't had time to stick dick back in trunks. I grabbed it, but he said to wait till later, and forced it down out of sight.

Pricked my ears up when he asked if Derrick used to take me on his bike.

ME: Derrick used to *take* me everywhere, he was that ready for it. At least, he was always ready as long as he didn't think there was anyone watching. Not much of a public performer, Derrick. Not like Joker and Heini.

CAPTAIN: Fancy a bit of a spin right now?

ME: Well, I'm supposed to be revising British Constitution, but it wouldn't do me much harm to get some powerful machinery between my legs again. Where can we go?

CAPTAIN: Oh, not very far – that's not the point. Round the lanes, and then perhaps we'll burn a bit of rubber out on the Upchester bypass. Just a joy ride.

Anyway, we went indoors and he zipped himself into his leathers – must have been like a sauna inside them, but it's cooler once you get moving of course. Took his camera with him and found spare helmet for me. Both helmets shiny black, just like Derrick's. We went round side of Lodge to bike. He spun back wheel and got aerosol can out of pannier (?) to squirt foaming white stuff called 'lube' on chain. Told him he could do that to me later, without using can. Noticed his Suzuki's quite a bit different from D's Yamaha – not so clean for one thing. He fixed what he said was a French number-plate over his yellow one, 'as a precaution'.

Captain stowed lube and camera in pannier and made me take off skirt so I could get leg over. Knowing how chilly it can be, I pulled socks right up over knees. Helmets on – he helped me buckle mine under chin. Then he got on bike and started it. Made me climb up behind him and told me to pinch his leg twice if I wanted to stop.

Slowly along rough track, then turned left into lane. Accelerated so hard he nearly left me behind. Had to shove myself forward, wedging crotch up against his bum. Even then the wind seemed to cut up inside bikini bottom. Squashed myself tight against his back. Shirt ballooned out behind me and started flapping with noise like helicopter, so undid buttons and managed to get it off without losing it. Tied sleeves round neck and let it stream out behind.

Local yokel cycling up straight stretch of lane towards us. I leaned right back and to left to give him something to see but gave him more than I bargained for – wind got inside bikini top and peeled it sideways so left tit popped out. When I looked round, yokel sitting on road scratching head, with bike lying beside him.

Captain slowed down for sharp bend. I reached behind me and unfastened top. Took it right off and tied strings round neck, along with shirt. Wind felt like needles pricking nipples when he got up speed again, so hugged up against his back and used both hands round front to hang on to love gun through soft leather. It stiffened up as he swung out into Upchester road.

Slowed down as we passed petrol station. No one in sight. Did U-turn, coasted into forecourt and pulled up at pump. Must be only garage in these parts without self-service – hardly any garages here, in fact, so people have to use it anyway and then get their windscreens cleaned and feel they have to give tip. Joker explained all that to me once. Anyway, Joker came out of office now in greasy overalls. Thought Captain was Derrick at first, and made lewd comment, quite uncalled for. Winked at me. Front of bike was just ahead of pump. Before he stuck nozzle in tank, Joker pointed it at my twat. I pulled bikini bottom to side and held myself open, telling him to 'fill her up'. Captain heard and twisted head round, but I'd covered up by then. Not that I could cover my boobs, of course.

Back into lanes with full tank. Pulled up by overgrown five-barred gate – he made me get off and wade through long dank grass and cow parsley to open it. Drove into field and stopped engine. He wheeled bike over flat piece of stone big enough to take weight, and put it on its centre stand as he called it.

When he took off his helmet and got camera out I knew at once what he wanted, and started posing with Suzuki. Warned me about not touching hot parts – told him in that case he'd better cool off himself.

CAPTAIN: Talking of cooling hot parts, I used to cycle to work on a push-bike. One really raw morning there were two young nurses riding side by side in front of me in their little caps and blue cloaks. We came to some red lights, and they got separated from each other in the traffic. I pulled up beside one of them and she must have thought I was her mate. Without looking at me, she pulled the hem of her skirt down. 'A bit cold on the cunt this morning, innit?' she said. 'I wouldn't know, madam,' I answered. 'Would you like me to, er, *chafe* it?'

ME: What did she say to that?

CAPTAIN: She said, 'I'd like you to *stuff* it, buster!' So I told her I'd got just the thing to do that with. 'Don't bother,' she said, 'I've got one of those already. Snipped it off the last punter tried to mess with me.' Then the lights went green, and probably my face too, and I never saw her again.

While he told this story he'd been taking a few snaps of me standing in front of bike in bikini bottom and helmet, some with visor up and some down. Then got me to put the little top on and pull bottom down round thighs. Shots of bum and pussy. Next he had to have me with bikini right off but wearing white shirt – kept helmet on all the time. Had socks pulled up for these – in others he preferred them rolled down to ankles. Sodding perfectionist, that's what he is! Instead of using bike as background, sort of draped me over it backwards with head hanging down and shirt turned back over face, clear of tits. Took his big leather glove (gauntlet?) off and laid it high up on right thigh as I sprawled back over saddle. Said it was meant to suggest 'ghost grope'. For last pix had me nude, except for footwear and helmet of course. I sat with head down and hands on handlebars as if riding. Then a couple of clever shots of me standing alongside and lifting leg to get on. Rather painful holding leg up for him to get proper focus on twat. After first one I had to play with myself a bit to get juices running and lips all puffy. Up with leg again, and he held it there for me while I pulled myself wide open. Agony when he stepped back to take picture, but two together ought to make nice contrast.

Then he opened one of panniers and took out folding tripod. Set it up beside bike – said he wanted to try one with self-timer. For this I took helmet off, so I could straddle bike, leaning right forward with chest on tank (ugh! metal really cold after filling it up!) and face up over dials in front of handlebars. Captain unzipped and cock jumped out looking very pale against black leather, though knob at end quickly got dark purple when he made me reach down with hand to stroke it.

'Ready!' he yelled. 'Stick your bum up!'

He pressed something on camera and a red light started flashing. 'Twelve seconds to blast-off!' he shouted, and jumped up on saddle behind me. Front wheel lifted up alarmingly as bike rocked back on stand. I pushed down on footrests to lift bum like he said, and felt tip of cock all hot between cheeks. Camera clicked, and he slid into cunt. Feel of leather against skin as he started screwing me. But I had other ideas and made him pull out. He seemed a bit hesitant at first when I explained what I wanted, but was desperate for a fuck and couldn't refuse.

He stowed camera, tripod and all my things in panniers, all except my helmet which he clipped on hook at side of bike. Then pushed bike down off stand, which sprang up with loud clunk. Bike seemed quite a bit lower now. Captain put on his own helmet and mounted, his cock still standing up out of leather fly. Turned key and pressed button on right handlebar to start engine. How I love that sexy roar! Now he had to keep both feet firmly on ground and hold machine upright while yours truly, in nothing but shoes and socks, lifted a leg right up and over tank. Got stuck halfway, with wet cuntleaves wedged open on icy tank. He helped by holding my sides and lifting me up with bike wobbling like the clappers till I was astride tank facing him. Then his hands went back to handlebars to steady us. Somehow I got both feet up on saddle (pillion?) behind him, so thighs were wide apart on either side of his hips. With arms round his neck I managed to lift bottom up from tank and sink down on his big dick. Felt it tear its way right up to bellybutton level or thereabouts.

I tried to keep head to one side over his shoulder so he could see where we were going. This was it! Bike swayed scarily as he lifted left foot to work pedal. Moved forward jerkily and did very slow and dodgy turn in long grass. Then out on to lane and up through gears, right up to sixth. Dust and little insects stung into my bare back like needles – bigger bugs like bullets. Though today was hotter than ever, wind seemed Arctic. Bored into my arsehole and cut up between saddle and bum as far as where Captain was plugging me. Because I couldn't see where we were going, every bend was terrifying and every bump nearly jumped me off his fat spike, but I clung on with him getting bigger and bigger inside me.

We hit a humpback bridge, and this time he really came right out of me, but amazingly I landed bang on target again. His prick stabbed in with such force it almost killed me, but damage might have been worse if it had missed opening. Not many people about on lanes, but every now and then we passed gobsmacked old gaffers, shocked pram pushers and hooting schoolkids who'd scuttled to side of road to get out of way. Of course, they couldn't see much of my rude parts, but they could certainly tell what we were up to. When we roared past pub on village green all heads turned in astonishment, spilling beer. But most exciting hazard was level crossing. Just as we went shuddering over it I felt his stuff spouting inside me – he threw head back howling and opened throttle wide as kind of reflex action. Lucky not to swerve right off road. Spunk started oozing out and running down inside of my bum cheeks – wind made it cold at once. All slimy with spillage every time my bottom bounced down far enough to touch place where saddle joins tank.

Thought Captain must have had enough by now, but no, this kind of joy riding seemed to be going to his head. He turned into a main road, and as we picked up speed he sort of accelerated into me and swelled up in another hard-on. Came to a roundabout. Went right round it twice, leaning over at forty-five degrees with him whooping at top of voice and me terrified, gripping his prick with my cunt muscles as if that would stop me falling off. Then out on Upchester bypass – really embarrassing for me when we overtook lorries, because I was left staring back at drivers who'd been able to look right down into lap as we passed.

Suddenly that awful wailing noise, and I could see the flashing blue lights emerging from hiding place by roundabout. What was I going to do without a stitch on me? Worked out story about Captain rescuing me from roadside rapist, but worried Captain might say something different. Then I realised he didn't mean to stop – this was going to be one of those high-speed chases.

Leaned back to relish grim expression on his face and he took advantage of move to stoop right over, pinning me down with back arched over tank and head on handlebars, to reduce wind resistance. My hair blew up across his visor. I couldn't see where we were going, of course, and neither could he for a moment. And in that moment we zoomed straight over top of another roundabout, flying on autopilot. He sat up straight – my hair came away from visor and streamed out over his shoulder again. Blue lights out of sight, hidden behind shrubs on roundabout – still hadn't appeared when we braked hard and went right round third roundabout to go back way we'd come. Vroom! Guys in police car must have been really fazed as we shot past them on other side of dual carriageway, but saw them do tricky U-turn over central strip and then they were suddenly much closer, dead keen to get an eyeful of me and maybe number of bike.

Back at middle roundabout Captain turned off on smaller road. Soon came to a lot of cars waiting at one of those temporary lights where half the road was being dug up and traffic from both directions had to take it in turns. We sneaked up on inside of line of cars and straight on over red light, slipping past traffic coming other way. Everyone hooting us, you bet! Then deep into maze of narrow lanes and high hedges.

On outskirts of some village we skidded through a gateway and coasted in through open door of a barn. Captain lifted me off his ramrod, which was still as stiff as – well, as a ramrod. He pulled off his helmet, and said they must have been after us because I was committing an offence by not wearing mine. We dismounted and I helped him to close heavy old door.

First he took off French numberplate, then chased me up rickety ladder to hayloft. Dusty, musty smell with golden specks swimming in rays of sunlight that came in through cracks between boards, just like in movies about sex in haylofts. But I wouldn't lie down on that dirty, prickly hay. Just stood leaning back with legs apart, knees bent and hips shoved forward. Captain peeled off leather trousers for this one, but I loved the feel of his jacket with its cold studs and zips rubbing against my belly and tits as he skewered me. Once his knob was in he lifted me up and I wrapped my legs round him. Thought he'd never have the strength to hold me up like that long enough, but he only had to shake me a few times before he came. Not quite what I wanted, so I made him kneel down as I stood with legs open and got him to lick me till I exploded.

Everything a bit of an anticlimax after that. Made ourselves respectable as far as we could – I put on shirt, helmet and bikini bottom – and drove quite slowly back to Cunlip with me riding pillion. No sign of the Law. In Lodge, Captain changed into shorts and T-shirt and washed my back.

It's getting late now, so can't go into more detail, but when he was walking me back to college we ran into Darcy and Susie and I had this Great Idea. But I do hope Captain isn't getting hung up on me. He's got to realise I like a bit of fun with him but he's not exactly my type or age group. How can I break this to him tactfully?

The Captain had just finished reading these pages when Melanie, who had been gone for ages, came out with two mugs of tea. She looked at him rather strangely, he thought, before sitting down beside him. Had she seen him from the upstairs window after all? It now seemed obvious that she had brought the diary here again because she meant him to read it, and especially that last part. Well, if she wanted to say anything he would find a

119

suitable response, but he had no intention of raising the matter himself.

An undeniable coolness hung over them as they drank their tea. Melanie sensed that he was aware of this, and said she was preoccupied on account of a French exam she was taking that very morning. After ten minutes of desultory chat as they sat there on the grass she stood up, smoothed the front of her dress down and said she would do her best to see him that afternoon. The Captain wished her luck in the exam, and made her stoop so that he could kiss her cheek while reaching a hand up to feel her knickerless bottom, which was cool, and her pussy, which was dry. Then she was off, turning once at the plank bridge, where she blew him a kiss and lifted her skirt, flashing her gingery tuft at him in valediction.

The Captain was left feeling slightly depressed, but he consoled himself with the thought that this unwelcome development in Melanie's attitude was probably the effect of exam nerves. And girls of that age were notoriously fickle, he generalised. All right, she had implied that she didn't fancy him because of his age and appearance. But if the passion of her lovemaking had all been simulated, the simulation was quite good enough for him, so what the hell? In any case, he had no wish to become emotionally involved with a young lady of decidedly sluttish disposition. He was only too familiar with the hazards of sentimental attachment to girls who insisted on holding themselves available for the pleasures they wished to share with all their youthful contemporaries. Moreover, when it came to appreciation of hard rock and kindred cultural phenomena, he could hardly compete and had no wish to try. Even in the field of Hard Cock his achievements didn't always rise to the standard of yesterday's performance. And apart from all this, he had to admit that every time he caught a glimpse of the haughty Gina, or heard her name mentioned, he felt the unmistakable pangs of jealousy which indicated that, if he was falling in love, this was the direction in which he was falling.

Such considerations soon restored the Captain to his usual level of buoyancy, and he felt delicious stirrings in his loins as he reviewed those events of the previous day that Melanie had been unable to record in fuller detail. On their return to the

Lodge he had made her lie down naked on her front in this same spot, and had brought a bowl of warm water, soap, a sponge and a towel out from the Lodge. The poor girl's back was in a state only to be understood by the analogy of what happened to the visor of his helmet during a fast drive over these lanes in the insect-ridden height of summer. It was splattered with green, yellow and red. In a few places, where more substantial objects or possibly creatures had made their impact, the red seemed to be her own blood rather than theirs.

Tenderly he washed away this leprous incrustation and the slight coating of greyish dirt beneath it. More effort was required to shift a few stripes of black grease on her calves where they had touched parts of the machine – she was lucky to have escaped burning. As the task approached completion, his attention wandered to the hemispheres of her bottom and the dark rift curving down between them.

He had slipped off his T-shirt and shorts and stretched out his body along her back, his legs astride hers, holding them in a firm but gentle grip. Lazily he licked her cheek. His penis rested comfortably between the soft buttocks, and slowly lengthened until the sensitive tip ran into hair; at the touch of this it swelled and pressed against dampness. Lifting one foot, he used it to lever Melanie's ankles apart so that he was able to force both his legs in between hers. His fingertips ran up the outsides of her thighs, over her hips and into the moist armpits. She stirred, and he slipped his hands under her flattened breasts, rubbing the nipples into prominence.

The Captain had clenched his teeth and buttocks, worming his way up into a vagina that fell open at his prompting. Her ear flushed crimson as he nibbled the lobe. Her cunt began to throb, exerting a recurrent suction upon his knob. With one accord and without losing their intimate contact, they rolled over on their right sides, the Captain's left thigh clamped between both of Melanie's. He lifted her left knee to give more play to his thrusting. Using the fingers and thumb of his right hand to play with her taut left nipple, he placed his other palm flat on the furry pad of her pubis and rolled it with a circular pressure against the bone. In response, the hair stood stiffly on end. The muscles of her thighs and stomach tensed as he squirted a thin,

121

continuous stream into her depths. It felt more like pissing than fucking – the relief was overwhelming.

After all their excitement, they had dozed a little (or so Melanie had claimed) in each other's arms. Then they had dressed, and he accompanied her for part of the way back to the college, not by the direct route up the avenue but through the woods and round the wall of the Secret Garden. Just before the point where the wall emerged from the coolness of the wooded slope into the sunlight that bathed the lower field and the Palace of Sweethearts, subdued whispers in the undergrowth off to their right had caused them to pause in their tracks. With great caution they edged their way through bushes and tall weeds until they found themselves peering into a small clearing, carpeted with pine needles. Generations of enamoured girls (and before them their predecessors, the 'moral degenerates') had supposed this to be their own private love nest.

On this occasion, however, the occupants were not a girlish couple but, the Captain decided after a second look, a boy and a girl. The boy, who appeared from his slight figure and girlish features to be no older than sixteen, had taken off his shirt, or (more probably) had let his girlfriend take it off, leaving him in faded jeans torn at the knees. The Captain recognised this girl, who was identified by Melanie as the Susie Freemantle he had already encountered, the friend of the wanton Nikki. She wore the usual Cunlip blue dress, and apart from a couple of open buttons her clothing had hardly been interfered with as yet. This young couple sat side by side in a rather awkward embrace, making a mess of kissing with wet but closed lips.

'That's Darcy O'Flammery,' Melanie whispered. 'Amazingly immature. They say he's being privately educated at home, whatever that involves. Spends a lot of time hanging about the grounds, just watching but not really understanding what's going on. First time I've seen him actually *touching* a girl. Let's see how far he gets – chances are he won't make first base with this Susie.'

The Captain was always keen to enjoy the manifestations of fresh young love as a spectator. His heart began to pound as Darcy pulled back from his partner and gazed, calflike, into her eyes. 'I love you, Susie,' the lad sighed, in well-spoken and surprisingly high-pitched accents without a trace of the brogue the Captain was half expecting. 'I want to – you know – stroke and kiss your legs.'

Susie sat back, leaning against a tree. She raised her left knee and stretched her right leg out straight; then she drew up the hem of her dress to the tops of her thighs, and the navy V of her knickers came into view. Kneeling by her right hip and trembling with excitement, her novice lover trailed timid fingertips up the inside of the leg nearest to him. Before he reached the hem of her dress he lingered, fondled the flesh of the inner thigh and descended again to squeeze the knee. His next move was to reach across to caress the soft underside of her left thigh, relishing the way it quivered when he patted it. During this part of the operation he lowered his mouth to the nearer thigh. Some saliva escaped and trickled down the skin. He slid his lips slowly upwards, leaving a wet trail as he went. Both hands now grasped her hips beneath the dress. Susie squirmed.

'That's enough of that,' she said, straightening her left leg and pulling her hem down. 'Now it's my turn. Lie down.'

Darcy did as he was told. She straddled his thighs and leaned forward to explore his bellybutton with the point of her tongue. She kissed the whole expanse of his firm white tummy, then moved up to lavish loving attention on his nipples. 'Look,' she giggled, 'they're sort of shrivelling up and getting all hard and pointed.'

This triggered a recent memory, and the Captain asked Melanie if Susie hadn't profited from Miss MacDonald's Physical Development classes.

'No,' she replied. 'Not all the lowest classes get it, though the MacDonald would like to change that. But in any case, they say the Freemantles won't let their Susie attend anything of that kind. Don't want her to get corrupted or start getting the wrong ideas.'

It looked as if the young O'Flammery was becoming aroused, and not just in his nipples. His loins were twitching restlessly between Susie's knees, and his cheeks were flushed. 'I want to – to *do* something,' he murmured thickly.

'What sort of thing?'

'Something rude.'

'Well, that depends,' the girl answered. 'You know I've told you what's out of bounds.'

Darcy bit his lip and took a breath before proceeding. 'I want to look at your bottom. And touch it.'

Evidently relieved, Susie dismounted, pulled her hem down and stretched out on her stomach, using Darcy's discarded shirt as a pillow for her face. Then she reached behind her and lifted the back of the dress up over the curve of her buttocks, before easing the knickers down to the tops of her thighs so that those curves were exposed in their resplendent white loveliness. Darcy hovered, fascinated, but unsure how best to glut himself on this unlooked-for feast.

First he prodded timidly, enjoying the rubbery coolness of those soft cushions and watching them quiver to his touch. On each buttock he then planted a restrained kiss. It was the Captain's impression that the nature of these caresses was determined by a mixture of rising lust and extreme reserve – for Darcy, the concept of *rudeness* which had been drummed into him was one that drew no line between the dark mysteries of sexual functions and the mundane familiarity of lavatorial ones.

'Take your jeans off,' Susie suggested.

Darcy complied, taking care not to let her catch sight of the tall erection that stretched the front of his emerald green Y-fronts, on which a damp patch had started to spread at the most extended point. She indicated that he should lie down on his tummy beside her, but facing the other way so that their faces were level with each other's behinds. She peeled his pants down over his buttocks and patted them reassuringly. Her handling of Darcy now proceeded with rather less inhibition than his of her, although in the eyes of the hidden onlookers it still fell far short of abandoned lasciviousness. With her palms flat on the cheeks, she pulled them aside to ventilate the cleavage between them, and closely inspected the pink orifice thus revealed. This she touched gently, and the boy's buttocks closed in scandalised reaction over her intrusive finger. And yet, as horror gave way to desire, his own fingers began to stroke their way down through Susie's cleft. Her thighs fell open, and the hand moved straight down to her sex pouch.

The Captain gasped, and as he gasped an insect flew into his mouth, causing him to cough. The lovers looked up in alarm. Melanie took his hand and led him boldly forward as if they had just happened to be strolling through the woods and had stumbled upon this amorous scene by accident.

'What do you two think you're up to?' she demanded, affecting a tone of shocked authority which made the Captain wonder if some kind of prefectorial system operated in the college. Was Melanie perhaps Head Girl? Did she enjoy delegated disciplinary powers? While these questions exercised him, the bashful couple had covered their exposed parts and risen to their feet, shaking and covered in confusion.

Susie was first to speak. 'Please, Melanie,' she mumbled, 'we were just having a bit of fun. Darcy's my boyfriend. I wanted to make him rape me, just to see what it would feel like.'

Melanie pretended to be shocked, and asked Darcy for his version of events.

'That's right, miss,' he said, apparently even less sure of her status than the Captain was. 'We wanted to see what it would be like to – you know.'

'To what?'

'You know – to commit adultery.'

'What exactly d'you mean by that?' asked Melanie, puzzled.

'Well, you know. We sort of wanted to play about a bit and, you know – do what grown-ups do. Adults.'

The Captain held back, an intrigued bystander, as Melanie demonstrated her remarkable improvisational skills. 'And you were going to let him do that to you, Susie – let him defile your body?'

Susie hesitated, her eyes downcast. 'I didn't want him to go all the way.'

'The whole hog?'

'That's right, the whole hog. I don't want to do that till I get married.'

'Now listen, you two.' The older girl was laying down the law. 'What we call petting is one thing – what we call *heavy* petting is quite another. Darcy, don't you be interfering with her again or I'll warn the Principal you've been trespassing and she'll get the Vice Janitor here' – she pointed at the Captain – 'to throw you out by the scruff of your neck.'

Stung into relative eloquence by this threat, Darcy protested. 'But that's not fair! We're sweethearts.'

'It's like that, is it? Well, in that case it sounds as if we must arrange something for you in the Palace of Sweethearts. Yes, we'll have a wedding, and then no one'll mind if you go the whole hog.'

'Oh, come on,' objected Susie, 'you can't have a wedding any old where like that. It wouldn't be legal.'

'Not in the world outside. But the law lets people have special emergency marriages in places like ships and prisons, just to get them by till they can make proper arrangements later. Anyone can do it, as long as the couple take their vows in front of witnesses. I know that from British Constitution. I'll try to fix it up before the end of the week, so poor old Darcy there won't get too heavy-bollocked.'

'Oh yes. Can I have Nikki as a bridesmaid?'

Melanie said this would be a good idea, and promised to liaise with Nikki about the practical side of things – the costumes and so on. The Captain had little doubt that this wedding would actually materialise. He understood by now that Melanie manipulated a mafia of minions whose mission in this microcosmic society was to make her dreams come true.

Darcy glanced at his watch. He gave Susie a shy peck on the cheek and shuffled off into the undergrowth. His dreams too were on the verge of being realised, and he seemed to be rather at a loss as to how he should comport himself. Melanie also had to go. She explained she had been promised some last-minute extra tuition from Miss MacDonald and hurried away, leaving the Captain with Susie. Since the latter was now in a state of embarrassed confusion and looking for an excuse for her own immediate departure, he hastened to put her at her ease by grinning and winking at her.

'Don't be put off by big words like Vice Janitor,' he said. 'I'm just a friend of Melanie's.'

'You're going steady? I thought she was with that Derrick.'

He tried to make it seem that he had ousted the objectionable youth without actually relinquishing his freedom to consort with whomever he fancied. This was a necessary preliminary to taking the pretty teenager in his arms and introducing her to a rather more advanced osculatory technique than she had experienced from Darcy's scarcely opening lips.

Moral conflict now surged up within his breast. He would have loved to gain possession of such engaging freshness by seduction or force. But in Melanie's eyes and her own, Susie was now affianced to Darcy, and he had no intention of upsetting that promising applecart. He contented himself, therefore, with placing one hand on her little bottom and squeezing her to him so that his cock, now rehardened to its old vigour, dug into her stomach. Susie gave no signs of realising what this source of discomfort could be. His other hand came to rest lightly over one of her newly springing breasts. She looked up at him with pleading eyes as the hand moved across and insinuated itself into the still unbuttoned opening in the front of her dress.

In the distance a handbell had rung out. Disengaging herself from the Captain's embrace, Susie had given him a delightful smile and excused herself before running off into the bushes.

Altogether it had been a pretty satisfactory day, the Captain told himself. His recollections, combined with the voluptuous influence of the midday sun, had brought him to a condition of high tumescence as he lay sprawled on the blanket, but he decided to save his powers until later. He had a date with Melanie that afternoon.

NINE

FREE FOR ALL

Two days later the weather had broken and it was raining heavily. Having used her TV monitors to check on the girls' whereabouts, Mary Muttock slipped up the stairs of the dormitory wing and returned to her study with the yellow exercise book. The approach to her outer door was overlooked (*guarded* would be too strong a word) by a cubicle crammed with antiquated office equipment. This was the kennel of that somnolent old body known as Grote, or 'the Bursar', whose function was to act as receptionist, telephonist, secretary and dogsbody to the Principal. Grote's gender and sexual orientation were indeterminate, or had long been forgotten even by those few who might have had occasion to know them. The bursar was thought to be a cousin of the dying janitor, and both were supposedly descended from illegitimate offspring of Sir Julius Cunlip himself. The college had inherited them, it was believed, from the old asylum, but rumour was vague and unreliable on the question of whether Snotty Grotty, to use the Cunlip girls' nickname, had haunted those grim corridors as an inmate, a warder or a doctor. The forbidding, not to say grotesque appearance of the bursar, who was in fact no more lethal than a neutered and toothless Rottweiler, made this ancient and marginally animate fixture of the college an ideal Cerberus. It could be said with truth, and in more than one sense, that hardly anyone penetrated Miss Muttock's sanctum without the knowledge and approval of Grote, who slept almost incessantly but always with at least one eye open.

As usual on these occasions, before locking herself into her study the Principal ordered Grote to divert any visitors or phone calls until further notice. To her surprise, the bursar reported a laconic message from Mr Hardbuckle, alerting her to the likelihood of imminent 'routine investigations'. Settled at her desk at last, bottle and glass to hand, she scanned Melanie's entry for Monday, and wondered whether it was the motorcycling incident that had prompted the interest to which the Deputy Chief Constable's warning referred. Then she turned the page and read on.

Got wind of some more whoring planned by Mags and that lot down at Palace of Sweethearts at 3.45 this afternoon, so picked up Captain as promised and took him straight there. Very close and sticky – clouds starting to build up, but still the right sort of weather for fun in the open air. Arrived in good time. Let ourselves in and waited. Captain showed me lots of spyholes he had made in shutters. A good thing veranda doesn't go right to end of pavilion – this means there's a window looking right down length of boardwalk. It was in shutter on this window he'd made most of his holes. Also in window at far end, with view of wall where Mags's tarts usually take their blokes.

Noticed floorboards very rough and splintery, presumably from spikes of running shoes. Will have to bring lots of rugs, blankets and extra cushions for Wedding. And candles of course, plenty of candles. Pity about reek of stale sweat. Must get shutters taken down and windows left open Thursday morning, and hope for best. Organisation already under way – have got Cathy and her friend Heini Hintenburger heavily involved in it. My only worry's that they're so heavily involved in each other they may forget they've only got two days to have everything organised. Got to be big surprise for Captain. Nikki Culpepper also going to help. They're all going down tonight to see what's needed and get things started. Wedding has to be Thursday because Darcy says he has choir practice Friday evenings. Let's hope his voice doesn't break!

While waiting, Captain said he was surprised Cunlip girls didn't get pregnant or catch things in this day and age. Think he was a bit worried in case he'd picked something up since being here. Explained how the MacDonald has supply of pills for girls who want them.

CAPTAIN: And the ones who don't want it?

ME: She keeps track of everyone's cycle and makes sure

she doctors their food on the right days. You won't find girls with heavy periods here. They all wonder why they have such a bad time when they go home for the hols.

CAPTAIN: That explains a lot. You'd expect a place like this to be littered with condoms, wouldn't you? But what about safe sex? If you ask me, it looks like a bit of a fool's paradise.

ME: I know. But we're a very closed community here. Most of the girls only fuck each other.

CAPTAIN: Dammit, you say that and yet here we are waiting to watch them being fucked by a gang of local studs. Could be lethal.

ME: Those boys are innocent. They get all they need here. Never need to go near the Upchester talent – much cheaper at Cunlip. Or free, even. No, you're the real danger right now.

CAPTAIN: Not to worry. I was living like a monk for quite a time before I arrived on this scene. Wouldn't let anyone lay a finger on me. And I had a proper test and checkup before I – you know, at my last place.

Had to stop chatting because clatter of shoes on boards of veranda announced that girls were arriving. We peeped through holes to see who'd come – more or less same as last time. Carla wasn't there. I think she must have been doing geography exam. Mags had her mate Wendy Mount puffing and sweating with her, and dear old Emily, who fancies Anne Amory, had taken advantage of Carla's exam to tag along with her little chum.

Wendy had brought a little broom and went round corner to sweep grass. Obviously cut out to be quite a high-class brothel keeper. Girls all wearing Cunlip outfits, but some had games bags with glam-rags to change into. I recognised what Emily got out – one of the costumes we made a couple of years ago for that French farce we weren't allowed to put on. Wondered how Em would manage to put bodice on now. She's a really lovely girl, but she's got quite a bit more flesh on her than when she was still sweet sixteen.

Well, she dropped her grey skirt and knickers and stepped into skirt of costume, which fitted quite easily, tying with tape

130

at waist. I'd forgotten how gorgeous outfit was. Skirt white silk, ankle length and very full. Took off her tie and shirt, and paraded proudly with those firm round boobs shining white in the sunlight and nipples so stiff they cast long shadows on skin.

Then she got Anne to unbutton her own shirt and take it off. She's got rather nice tits too, considering she's not seventeen yet – expect they get a lot of attention from her Carla! It was Anne who had to put on top part of the costume, a sort of tight-fitting sleeveless bodice, very pretty, which Em made her leave open at front. Then she took off shoes, socks, knickers and skirt. Through peepholes we had close-up views of her slim but nicely shaped legs and lovely little bottom, its own kind of white silkiness contrasting with the real white silk of the top she was wearing. And Captain gasped when she turned round and we saw the tiny triangle of blonde fur, too fair and fine to hide the pretty slit of her snatch. As final touches, Emily got a dainty white parasol out of her bag and Anne put on her straw boater, and they stood there arm in arm waiting for the customers to roll up.

That tired-eyed slut Helen hadn't brought anything special to wear. Suppose it was quite bold of her to be doing it again after what happened here other day. Everyone says she and Carla got a right muttocking! They yelled out so much Snotty Grotty came bumbling into study to see what was up. Today she'd come in just her navy knickers and white vest – all she did now was take the vest off and roll the knickers into a sort of G-string, very low round the hips and disappearing into the crease of her bum. She kept her socks and trainers on, which gave her thin legs a rather delicate look, kind of fragile. Got her teddy bear out of bag and took up position on corner of veranda so she'd be able to spy on action out there on swept grass – stood with weight on one foot, sucking thumb, holding teddy by foot in other hand. Reminded me of *Lolita* the MacDonald lent me last year, although Helen's really sixteen of course.

Celia's seventeen, quite tall and slightly on the thin side. When she undid front of dress saw she already had on red boob tube and black hot pants, same as on Sunday. Something a bit stiff about way she walks – can't help wondering if being victim of gangbang has anything to do with it. Anyhow, it doesn't seem to have put her off the so-called stronger sex.

Young Nikki peeled her dress off. Not a stitch on underneath it, but she had two yellow chiffon scarves in her bag. Rolled one to make it small, and tied it round her flattish chest – other one round narrow hips. Her bottom was completely bare and cunt just hidden behind point of scarf hanging down in front. Nikki was standing really close to my peephole. Funny feeling – she was so close I could have touched her if wall of Palace not there between us. Could see every detail, every little hair on forearms, every freckle and mole on back. Slightly hollow curve on nearest cheek of bottom when she shifted from one foot to other made me want to slide palm of hand over it and trail finger down crack of bum. How I envied the yellow chiffon hugging that delicious skin!

Whores lined up on veranda ready, but no sign of customers. Wendy spoke to Emily and Anne, and they went off hand in hand round corner and settled down on smooth grass. But they weren't doing much, just peering into each other's eyes and waiting.

On dot of 3.45 blokes started to show up – not exactly crawling out of woodwork, but out of woods. Popped out at different places, but got together as they crossed Lower Field. Quite menacing, chewing away in leather jackets with hands in pockets of jeans, but sat down good as gold in front of pavilion. Wendy made little speech. Hard at first for her to make herself heard – guys hooting and telling her to 'get 'em off'. She shut them up by opening front of shirt and yanking one of her great knockers out of bra. Jiggled it about a bit then held up hand and called for hush.

WENDY: Thank you, gentlemen, thank you very much. Now, today we have a little surprise for you.

YOUTH WITH ACNE: You're going to give us a belly dance.

WENDY: Just listen, will you. Mags here is the oldest student in this college. Today's her birthday – she's nineteen.

YOUTH WITH SHADES: Congratulations, you fucking old cow!

Others shut him up and began singing 'Happy Birthday', but broke down after a couple of lines.

WENDY: Listen, will you. To celebrate her birthday we're laying on a special live show to warm you up. Absolutely free. And after that, when we start trade, all proceeds go to Mags's birthday fund. OK, then, gentlemen. I'd like you all to step round the corner to be entertained by the very lovely Emily and her delightful partner, the bashful but, er, *naughty* Anne.

Boys trooped round side of Palace and tarts followed them. Me and Captain moved to spyholes in end window. He'd made them one above other, so he was able to sit on chair with me on lap. He had shorts down round ankles and lifted my dress up so I straddled his thighs with bare quim. Stiff cock stretched up my back. He held me by tits and fingered them through dress. Lads and lasses sat on grass to watch fun.

Wendy switched on Sony she'd brought. Instead of usual rock or C & W, one of those schmaltzy (spelling?), old-fashioned Viennese waltzes with silvery swooning violins and a tenor warbling away in German. Anne and Emily stood up and blew kisses to audience. Anne took off boater and fanned it about in front of fanny. Em stopped twirling her parasol, closed it and started poking at Anne's crotch with point while Anne used boater as shield. After messing about like that for a bit, in time with music, they chucked the things away. Em put one hand round Anne's waist and held her other hand stuck out as if they were going to dance. Anne had a hand on back of Em's neck and they put their cheeks together.

Grass not much of a dance floor, but didn't matter because they didn't actually dance, just stood there snogging more and more passionately and moving their bodies about to sort of *mime* waltzing, sometimes turning round where they stood but mostly facing audience to give good view. Em took lead. Kept rubbing up against partner and bending her over backwards so her twat was stuck forward with the lips open. Em would shove one of her lovely round thighs against it so that silk of skirt was kissing Anne's cunt.

Captain's hand had undone some of my buttons and was

wandering round inside front of dress. Found a nipple and started pinching it and pulling it out like tag of hard leather. Other hand crept up thigh under skirt and did same to clit. Felt head of his cock creeping up my back.

Music ended and girls got down on swept patch of grass. Just lay there at first smiling naughtily at each other. Anne knelt up with front hanging open to show her nice tits, uncovered Emily's bare bum and stroked it. Lots of wolf whistles when she pulled cheeks of bum apart and buried face down there.

I dragged Captain's hands away from clit and tit so I could stand up, turn round and sit down on lap again but facing him. As I bent knees and lowered myself, great fat prick slid up me like thumb into soft butter. He undid more buttons and dress slipped down off shoulders. Captain stopped watching show to nuzzle wetly all over chest and tummy while fingers of both his hands rummaged in cunt-thatch and plucked at clit, but I kept an eye pressed up against peephole.

Em rolled over on back, skirt right up round waist. Anne got down over her in sixty-nine – you could see they were at it for real, not just mucking about, and all the blokes clapped and cheered when they came, just as I did. Captain still rammed up inside me and growing bigger, so I started jigging slowly up and down.

The lovebirds had collapsed in each other's arms, too bombed out from their orgasm to get up and take a bow. You wouldn't think Anne's supposed to have such a pash on Carla Merryweather! Wendy announced that everyone should go back to veranda so trade could begin, but ringleader of lads got up and said no, they'd each put £1.50 in kitty – the 50p a bonus for Mags's birthday – and take all the girls together, including Wendy and Mags, in a general free-for-all. And that's what they did. Ringleader and his best mate dived straight down and started fumbling Anne and Em. Others grabbed a girl each, grappled with them and got them down on top of the others. Wendy and Mags, with all their extra weight, soon worked down to bottom of pile – being small, Nikki and Helen with their partners finished up on top. Well, I say partners, but this was a proper orgy and nobody had an actual partner more than a couple of minutes. It wasn't a one-on-one situation at all, because as far as I could make out with all that writhing and threshing about, each of the girls was usually doing things to at least two of the boys and having things done to her by at least three of the others. I reckon it worked out something like that because there were more boys than girls. But in fact that may not be quite right because nobody seemed to be paying much attention to which sex they were groping or screwing. Garments kept being thrown out from heap, so circle of boots, jeans, jackets, underwear and girls' things piled up round edge of swept area. They made quite a row, going at it like animals. First mostly shrieks of laughter, hooting noises from guys and high-pitched squeals from girls. Then more of a continuous grunting from so many sweaty bodies on the job together. Finally gasps, moans, sobs and yells as they exploded in orgasm, some more or less together and others one by one. Was reminded of finale of firework display – Captain's own Roman candle went off deep in my insides just as they started calming down. And I came too. And came again. And again. Invited him to join dorm feast tomorrow night.

No time to write any more now, but that was about it anyway. Big Mac's asked me to go to her room for some reason. I *wonder* what she has in mind! Am on my way.

In perfect synchronisation with the exploding fireworks about which she was reading, Miss Muttock's own pent-up sexual energies erupted as her internal muscles locked on the finger scouring her vagina. She adjusted her clothing and checked on her monitor that Melanie's dormitory was still unoccupied, as indeed the rules insisted it should be at this time of day. Then she unlocked the study door and nodded curtly in the direction of old Grote as she hurried upstairs to replace the diary in its secret repository.

Egg and chips, the Captain told himself, should form no more than a small part of an active man's diet. He stubbed out a cigarette on the greasy plate, dreading the chore that lay ahead of him downstairs in that unsavoury kitchen. At least he had found it fairly easy to give up smoking, or almost give it up (the odd cigarette after a heavy meal being the allowable exception) once he had persuaded himself that abstinence boosted his sexual potency.

Certainly his potency this afternoon, with Melanie seated on his lap down in the Palace of Sweethearts, had been undiminished, in spite of the extent to which it had been taxed of late. Perhaps it was the long, enforced abstinence from sex itself he had so recently endured before coming to Cunlip, rather than the concurrent nicotine deprivation, that had brought him to such a peak of condition. He lit another fag.

It would be hard to sustain the view that Melanie was losing interest in him, as he had feared. His fingertips had become so accustomed to the velvety sheen of her flanks that she seemed almost to have become a permanent extension of his own body, and that, surely, was through no particular effort on his part; she had thrown herself at him and clung to him, letting him fuck her every day.

Pleasant as the afternoon's intercourse with her had been, the image which now burned most brightly in the Captain's memory was that of Anne and Emily, draped in white top and white skirt respectively, pretending to waltz to the strains of Wendy Mount's cassette player. '*Wien, Wien, nur du allein,*' the Tauber-like tenor had cooed in celebration of the saccharine, *sachertorte* charm of his dream city, as Anne's soggy genitals were displayed to the enthusiastic crowd, '*Du sollst die Stadt meiner Träume sein.*'

The Captain's dreams, as his cheek sank down to the table top, were not of Viennese frippery but of homegrown orgies in which mountains of heaving flesh were surmounted by a pair of pretty rumps pointed at him, a pair of lean arses he readily identified as those of Helen and Nikki. 'The sun,' he mumbled, dribbling on the table, 'the sun – both the suns – out of both their elbows. More power – more grease – to their arseholes, is what I say. Is what I mean.'

He opened one of his eyes and lifted his right elbow from the cold grease and ash on the plate. Hadn't he just been dreaming about elbow grease or something? Night had fallen, a moonless but starry night. What had awakened him was a cold, mobile light shining on the wall and ceiling. He staggered to the window.

Most unexpectedly, the twin headlamps of a car were proceeding with caution down the avenue. The vehicle halted at a point which must have been just above the plank bridge, and lights and engine were switched off. At this moment the Captain's attention was caught by another unexpected light over to the right: the door of the Palace of Sweethearts stood open, and the interior was illuminated. As he watched, a dark figure closed the door, but points of light spilling through the numerous perforations he had bored in the shutters suggested that the person or persons responsible had shut themselves inside.

Interesting proceedings were afoot. The Captain pulled on a pair of shorts, hurried down the stairs and slipped out into the warm night. Instead of crossing the bridge to investigate the mysteriously parked car, he made his stumbling way up the overgrown path on his side of the stream. Where the stream flowed through the bathing pool, the path left the water to skirt the thicket, and it became even more difficult for him to find his way. But he persevered, and after five minutes or so he again stood beside the rustling water. Gazing up the slope, he beheld the dark outline of the Palace of Sweethearts with its points of leaking light.

Clutching his sandals in one hand, he paddled, waded and staggered through the cold current and hauled himself out on the other side. To avoid being seen, he clung to the hedge that marked the right-hand limit of the Lower Field and then scurried across the open ground separating him from the wall of the Secret Garden. This gave him some sort of cover until he reached the level of the pavilion, from which he heard rumblings as if heavy objects were being shifted, as well as raised but indistinguishable voices. Cautiously, he crossed the strip of grass on which that glorious orgy had so recently taken place, and searched for the holes through which he and Melanie had witnessed the sport.

Something was wrong. He found the holes, but no light shone through them. Large objects, probably some of the old lockers, had indeed been moved and now blocked his view in through this side window. Very quietly he moved to the corner of the building and peered along the length of the veranda.

What he saw made him drop to his knees. The night, he felt

sure, was dark enough to render him inconspicuous in this position, but the stars, assisted by light shining through the unobstructed peepholes in the shutters on this side, were just bright enough to show two dim figures standing side by side and peering in. As his eyes became more accustomed to the level of illumination, he formed the distinct impression that these were emissaries of the local constabulary, and that one of them was female. Yes, that was the jaunty little cap they wore. But it was mainly from the white shirts with black epaulettes they sported on this oppressively hot night that he was able to make them out.

The WPC spoke, softly but distinctly. 'We better go in there, sarge. We better sort them out before the others start sleeping with him too.'

'Don't be soft, Jives,' came the sergeant's reply. 'Orders is orders, and in this particular instance our orders is straight from the Deputy Chief. Might not let me own kids muck about like this, mind. But it ain't so different than what happened at your induction when you was assigned to this patch. Anyways, these toffee-nosed little bastards – cor, see what she's doing?'

The Captain realised that as he uttered these words the sergeant's large hand had come to rest on WPC Jives's behind. A little fiddling with the fastenings, and her skirt slipped down to her ankles. The burly officer, his pale truncheon already released and bobbing up and down, took up his station behind her. He dragged down her black tights and panties and applying himself to the plump, starlit buttocks drove straight into the delights lurking between them.

'You just keep your eye to that hole, Jives,' he growled, 'while I concentrates on this one. Let me know what they're doing to him, the smutty-minded little cows.'

'I couldn't. It's just too dirty for words. I never saw such red hair – he's got it all over him. And the size of his . . . Did I *say* you could sleep with me on duty, Albert Raddle?'

Sergeant Raddle's response was immediate. 'Your duty, constable, as long as you're with the force, is to take orders from your superiors. Right now that means me.'

'But you're killing me, sarge. It's too frigging tight. Hey, she's doing it with her tongue.'

Raddle, meanwhile, was doing it with his prick, and doing it so vigorously that the veranda boardwalk creaked and groaned and threatened to give way beneath them. The Captain was saddened by a sense of waste as this enforcer of order and orders shot his load into the quivering quarters of his subordinate and instantly withdrew and zipped up. Raddle and Jives, it seemed, had no more joy from their congress, and hardly more awareness of it, than a pair of rutting animals.

'Can we go back to the car now?' asked Jives, as she made herself decent.

'No. Our orders is to hang round here, my dear, till they all goes away. Just remember – my report goes straight to County, to old Hardbuckle himself.'

The Captain, however, saw no point in hanging around, and after tiptoeing back to the wall of the Secret Garden crept along its base until he was concealed not only by the blackness of the night but also by the dense boskage of the wood. He felt his way forward as rapidly as he could, but the lack of light and the overgrown condition of the path hindered his progress. It seemed ages before he stumbled into a large tree trunk he remembered as being close to the love nest where he and Melanie had discovered Darcy and Susie the day before. He drew back, rubbing his nose, and stumbled again, this time on a couple lying and embracing beside the pathway.

'Oh, it's you,' said Melanie, who had no difficulty in recognising him in the dark and seemed not at all surprised that he should be prowling in the woods so late at night. 'It's time you met Miss MacDonald. Miss MacDonald, this is the Captain. You may have seen him around – he's taken over from Derrick.'

'I can't see your face,' said the older woman calmly, 'but yes, I've seen you around. A netball fan, aren't you?'

'Let's say I take my pleasure where I find it. Do you fuck?'

He didn't bother to wait for an answer, but kicked off his shorts and stretched out beside the two of them. With his left arm he hugged them all together. Their three tongues touched tips, and each tip splashed over the other two chins. The Captain's lengthening and thickening cock was squeezed tight, at an enforced downward-pointing angle, clamped between the two cuntpads. As he felt their bodies he established that Melanie's dress was unbuttoned all the way down the front, and she wore nothing underneath it. Miss MacDonald was stark naked. Her hard muscles and firm breasts delighted his touch, and his seed was gathering in readiness to flood the tight space between their six thighs when she broke away from the embrace.

'Sorry,' she explained. 'I've just got to have it in me. Now.'

She pulled the Captain apart from Melanie and forcefully rolled him on to his back. Placing her athletic thighs on either side of his hips, she lowered an unseen but hotly burning, oily cunt straight down on his erect tool. Her mouth touched his, and her tongue probed his lips while her hardened nipples brushed against the hair of his chest.

The Captain was something of a moralist, and was not willing for his ardent Melanie to be left out of this engagement. He cupped the MacDonald's breasts and pushed her gently up so that Melanie could take a position facing her astride his chest. The two women moaned and kissed, and he knew they were doing wonderful things to each other's tits. Placing his hands on Melanie's soft flanks, he lifted her bottom and brought it back until the reek of wet cunt was sharp in his nostrils. He directed a stream of breath upwards. The girl responded by pressing her open flesh down over his mouth. Hair tickled his chin. His tongue washed the inner surfaces of the petals and plunged into her tight love tube, while he reached his hands round her body, stroking her belly with one and tormenting her swollen clitoris with the fingers of the other. The Big Mac bucked up and down in sudden orgasm, and he brought Melanie to her climax at the very moment that his loins contracted and he slowly injected thick slugs of come into the proponent of Physical Development's vagina.

On his way back to the Old Lodge he paused at the plank bridge. Pale lightning flooded the scene, the herald of distant thunder, but there was no sign of the police car. Wearily he climbed the stairs. The washing-up could wait until morning. When he looked up the valley from his window the Palace of Sweethearts was in darkness.

140

TEN

RAINY DAY, STEAMY NIGHT

Overnight the thunderclouds had built up steadily, and by Wednesday morning the storms had broken. Rain lashed against the rattling windows of the Old Lodge, and the Captain felt a sense of emptiness and depression as he stood at the earthenware sink tackling the congealed grease of last night's meal. Outside, everything looked grey and sodden. The temperature had dropped like a stone. Had the long days of flaunted beauty and open-air sex finally come to an end? Officially banned from the main building of the college, what opportunities would he find for continuing to enlarge his circle of delightful young friends and for developing his growing intimacy with them? The rain poured down, and even his collection of erotic fiction failed to hold his attention. What was more, he had no waterproof clothing apart from his motorcycling leathers.

Around the middle of the morning, however, the clouds parted and the sun struck through, clear and brilliant. When he stepped outside, the long, wet grass clung to his ankles. The air was fresh, and all the clogged oppressiveness that had been thickening suffocatingly over the last week had been washed out of it. Breathing had become a rediscovered pleasure. And in contrast to the coolness of the light breeze, the rays of the sun when the breeze lapsed were as strong as ever. The Captain went indoors to get dressed, inspired with intimations of a new start. Intimations ... 'All things that love the sun are out of doors,' he declaimed aloud, remembering a fragment of Wordsworth.

Patches of sunshine chased the shadows of the clouds across the valley, and were chased by more clouds in their turn. Through the open window the stream could be heard, enlivened by the recent downpour, chattering over its gravel bed below the plank bridge. Surveying the sky, he reached the conclusion that although the blue was gaining rapidly on the fleecy stragglers racing across it, a dark bank of swag-bellied cloud looming up on the left might still be the determining feature of the day's weather. If he got a soaking in his overalls he would feel miserable. He would venture forth in shorts and T-shirt, easily discarded and easily dried.

As he crossed the plank bridge, he paused to enjoy the sun sparkling on the laughing current, and noticed the fluttering of a blue dress which immediately withdrew behind the oak tree downstream. A casual approach seemed best under the circumstances. He sauntered a few yards up the avenue, his lips pursed to form a silent whistle, casting his eyes in idle rapture from the dusty pathway up to the racing clouds and down again. At precisely the right point he turned his head towards the tree.

Even without seeing their faces, he knew by now who these girls were: Susie Freemantle and Nikki Culpepper. Both wore their blue summer dresses. They stood beneath the oak in a tight embrace. Susie's back was towards the Captain. The hem of her skirt had been lifted and her navy pants pulled down to her thighs by Nikki, who was stroking her bottom. On catching sight of him, Nikki put a finger of her free hand up to her lips, warning him not to let her friend know he was there. The Captain stopped in his tracks, fascinated, as the stroking continued and the caressing hand was slowly insinuated between Susie's delicious thighs.

The direction of the breeze favoured his overhearing scraps of their conversation. 'Ouch!' cried Susie. 'You're not supposed to go in there.'

'No, and I wouldn't have to, would I, if you'd only do as Melanie told you. You've got to do it with your own fingers, and you've only got till tomorrow night.'

'But it bleeds when I try to do it.'

'Good,' replied Nikki. 'That's what's supposed to happen. You must be nearly there by now. Just a little bit more and you'll be all nice and ready for him, and nothing's going to hurt any more. Let's have a nice kiss.'

Susie wriggled in her companion's arms. The position of their heads changed, and she became aware of the Captain's interested gaze. He waved to the girls and plunged into the dripping undergrowth, heading in light spirits towards the pool.

So early in the day he was not expecting any sport in that particular neck of the woods; he was happy just to commune with nature. All the same, as he drew near the expanse of water he exercised an automatic caution, moving with silent steps and remaining concealed in shady foliage.

His prudence was rewarded. On the end of the little jetty projecting from the opposite bank, resplendent in the dazzling sunshine, sat Anne Amory, her legs swinging in the water. As usual, her blonde curls were adorned with her fetching straw boater, which she now wore tilted back at a jaunty angle. Her bosom was not available for the Captain's admiration, as she sported a voluminous, bright red sweater. His eyes were thus drawn down to the pale, parted thighs, between which he could distinctly make out the line of pink dividing the dusting of fine yellow down. She splashed her feet in the water and blew a condomlike balloon of bubble gum.

At this moment her friend Carla emerged from the shadows to stand on the sunwashed, steaming lawn behind her. The dark, flat-chested girl was wearing nothing but a Walkman. She stood with her feet together and her hands clasped behind her neck. Her armpits sported little black tufts, and she swayed her slim loins, with their patch of black fur, in time with the music. Then she broke into an uninhibited dance, pirouetting, high-kicking, turning cartwheels and floating gracefully over the buttercups, daisies and dandelions, her trained limbs supple and expressive. The Captain recalled and silently articulated another snatch of Romantic poetry: 'Heard melodies are sweet, but those unheard are sweeter'. Wasn't that the ode in which 'loth maidens' were struggling to escape the 'mad pursuit' of men or gods? The idea of such a chase was most appealing – he would mention it to Melanie.

Real artistry informed the balletic display, which took on an increasingly erotic character as Carla's body swayed, gyrated and undulated. Her performance was wasted on Anne, who continued to sit with her back to it, noisily popping bubbles of gum. On the Captain, though, it was certainly not wasted. The tip of his penis had crept down to emerge from the leg of his skimpy shorts. A string of clear, sticky fluid snailed its way down the hairs on the inside of his thigh. Carla's skill was such that, as he watched with thumping heart, she seemed to be transformed from a naked girl with long legs and a little cunt into an open,

143

inviting cunt supported by the flashing white flesh of a small body and its flailing limbs. It was the cunt that was dancing, in celebration of its own allure, in proclamation of its carnal hunger.

The dance ended. Carla stepped on to the jetty and stood behind Anne, her legs apart. She removed the lightweight headset, and faint strains of Tchaikovsky drifted across the pool. 'Come and dance,' she said, stooping to lift Anne's sweater and let the sun fall on the snowy breasts.

But as her friend looked up, smiling, the sun went in and a chill breeze ruffled the surface of the pool. Heavy drops fell on the Captain's head and shoulders, shaken from the branches above him. His manhood, uncomfortably pinched by the leg of his shorts, was cooled into detumescence. The spell was broken. Both girls were hurriedly dressing, and in no time had moved off, arm in arm, downstream.

Instead of following them, the Captain went the other way, seeking the shelter of the Palace of Sweethearts. Just as he reached the veranda, the rain began to fall in earnest. A powerful gale was blowing. Fortunately, the wind was coming from behind the building, so he could stand on the boardwalk, chilly but dry, as sheets of water bucketed over the roof and chased each other in shaking curtains across the field to the straining woods. He took out his key and went inside.

The shutters rattled intermittently, and when they were not rattling a steady dripping and splashing sound was indicative of the disrepair into which the pavilion had been allowed to fall. It seemed darker than usual, and this was not just because of the absence of sunshine. As he had guessed the night before, the large lockers had indeed been shifted to leave a clear space running the whole length of the room. They now stood along the walls, close to but not right up against them, obstructing the rays that entered through the chinks and spyholes. Because of this rearrangement, he no longer knew which locker contained the pornographic material with which he had hoped to beguile the time during the storm. He had examined only a few of them, all of which turned out to be either locked or empty, when a clatter of feet and babble of voices announced the arrival of a party seeking shelter. The Captain was glad he had locked the door; after all, the newcomers would be protected from the rain out on the veranda. He tiptoed round into the narrow space between lockers and windows, and applied his eye to the most suitable holes.

Half a dozen bedraggled girls, their bare legs spattered with mud, huddled there shivering in singlets and navy knickers. They had evidently been out for a run under the supervision of Miss MacDonald, who stood beside them in a soaking tracksuit, wringing the water out of her dark hair. The condition of their hair was indeed the immediate preoccupation of all of them, and its saturation, as well as the fact that they tended to stand with their heads hanging down and their eyes screwed up, made it a little hard to recognise them. But this, undoubtedly, was his lovely, freckled Gina, and the girl quivering next to her must be her friend Jane Jewkes, wielder of the famous salami.

Not without difficulty, Miss MacDonald had dragged the heavy top of her claret-coloured tracksuit over her head. The nipples that crowned her fine white breasts had gathered themselves into hard, glowing coals, a fierce orange-red among the surrounding goose pimples. 'Get out of those wet things, girls, everything except your trainers,' she ordered, lowering first the bottom half of her tracksuit and then the white silk briefs she wore under it. An innocent observer might have wondered why she found it necessary to remove this last garment. Beside the streaming flesh of her young charges, the Captain found it slightly incongruous that her pubic curls formed such a dry, fluffy bush on the mound between those athletic thighs. Naked and fanatical, she now devoted herself to helping the girls to peel off their drenched clothing. The chattering of teeth was punctuated by squeals of laughter.

The lurid untruths Melanie had told the Captain about Alexandra Fellowes, the young lady with the virginal reputation who had sex with her own brother, had stuck in his memory, and he recognised her even before Miss MacDonald rolled the navy-blue pants down over the girl's thighs. The familiar, ample bosom of cuddly Emily identified *her* readily enough as the vest was pulled over her head. Celia Prout was also known to him by now, but who was this handsome, snooty-looking, sixth girl with narrow white belly, sodden black cunthair and long thighs?

'Off with that vest, Josie Greene!' the MacDonald's voice called

145

out in answer to his silent question. The bottom of the clinging vest was raised, and the nipples, which had pushed out proudly through the thin and by now almost transparent material, were exposed in their full glory, hard, long and thick. In lifting her arms to remove the vest, Josie revealed the growth of brown hair adorning her armpits. Of course: Josie was the girl who had been fucked in the shower by Joker Jennings.

Briskly, Miss MacDonald lined the girls up in three pairs, one behind the other, and stood in front facing them at the end of the veranda. 'No towels to dry ourselves,' she shouted above the wind, 'so we'll do some exercises to get warm.'

The Captain moved along the line from peephole to peephole, relishing the rippling of muscle under wet skin, the tensing and relaxing of buttocks, some lean and some plump but none of them excessively fleshy, and the jiggling of assorted boobs. On the whole the operation was being conducted in a good-natured spirit, but it was very plain that Gina and Josie, who formed the last pair, did not find each other's company congenial. At every opportunity the arm of one would swing round into the other's face, or an elbow would nudge spitefully into a breast.

For ten minutes or so the party was drilled in conventional exercises of the toe-touching, hip-swinging, arm-lifting kind, until they were all rosy and panting. The order was then given for the couples to turn inward, facing each other, and for each girl to raise her left leg and place it on her partner's right shoulder. For a moment they all stood looking at each other in disbelief. Jane and Celia, who occupied the middle position, then attempted the feat with some assistance from their neighbours, who had to hold them together in a lewd embrace, cunt jammed against cunt. Seeing that it was physically possible, Alexandra and Emily followed suit, while Miss MacDonald ensured that the two couples leaned lightly against each other for mutual support. She urged the reluctant Gina and Josie to complete the tableau. The result, of course, was disastrous, and all six girls collapsed in a gasping, giggling heap, although the giggles came only from Alexandra, Celia, Emily and Jane.

When they had recovered, the MacDonald consulted her watch. 'Right, girls,' she said. 'Twenty minutes left before that revision class you've all got. Just time for a quick competition.

The rain's not going to stop, so we'll do it out there – the main thing's to keep warm. All know what an *orgasm* is, don't you?'

An embarrassed silence was taken to signify assent.

'Has anyone here never had one?'

Alexandra raised her hand, but quickly converted the gesture into one of scratching her ear when she realised she was alone.

'We're going to have an orgasm race,' Miss MacDonald continued.

'What's the prize?' Emily demanded.

'Dinner in my room.'

Celia sneered. 'In that case,' she said, 'they'll all cheat. Anyone can *fake* it.'

But Miss MacDonald was ready for that one. 'It's not the first to come, silly, but the last. Come down here – and you, Jane – and I'll show you how we're going to do it.'

The three of them stepped out into the rain. Jane Jewkes was made to stand with her feet apart and her hands raised above her head. Steadying her with one palm on the small of Jane's back and the other cupping a breast, Miss MacDonald helped her to bend backwards until first her hands and then her head touched the ground. The curve of her belly now formed a glistening dome, on one side of which her pink-tipped tits flowed back towards her armpits. On the other side a pouting pussy was offered to the rain, which saturated the black sponge of her pubic hair and trickled down the central runnel between the tensed thighs. Celia was then placed standing with her back to Jane, some eighteen inches in front of her and slightly to one side. She too was put through the backward-bending routine. Standing between her legs and grasping the concavity of her buttocks, Miss MacDonald manoeuvred her until her face hung directly underneath Jane's cunt. Once she was in this position, it was possible for the older woman to support and raise the nape of Celia's neck while the girl reached up to find a secure hold on Jane's hips. Miss MacDonald stood back. 'Just let your head hang right down,' she ordered. 'Now check whether you can pull yourself up and press your face back so that you can lick up her labia to her clitoris. Yes, that's fine. No, stop licking now or you'll have an unfair start.'

The other four girls were called down from the veranda, and

147

the difficult operation performed by Celia was repeated by them in turn. Emily was positioned between Celia's legs, Alexandra between Emily's, Josie between Alexandra's, and finally, protesting loudly, Gina between Josie's. Thanks to the angle at which each girl had been placed relative to the one she was going to lick, they now formed not a line but an almost perfect hexagon. It only remained for Miss MacDonald to seize Jane by the armpits and lift her into position between the thighs of Gina, whose complaints died away when she felt the girl's hands on her hips and her breath on her groin.

This ingenious formation was evidently putting a huge strain on the poor girls, especially on the muscles of their legs; it was only the way they interlocked, and their powerful motivation, that allowed them to remain in place. As he watched the rain rebounding from their taut bellies, the Captain longed to sink his throbbing member into a moist sheath. The order was given: 'Lick !' Six eager tongues lashed into six reluctant clits – although in some cases the slavering Captain had the impression that the reluctance was quickly overcome. Who would be the last to succumb to this outrageous titillation?

Who succumbed last, or first, or whether indeed they all succumbed at the same moment, was impossible to say. What was clear, though, was that the first orgasm or orgasms caused convulsions that overthrew the whole cantilevered structure. The six girls sprawled on the wet grass, spending or spent, and the contest was declared a draw, with *tête-à-tête* dinners promised for all of them in the coming days.

Miss MacDonald clapped her hands. 'On your feet, my poppets,' she shouted. 'No time for a hot shower, I'm afraid. That'll be my reward, but you've got work to do. When we get to the bathhouse just grab your towels and take them up to your dorm to rub yourselves down before you put on dry clothes.'

Led by their popular and talented mentor, the girls gathered up the wet things they had left on the veranda and jogged off with stiff limbs down the Lower Field, heading to their right along the bank of the stream. The Captain locked the door behind him and followed them at a distance of some twenty yards, far enough behind for them not to sense his presence but close enough, even in the driving rain that quickly soaked through his T-shirt and shorts, to enjoy the view of their bouncing bottoms. Their vulnerable nakedness shone wetly, and on those of them whose hair was long the tresses were plastered down their backs. Bits of grass stuck to their thighs and buttocks from the collapse of their orgasmic circle, and the backs of their legs were splashed with mud as they ran wearily round the pool and up the avenue.

As they approached the building, the Captain dodged into the shrubbery and waited in increasing discomfort for a few minutes after they had all entered the door of the bathhouse. Then he let himself in quietly and looked around, shivering. The girls had disappeared, but he could hear water running and saw clouds of steam issuing from one of the shower cubicles. This hint of luxury proved too much for him. He peeled his wet clothes off and advanced purposefully towards his unsuspecting quarry.

Before entering the shower, he stood for a moment waiting for his prick to stiffen while he admired the MacDonald's long back. The ridge of her spine as she bent forward to wash her hair divided the pale, muscular hardness that gave way below her waist to the tight, ripe cushions of her buttocks. Below them gleamed the athletic thighs, and between them the dark rift through which he could make out a dark mass of dripping hair.

This prospect had done the trick. As he stood on the tiled floor his penis had extended itself so far that the head, bursting out of his uncomfortably tight foreskin, almost touched the desired flesh. He stepped into the shower, delighting in the warm caress of the water, and pressed himself against the woman's back. She neither looked round nor straightened up. Instead, she reached a hand back through her parted thighs and grasped his tool. Her other hand followed, and eased open her dark-fringed lips. He entered her and started to fuck. It's got to be once only, he told himself, if I'm going to last the course at Melanie's party in the dormitory tonight.

Miss MacDonald lowered herself to a kneeling position, taking the Captain with her. Deliciously warm water streamed over his back, down between his buttocks and over his balls. One of his hands explored and briskly fondled the hanging breasts with their distended tips, and then slid along the smooth, hard stomach to find the sopping fur-pad. With thumb and middle finger in her groin channels, he squeezed the vulva hard until he could feel the pressure on the stem of the cock that filled it. Still holding her like this he pistoned in and out. His index finger ran upwards between her fleshy love lips and found the enlarged clitoris. He pressed the fingertip hard into this pip and rolled it from side to side.

He breathed thickly into her ear. Without turning for visual confirmation of the identity of her ravisher she murmured, as he pumped harder, 'Oh, Captain, do you call this netball?'

'I call it Physical Development,' he riposted. His wad of hot spunk shot straight up her womb at the very instant that her own ecstasy convulsed her limbs and left her howling into the white porcelain.

The temperature and humidity rose as the day wore on and gave way to an oppressive night. At eleven o'clock precisely, the Captain was waiting on the steps of the main entrance. The clouds had parted for a moment, and the scene was steeped in moonlight. He gasped as Melanie appeared in the doorway to welcome him. Her fair hair and pale limbs were lustrous in the strange light, and a sense of coolness was communicated to him as he took in the costume she had chosen for the dorm feast. It was of pale blue cotton material: a little, bust-hugging top with shoulder straps and a trimming of white lace above the bare belly, and high-cut knickers, loose round the hips but snug at the crotch, with lace at the waist.

She took his hand and led him into the building and up two flights of stairs to the room she shared with Emily, Honoria and Priscilla. Neither he nor the girls had any inkling that their activities and conversation were being monitored in close detail by the Principal, who was sitting up late in her study. Mary Muttock wore nothing but a lacy black negligée on this occasion, and her wet vagina was stuffed with about two-thirds of a solid rubber dildo, its straps hanging loose, which was usually kept for demonstration purposes in Miss MacDonald's lab. Miss Mac-Donald was unaware of the Principal's habit of borrowing this instrument for her own pleasure, and of course neither woman had any idea of the part designed for it in the nuptial rites

Melanie had planned for the following night. Concerning that occasion nothing was said now by Melanie, as it was meant to be a great surprise for the Captain.

Melanie's room-mates greeted him enthusiastically, and they all sat on chairs at the end of a bed on which the feast of cakes and fruit had been laid out. A bottle of Bulgarian Cabernet Sauvignon was passed round, and a second one. Eating and drinking gave the Captain time to admire these young ladies at close quarters. Emily attracted him more each time he encountered her. Tonight she wore a man-sized pair of striped pyjamas. Most buttons on the jacket were undone, and glimpses of her glorious bosom were freely bestowed whenever she leaned forward for the food. The punky Honoria also sported male attire, a rugby shirt of her brother's, maroon with a white collar. Priscilla sat there, demure in a white cotton nightie with wide openings under the arms through which the curves of her breasts could be seen. It seemed to be so contrived that the frills could easily be slipped down over the shoulders. Her long, black hair was tied back with a red ribbon.

The remains of the feast were cleared away, and the Captain followed his hosts to the Main Ward, as it was still called, which accommodated the younger girls in institutional austerity. There they moved between the iron bedsteads, selecting four playmates. At once, and without ceremony, they led them back to the smaller room. Not a bad selection, the Captain thought: Helen, Nikki, Anne and Carla.

Events now moved briskly. The four young concubines were ordered to strip naked. Melanie took Anne to her bed, Priscilla took Nikki, Honoria grabbed Carla and Emily seemed happy enough to be left with Helen. The Captain moved from bed to bed, watching the couples as they sported on top of the covers, every now and then sitting beside them and assisting with judicious applications of finger or tongue. Throughout these proceedings, the older girls retained their nightclothes, although Helen soon removed Emily's pyjama bottoms. Prissy's nightdress slipped right down to her waist under Nikki's lustful scrabbling for her breasts, and Honoria's rugger shirt gathered itself up under her armpits. Melanie alone was still relatively untampered with, at least in this respect. Her pretty outfit was designed to

151

attract and receive amorous advances without disturbing its general appearance – the close-fitting top encouraged the luxury of fondling through the material, and the knickers allowed the easy access at hip level of a hand which could slide down the front to the crotch or behind to the anus.

No sooner had all eight girls achieved their climax than they stood up, moved the bedside cabinets out of the way, and pushed the four beds together. At this point the Captain, as guest of honour, was brought more actively into the picture (a picture which, reduced to black and white, was affording Miss Muttock considerable diversion). Melanie, who as usual directed the operation, lay on her back. Next to her lay Honoria, then Emily, then Prissy. Their arms were stretched back above their heads. The four concubines were ordered to kneel straddling their chests, crouched so that their genitals brushed their mistresses' mouths while their own tongues could work the recumbent clits. The older girls then reached round with their hands to work the younger ones' breasts (although only Anne had any real development there) and the pubic regions. At first the Captain saw no opening for himself, until Melanie demonstrated her idea. Pushing little Anne's head up from her crotch, she made her rise to an upright position. Our hero, who had already undressed, then mounted between Melanie's thighs, pulled aside the cute knickers and shoved his hard cock up her cunt. Cupping his hands round Anne's buttocks, he licked into her moist slit while fucking Melanie.

'Go steady!' cried the latter, her voice muffled by Anne's bum. 'Let's see if you can get it into all eight of us before you have to come.'

Inspired by this suggestion, he withdrew, and Anne changed places with Melanie. There is something poignant in the sight of an erect phallus prematurely withdrawn from a willing cunt, but in this case precautionary *coitus interruptus* was not the object. Glib with Melanie's spendings, the instrument was slipped with ease into Anne's small but elastic sheath. The pumping action was resumed, but only for a few strokes. Following exactly the same routine as with the first couple, the Captain bestowed his favours in rapid succession on Honoria and Carla, Emily and Helen, and Priscilla and Nikki. Each time he felt the semen gathering at the root of his prick, he drew out and took a breather before mounting the next girl.

It was while his tongue was nipped by Prissy's labia and his prick by Nikki's cunt muscles that he discharged, having just managed to service all the girls. As he came, he recollected for the third time that day some lines of Romantic verse:

A mighty fountain momently was forced
Amid whose swift half-intermitted burst
Huge fragments vaulted like rebounding hail
Or chaffy grain beneath the thresher's flail;
And, 'mid these dancing rocks, at once and ever,
It flung up momently the sacred river.

Instantly he was torn from Nikki's deep, romantic chasm and thrown on to his back. All eight of them were at him with hands and mouths, and no part of his body was spared their attentions. Nikki, delighted to have been the recipient of a tribute now running copiously down her thighs, insisted on kissing him and mumbling endearments into his ear. 'I'm really getting off on *Adventures of a Naked Girl*, mister,' she confided. 'Just love that bit when she's stretched out on the bough of a tree and the boy flops down on top of her.'

By now, the Captain's member was once more the dominant feature of this animated scene, its shining purple head straining towards the smoke detector above them. He thought there was something not quite right about that rather unexpected piece of technology; it had the appearance of an eye gazing down on them from the ceiling. The conflagrations raging below, however, would not require a sprinkling triggered by that dubious source to quell them.

As he lay glorying in the potency of his restored erection, the girls straddled him and shafted themselves one after the other, each bouncing up and down six times before surrendering the saddle to her successor. Melanie, Anne, Honoria, Carla, Emily, Helen, Prissy and Nikki all took his tower of strength into their vaginas and exercised it furiously while he played with their nipples. A second round began, and he had got as far as the lewd young Helen with her dark-ringed eyes and corrupt grin

153

when his pent-up reservoirs burst open and poured another mighty fountain into a canal too tight to contain it. But before the surplus had time to spill into his pubic hair he was asleep.

Miss Muttock plucked out the dildo and slumped back in her chair. Then she too slept.

ELEVEN

THE WEDDING

Late on Thursday evening, the wedding party assembled in the Palace of Sweethearts, the darkness of which had been seductively illuminated by two dozen or so candles on saucers and tin lids set on benches and lockers around the room. A pair of tall candles stood on an old table meant to represent the altar. Between these a large rubber phallus had been placed erect, destined to play a minor but active part in the licentious service.

Among those present, the role of the Captain was slightly anomalous. Strictly speaking, he was not accounted one of the guests but held the humbler status of photographer. Some licence had been promised him, but his sanctioned participation was confined to flitting about among the more honoured personages, flashing Melanie's camera. Like everyone else, he was dressed for the occasion. He was rigged out in a long black academic gown wrapped tightly round him for decency and secured with a cord round the waist. His features were concealed behind a black mask.

The first picture he took was of Melanie herself, seen from the side as she stood there as officiating priest. Her sacerdotal function was acknowledged in the way she held aloft a chalice – actually a netball trophy containing unconsecrated Babycham, to be liberally dispensed at intervals throughout the nuptials. It was also reflected in her costume, comprising a pair of starched linen bands attached to a cloth around her neck to represent a dog collar, and in the long black silk scarf hanging down her front as a clerical stole. This concealed her nipples but not much else of her pointed breasts. Here the ecclesiastical guise stopped, for the rest of her costume consisted of black sandals and a tiny black silk G-string. As he activated the flash, the Captain reflected with some dissatisfaction that, since the picture would not give a view of the cleft of her behind, anyone who had not been present might mistake this G-string for the bottom of a mini-bikini.

Next to be taken were the youthful couple themselves. What a charming sight they presented standing there bashfully, hand in hand! The radiant Miss Freemantle was draped from head to foot in a gauzy veil falling down her back from a headdress of artificial white blossoms fastened to her golden curls. The edges of this veil lay over her bare shoulders, and down the front it hung wide open, showing off the bridal costume Melanie had devised for her. Her neck was adorned with one of the few non-white touches in the outfit, a black velvet choker with a red rosebud fixed at her throat. A flimsy suntop, sleeveless and unbuttoned down the front, but not quite revealing the little breasts to each side of the opening, reached to just above the level of her navel. Its dazzling whiteness furnished a charming background for the other departure from bridal white: two little red bows on the ends of the pigtails falling forward over her shoulders. Low around her narrow hips was tied a white ribbon; attached to this, back and front, were a pair of small, spotless white handkerchiefs, producing something of the effect of a microskirt open at the sides to show as much flank and bottom as was needed to maintain a male spectator in a state of semierection. The beautifully rounded thighs invited the photographer's touch, which had to be restrained by a slap from Melanie. The well-formed white legs were bare, apart from a saucy white and blue bridal garter halfway down her left thigh, and her feet were neatly attired in white sandals and ankle socks.

The general effect of young Darcy's costume was similar to that of his bride's, but, being unveiled, less encumbered and with more firm young flesh exposed. His modesty, like hers, was covered by a pair of handkerchiefs hanging from a low-slung ribbon round his hips, and his dark brown hair and blushing cheeks were offset by the choker and rosebud fastened prettily round his neck. Otherwise he stood smooth and naked.

The other people present were the two guests, Cathy and Heini, both attired in white nightshirts, and two little bridesmaids, one of whom was Susie's wanton friend Nikki. Apart from flowery garlands around their necks, and colourful chaplets on their heads (the flowers being artificial blooms borrowed from among the college's theatrical costumes), these attendants were stark naked. Their bodies shone in the flickering candlelight, Nikki's white and her companion's suntanned, and both of them were hairless, as Melanie had taken pains to shave all traces of youthful down from their bodies.

Melanie instructed the somewhat apprehensive couple to face each other, and clasped both their hands between her own. At this point they were to exchange vows, repeating the words after the priestess, of whose lubricious imagination they were the product.

'Repeat after me: I, Darcy O'Flammery . . .'

'I [*cough*], I, Darcy . . .'

'. . . do solemnly promise . . .'

'. . . do solemnly promise . . .'

'. . . to take you, Susie Freemantle . . .'

'. . . you, Susie, Susie Freeman . . .'

'. . . to be my unlawfully bedded wife . . .'

'. . . [*mumble*] unlawful wife . . .'

'. . . to handle and hold, to frig and to fuck . . .'

'. . . to – frigging fuck . . .'

'. . . till my sperm overflows from your cunt.'

Darcy, whose sheltered education had kept him ignorant of the meaning of many of these terms although he had often heard them used by older boys in a salacious context, was by now blushing and giggling almost uncontrollably. He just managed to blurt out '. . . overflowing cunt.'

Susie, shy, subdued and hardly audible, was then taken through a similar litany with appropriate modifications. It seemed to the Captain that she understood rather more of their import than Darcy, which would have explained why she seemed so fearful. 'I, Susie Freemantle, do solemnly promise to take you, Darcy O'Flammery, to be my unlawfully bedded husband, to handle and hold, to frig and be fucked, till my cunt drains the last drop of sperm from your balls.'

'Dearly beloved, let us proceed to the consecration of the chalice,' Melanie intoned. She held up the trophy above her head, which she tilted back so that her hair, unbraided, cascaded down her back. Her legs were wide apart, the narrow strap of the G-string lost between the cheeks of her bum. Bride and groom waited on either side of her. As they knew from the thorough schooling they had received from her, this was the moment before they were required to kneel and each of them kiss one of her buttocks. This they did, presenting a demure scene to the Captain's viewfinder.

But just as he prepared to take another picture, the choreography which had so far been adhered to with fluent ease suddenly cocked up. Darcy crawled round to the front, while Susie took up a central position at the back. What they had been taught to do was to support themselves, still kneeling, with their hands on Melanie's hips, and push their faces between her open thighs until their mouths met and they could kiss. But in his eagerness to perform what was required, Darcy somehow put too much weight on Melanie's hips and at the same time thrust his head too vigorously between her legs. The result was that she lost her balance and subsided backwards on poor Susie, whose face was partly buried under her behind. The boy did his best to kiss the mouth which showed, with the tip of the nose, beneath the black triangle of the priestly G-string, but being unable to reach that far, he nuzzled into the G-string itself. Forgetting himself and prompted by nature, he then slid his face a little upwards, grabbed to top edge of the garment between his lips, and dragged it halfway down over Melanie's gingery curls, into which he darted a wet tongue.

She gasped with surprise, but the well-built Heini, laughing, stepped forward and hoisted him to his feet. As Darcy stood there sheepishly, watching the bigger girl get up and recompose her attire, all present could see the effect this adventure had had on his own composure: his front handkerchief had lifted to expose a tight pink scrotum.

Melanie turned to the Captain and whispered rapidly in his ear. 'Think we ought to do something about that?' she asked.

'Well, it would be a kindness to put him out of his misery.'

'We don't want to spoil his appetite for the main course.'

'At his age,' replied the Captain with a somewhat wistful air, 'a quick wank will do no more than dampen his ardour for a couple of minutes, and will make him even keener for what's to come.'

Grateful for this advice, Melanie grasped Susie's hand and placed it over Darcy's risen foreflap, bending the girl's small fingers to clasp the hidden stiffness. Her reaction was one of fascinated horror.

'What's this? she stammered.

'Just his thingie,' Melanie replied. 'With big boys and men it gets like that when they need to make love. Keep holding on to it.'

Darcy seemed embarrassed. 'That's rude!' he exclaimed.

'It was pretty rude of you to stick your tongue in my cunt just now! But when you're married she'll be allowed to do rude things as much as she likes – much ruder than this,' laughed Melanie.

'And will he be able to do rude things to me?' his bride demanded.

'Of course. You can both do rude things to each other.'

'What, really dirty things?' inquired Darcy. 'Like – like sticking my willie in her wendy?'

'That's exactly the sort of thing I mean,' she replied. As she spoke, she pushed Susie down on her knees, and made her lift the lad's handkerchief, which he then held up for her convenience. Now for the first time they all saw the little chestnut-coloured bush sprouting round the root of his pink-headed prick. 'There,' said Melanie, guiding one of the bride's hands to cradle his testicles and the other to grasp the base of the long, slim penis, 'you must kiss it, lick it and suck it like a lollipop.'

Blushing deep crimson, Susie did her best to carry out the first two orders, confining her attentions to the shaft, and as she did so a droplet of clear liquid was observed to gather on the tip of the cockhead. Perhaps it was this that made the third task too much for her, for she bashfully turned her head aside. At this moment Darcy's loins bucked forward as he ejaculated, drenching the face and body of his coy bride with a liberal spattering of creamy white semen. The Captain's nostrils widened at the fresh tang of sex, and he quickly took a photo of the wet penis. It had already wilted to boyish dimensions, a last thread of viscous fluid dangling from the tip. Darcy still held up the handkerchief, but was about to drop it to hide the shame that threatened to overtake him.

The horrified exclamations he had uttered as he came strongly suggested that this was a virgin ejaculation. Melanie had to reassure him that the spillage was simply the evidence that he was mature enough to be married, although really the sticky fluids ought to have been delivered inside Susie. This, she exclaimed, was the *sperm* referred to in their marriage vows.

'But I thought you just had to wee in their wendies,' he objected naïvely.

Adopting the tones of a strict schoolmistress, Melanie insisted that Darcy should 'clear up the mess' he had made on the poor girl by licking her clean. At first, he evinced some distaste for such a chore. The initial gob of sperm had caught her on the left cheek as she turned her head aside. Fortunately the elegant choker and rosebud had been spared, and it was the bare flesh of her chest and tummy that had been puddled with the rest of the sticky come, now beginning to run sluggishly down the skin to unite in one long trail.

'Start with her face!' snapped Melanie, hauling the drooping Susie to her feet and forcing Darcy down into a kneeling position, his hands on the girl's bare flanks. Gingerly, as she stooped over him so that he was partly hidden in her veil, the tip of his tongue flickered on Susie's polluted cheek. Far from disgusting him, the taste and smell of his own secretion seemed to arouse fresh interest in the operation. His lips followed his tongue, and from sucking her cheek they slid to her mouth, on which he forced a passionate kiss. It did not escape the Captain's notice that his hands, resting on her hips, had begun to move a little – without lifting them from the skin, under the partial cover of her back-flap he was gently kneading the undersides of her buttocks with his fingers.

Not yet ready to honour her vows, the bride snatched her lips away. Her groom proceeded downwards, and starting at the lowest part of the slippery trail, just below her navel, relished his salty pleasures with both tongue and nose on his upward progress. The speed of this progress varied. At the tummy-button, the concavity of which had furnished a reservoir for the steaming flood, he lingered until he had licked and sucked it not only clean but quite dry. And at the upper end of the trail, by now perfectly clear (the thick white constituents having run down to a level at which they had already been licked off), he seemed reluctant to back away from her. He nuzzled his right cheek against her chest and manoeuvred it sideways until his ear, pressed against the open cotton suntop, could feel her left nipple. At this point he had to be pulled to his feet by Heini. In his standing posture it could be seen that his front handkerchief was again beginning to stir, moved by signs of renewed arousal behind it.

'You scamp,' cried Melanie, 'it's not your honeymoon yet!'

After the distraction occasioned by this emergency operation, the regular order of service was resumed. The smaller bridesmaid brought forward three cushions and laid them on the floor before Susie, one of them in front of another, and the third on top of the cushion nearest the bride. The latter was ordered to kneel on the raised cushions with her knees slightly apart and her bottom up in the air, her head down and her right cheek comfortably supported on the lower cushion. Darcy was then invited to gather up the gauzy veil covering her and lay it to one side, and then to lift her handkerchief so that it rested on her back. Timidly he took a corner between two fingers, and exposed the curve of her buttock inch by inch.

'Oh, no,' he exclaimed, 'she hasn't got any knickers on!'

'So what?' said Melanie. 'Neither have you.' And she lifted up his own back-flap to dart a hand between the thighs and squeeze his genitals.

The Captain positioned himself for what promised to be a most successful picture: Susie's slim white thighs surmounted by a delicious little bum, beyond which could be seen hints of the bridal white of the garments covering her upper parts. He took care with the angle of the shot, so that it would be possible for the viewer's eyes to follow the cleft between her cheeks right down to the plump and, from this rear viewpoint, hairless cunt. As yet it remained modestly closed, the slit a neat line dividing the outer lips.

The next step was reserved for the priest, but before taking that step, Melanie asked the bridegroom as an endearing afterthought if he would like to fondle Susie's bottom and 'feel her up'.

'What!' he cried indignantly, seemingly forgetful of his pleasures a few days earlier, 'touch a smelly old bum?' Probably, the Captain thought, he was inhibited about repeating those delights in public.

'Hey, that's not fair,' retorted Melanie. 'She had a bath this evening before coming here, and I checked her very carefully when I dressed her. She's squeaky clean; I'll prove it.'

So saying, she knelt behind the slandered young lady, the cheeks of whose bottom she parted to reveal a rosebud as neat and pink as those on the couple's throats. Then, extending the tip of her tongue as far as it would go, she ran it up the slit, which was just beginning to slacken and open itself, until she reached the rosebud, which she proceeded to lick thoroughly and with evident relish. The girl's giggles showed that, though ticklish, she was not averse to these lewd ministrations.

As Melanie stood aside, Darcy made to follow her example, but not wishing him to get overexcited at this stage, she insisted that hands only were to be applied, and only briefly. So he contented himself with kneeling on the cushion to stroke both buttocks and prod them with his fingertips before timidly touching her femininity, a part which Melanie's timely intervention had deprived him of when she and the Captain had caught them in the woods.

'She feels wet,' he announced, and butted his front handkerchief and the visibly stiffening rod behind it hard up against the central rift.

'That's enough, you rascal!' laughed Melanie, roughly tugging him away. 'It'll soon be bedtime.' And to the bride: 'You OK, dear?' A rather subdued murmur from poor abused Susie, her face half hidden in the cushion, assured her that the ordeal was being borne bravely.

Now was the moment when the monstrous pink dildo which had graced the altar was to serve its ritual purpose. Melanie strapped it to her loins over the G-string and glanced lustfully at the girl's bum. For the pretended reason why Susie had been placed in her upended posture was to make sure that the bridegroom would find an unobstructed passage to the joys of manhood, and that the vigorous finger exercises in which she had been schooled had left no scrap of membrane to impede the rites of the absent Hymen.

'Isn't that a bit big?' the Captain asked. 'Don't you need Vaseline or something?'

'I've thought of that, and I've got a better idea,' she replied.

'Heini, we're going to need some high-grade lubricant – you remember how we said.'

Two more cushions were then placed alongside those on which Susie was still kneeling, and the delicate Cathy was requested to lie down on them. The two bridesmaids were called on to unbutton her nightshirt down to her waist, exposing her breasts, full but standing up firmly, with their small, dark nipples. Heini knelt astride her and pulled up his own nightshirt to reveal his ginger-fuzzed thighs, flaming bush and half-erected tool.

Melanie then whispered some instructions in Nikki's ear. With a grin, the naked girl threw an arm around Heini's neck, fastened an open-mouthed sexual kiss on his lips, and with her free hand fondled his balls. His cock reared up to its full glory. Nikki clutched it in her little hand and brought to to bear on Cathy's bosom just as the latter squeezed her breasts together to envelop the head in their warm grasp. Nikki slipped her hand back under the testicles, whereupon the hot white fluid gushed from between Cathy's breasts to flood the whole expanse of skin up to her throat. Heini and Nikki now withdrew, and Cathy's breasts fell open, allowing the thick puddle to spread; the reek of spilt seed was overpowering, and went to the heads of all present. The smaller bridesmaid was made to scoop it up in her hands so that both palms were brimming with it.

One of these was applied to the dildo, giving it a completely slippery surface. The other hand was taken by Melanie and rubbed hard against Susie's private parts, which were now pouting wide open, bringing her pretty pink wetness into full view for the first time. Finally, having wiped her hands on Nikki's buttocks, the girl was given permission to lick that firm white bottom clean. This she did with alacrity.

Before the fluids smeared on the girl's pussy and the great rubber phallus had time to dry, Melanie knelt and swooped forward to seize her bare hips. Without preliminaries she rammed into the tender cunt until the fronts of her own thighs pressed against the backs of Susie's, and the Captain's view of Susie's behind was replaced with that of hers, the little G-string cutting between the quivering cheeks and the pouch containing her pussy fully visible. Susie screamed. Then she moaned, sobbed and whimpered.

Leaning forward to let the girl's rump take the weight of her slender body, Melanie reached both hands around her. With one, she stroked first the fronts of the upper thighs, and then the tummy, while, with the other, she caressed the unseen young breasts concealed within the white suntop that hung wide open. The whimpering now ceased, and the Captain even thought he caught a hint of a smile at the corner of Susie's mouth, half-buried in the cushion.

'There,' said Melanie, 'it's not all that bad, is it? I'm only doing it so you'll get really lovely feelings when Darcy puts his willie inside you.'

'It's quite nice now, actually,' the girl replied.

'But nothing like as nice as what's coming to you when you get a real one up you,' breathed Melanie, who then reached behind herself to unfasten a buckle and disengage the dildo from her loins. Little more than half the length of the huge instrument was now seen to have been accommodated by the girl's vagina. Before unsheathing it, Melanie worked it rapidly and vigorously in and out a dozen times. Each time it was partially withdrawn, it dragged back with it the tender pink lips which had stretched to cling to its circumference. When finally pulled out with a sucking sound and displayed to the congregation, it looked even wetter and more slippery than before it was inserted.

Melanie's next action was unscheduled and took everyone by surprise. As if seized with mania, she threw herself down on the cushions beside Susie, her body arching back and her thighs opened wide. One hand tugged the black silk triangle aside and splayed the wet labia, while with the other she wedged the slimy dildo up between them to its furthest extent.

'Susie! Darcy!' she gasped. 'Quick! Kiss my tits!'

Astonished, the young couple adopted a kneeling position on either side of her and moved away the scarf which lay on the breasts of this sacrilegious, frockless priest. The nipples stuck out in their pride, and were instantly taken between the lips of the child bride and her eager groom. Meanwhile, Melanie herself was agitating the dildo even more furiously than she had applied it to Susie. In no time at all she screamed aloud, threw up her hands and hugged her two attendants, crushing them to her breasts as she wailed, sobbed and shuddered in repeated spasms.

Another photograph was attempted, a close-up showing the faces of the happy if embarrassed pair, now pronounced man and wife. Darcy was then told to kiss the bride 'in threefold greeting'. If the first part of the rite had been performed successfully in accordance with the priest's instructions, the shot might have been less appealing, as the close contact would have hidden much of the pretty countenances from view. But Susie, clasped in her husband's tight embrace, forced her lips from his after the first touch, so that the Captain caught the couple in his viewfinder cheek to cheek, the boy's tongue extended and his eyes mad with lust as the girl flinched from him bashfully. The flash of the camera illuminated a trail of saliva smeared over her cheek from the corner of her mouth by his tongue.

Probably the intimate face-to-face contact of a kiss on the mouth had been too much for her in such a public setting. But she offered no objection or resistance to the second and third stages of this nuptial greeting, which were carried out smoothly under Melanie's efficient direction.

First, the smaller bridesmaid stepped forward and positioned herself behind the bride, who stood with her legs slightly parted. She reached her hands forward beneath Susie's arms, and drew the suntop fully open to expose her breasts. The Captain had already had chances to observe these from a distance on earlier occasions, and indeed to feel them through her dress, but not so Darcy, who was thrilled, and expressed his excitement in a high-pitched cry. 'Look, she's got proper little titties on her!' he gasped.

This was indeed partly true. The hemispheres themselves were as yet no more than plump ripenings on the ivory chest. No semicircles demarcated their lower limits, and an unskilled artist might have found it hard to indicate their swelling contours in a frontal drawing. What had engaged Darcy's enthusiasm, surely, was the far more developed appearance of the nipples. So pale that their pink was only slightly darker than the smooth skin in which they were set, the areolas were large and puffy, textured with a profusion of tiny bumps clustered around their central protuberances. The latter, too, though not yet engorged through the stimulation they were about to be subjected to, were more prominent than the Captain had expected. He could easily make out the small slotlike depressions, resembling in miniature the opening of the head of a penis, in which the tips terminated.

At a wink from the mistress of ceremonies, the bridesmaid grasped the right breastlet in an 'O' formed by her thumb and fingers and squeezed it so that the teat was thrust forward into Darcy's mouth as he inclined his head to meet it. With his own right hand he clutched and rubbed her other breast so roughly that the Captain was afraid she would find this as distasteful as the kissing of her mouth. But the nipple rapidly grew darker, growing hard and elongated, and now her face lit up with every sign of rapture.

'That's enough for that part,' said Melanie.

As the lad dropped to his knees, everyone saw that Susie's right nipple was now even more aroused than the one he had fondled, to which it offered an interesting contrast in its gleaming wetness.

The bridesmaid was reminded that it was now time for her to execute a duty the guests had anticipated with impatience, although the girl herself, because of her position standing behind the bride, was unable to see what provoked their gasps of admiration. Reaching round to the front of Susie's thighs, she took the corners of her handkerchief in her fingers and raised it to cover the belly, revealing for the first time to the assembled company, including the husband, a front view of the venereal mound, as yet unconquered by manly flesh.

The vulva itself was plump, white and smooth, bisected by a simple vertical line betraying no hint of her recent mauling by the sacred dildo. It had been shaved to look like the smooth pussy of a little girl, and distinguished only by the yielding softness the Captain's imagination credited it with from the firmness of the inner thighs between which it was displayed. But immediately above the slit, at the base of the belly and only just uncovered by the uplifted handkerchief, a silky tuft of golden fur proclaimed her nubility.

Darcy rested his hands on her hips and kissed the tuft, grinning as it tickled his nose. Then he kissed the slit.

'What does it smell like?' asked Melanie.

'It doesn't. Well, sort of fresh. Like scented soap.'

'See if you can open it a bit with your tongue.'

Driven by curiosity, he inclined his head so that it hung sideways, and ran the tip of his tongue slowly up the cleft. This had the effect of slightly parting the outer lips, so that the moist inner ones were revealed.

'Now it smells like – like biscuits,' declared the puzzled boy.

'Lick a bit more,' ordered Melanie. 'See what it *tastes* like.'

As the tongue executed a second pass from the vaginal entrance to the clitoris, it separated the delicate inner lips, and moved down again to penetrate their recesses.

'No, I can't think what it tastes like,' he announced, backing away to breathe. 'But it's scrupulous.'

'Scrupulous? Don't you mean scrumptious?'

'That's it – scrumptious. Can I go on doing it to her?'

Once more in a state of conspicuous tumescence, he was told to back off and wait for everyone else to take their turn at kissing the bride, as prescribed by custom and practice. The congregation lined up, first the bridesmaids (Susie now had to hold up her own handkerchief with one hand while squeezing her right breast with the other), followed by Cathy and Heini, then Melanie and finally the photographer. For these kisses, Susie was permitted to avert her mouth and present a coy cheek to be pecked. The only restrictions imposed on the second and third elements of the threefold greeting were temporal ones, no more than ten seconds being allowed to each part.

It was a pretty sight to watch the younger bridesmaid rise on the tips of her toes to kiss Susie, who was slightly taller than her. A blush suffused this girl's cheeks when a pink nipple was offered to her lips, and her cunt-kiss appeared to consist of no more than a nudge with her nose. She skulked off the edge of the group, overcome with modesty.

Unsurprisingly, Nikki was bolder. The attention she devoted to her friend's proffered breast was a sucking so vehement that she left the nipple twice as long as she found it, and dripping with saliva. And in her tonguing of the slit, by now well lubricated and sagging open, she showed even more passion than the bridegroom. Rising to her feet, she turned away reluctantly, made for her bashful colleague and hugged her, squeezing the little buttocks in a frenzy as their bellies rubbed briskly together.

It was now Cathy's turn, and a marked difference in approach was evident. All three kisses were quick, light and chaste, but she began and finished by hugging the girl to her generous bosom in a gesture of real affection.

Less lascivious still was Heini's attention. Kiss, kiss, kiss, and that was it. He withdrew to rejoin his darling Cathy.

How would the fiery and unpredictable Melanie make out? As she stood in her outrageous canonicals before the bride, the Captain guessed that she was about to take some advantage of the ritual she herself had devised. First she threw her left arm round Susie's neck and, bringing her lips to the girl's right ear, whispered something in it that made Susie simper and blush. She then proceeded to her own version of the threefold greeting. Her actual kisses were as chaste as those of Cathy and Heini, though more prolonged. But while she administered them, her hands were employed less innocently, being planted firmly on Susie's bottom under the back handkerchief. During the kissing of the pubis, the girl winced, and it was not hard to guess that probing fingers were at work in a private place between the cheeks.

At last Melanie got up, and it was the Captain's turn, although strictly speaking the photographer had no right to this familiarity. When he laid his hands on the bride's shoulders, he realised they were quivering. Indeed, her whole body was shaking, not visibly but quite evidently to his touch. Planting his lips on her forehead, he drew her towards him, and felt the head of his cock press through its black covering against her belly. He dropped to his knees, opened his mouth and took a whole delicious breast into it, swirling his tongue around a nipple that hardened in shocked response. Finally, he rested a cheek against her mound, rubbing it across the silky down as his nose sought contact with her cleft. Ecstatically, he just flicked the lips with the very tip of his tongue, then withdrew and stood up. How charmingly she blushed! Nor was it merely a coy blush – he was sure she darted a momentary glance of the most lascivious naughtiness at him as he turned to retrieve his camera.

For the next picture, which was to display their genital areas from the same close range as the portrait shot, Susie had to be adorned with a red carnation. The stalk was woven into her tuft by Nikki's nimble fingers, so that the bloom hung downwards over the upper end of her rift. At the same time, Nikki's little colleague had taken Darcy's cock, now perked up again to full erection, slender but rigid as an iron rod, and garlanded it with a daisy chain fashioned into a ring.

By this time, the most formal part of the proceedings was over. At a sign from Melanie, the bridesmaids stripped the new Mr and Mrs O'Flammery naked, except for their rosebud-adorned chokers. The carnation and daisy chain, only produced for the picture, were snatched off. Darcy took his wife's hand and led her boldly to the other end of the room, where the nuptial couch awaited. His penis pointed the way, a growing drop of clear secretion on the tip glistening in the candlelight.

TWELVE

THE BEDDING

Feeling somewhat overheated, the Captain emptied another bottle of Babycham into the chalice and gulped it reflectively before following the others, who now stood, sat or sprawled, panting with eagerness, on piles of cushions and a couple of chairs around an old king-size mattress. Illuminated by repositioned candles, the couple lay ready for the fray.

Stark naked, the bride exhibited her prostrate charms, her cheeks burning with expectation. Against the purple sheet her body looked purest white. These two dominant colours delightfully set off the few contrasting details: dreamy blue eyes; two golden plaits (one on the sheet, the other draped forward over her shoulder) with their scarlet ribbons; the black velvet choker with its red rosebud; the lighter pink rosebuds of her parted lips and her nipples; the shining gold tuft above the bare slit. She lay with her right arm thrown back above her head to expose a childish armpit. Her left palm rested on her lower belly, the fingers spread out so that the index and middle ones, forming an inverted V, masked the edges of the tuft, their tips just resting in the creases between mound and thighs. Thanks to the way she sprawled with legs wide apart, her labia were displayed, moist and slightly open, adding a final touch of pink to the delicious scene.

While the ensuing drama was acted out, the Captain staggered and crawled about trying to capture some memorable moments with his camera. To begin with, Darcy, rod fully extended, knelt between the thighs of his darling wife and began to poke at her cunt. Like most novices, he aimed rather too high, and the first picture taken in this series promised to show, in close-up, the forfeit he had immediately had to pay for his overheated impetuosity: hanging from the glowing head of his tool, a viscous white column which formed a vertical connection, some two inches long, between the glans and a now sodden pussy. The lower tummy and tuft were awash with his hot white jelly, already beginning to run down the channels of her groins.

This time Darcy needed no instructions. Placing his hands under her bottom, he buried his face in the steaming puddle. He slurped away until his Susie was as clean as she had been brought to him, even though, as was seen when he raised his head to inspect his work, the effect of that silken tuft was now ruined, the hairs being darkened and slicked down on her skin. Otherwise, all traces of his second ejaculation had disappeared. But this did not seem to satisfy him, and he resumed his licking, at the same time kneading the little buttocks vigorously. The Captain noticed that the centre of his attentions was now rather lower – it was evident that the tip of his tongue had discovered a most sensitive point.

The newly married bride was showing signs of approaching throes of bliss. Her eyes were closed, and her mouth set in an expression of intense concentration as she tossed about on the mattress, oblivious of her audience. The dark blush on her cheeks hurried downwards over her chest and stomach; she stretched out her legs at a wide angle and thrust up to press the yearning flesh into her husband's face. With a sudden cry and a convulsion which threw her loins so violently upwards that Darcy was toppled sideways from his kneeling position, she gave herself to the rapture of her first connubial orgasm.

However, the satisfaction she derived from this seizure (and her bashful smile as she lay back gasping testified to its potency) lasted for a short time only. Her eyes found Melanie's, and she appealed to her in evident bewilderment. 'That was nice,' she said, 'but when am I going to get fucked?'

By this stage the Captain was so well primed that he would have been glad to step forward, hurl himself on to her and bore deep into the moist cunt she displayed invitingly to the bystanders. But he was held back by a reluctance to disrupt the ordained progress of these solemn rites, and also, perhaps, by a recollection that Melanie had given some vague promise about the bride being made available to the wedding guests once the groom's needs had been sated – a provision, he had remarked, that might enliven many a more orthodox wedding.

'Oh, he'll fuck you as soon as you get him hard again,' she assured the girl.

'How am I supposed to do that?'

'You can try kissing and licking,' she replied, lifting the boy's limp, wet prick with one finger.

Excellent and seemingly clear though this advice was, Susie managed to misconstrue it. Rising to a sitting posture, she took Darcy by the shoulders and brought her open lips to his mouth, dribbling and trailing her tongue over his chin as she sought out the best angle from which to engage him in a long and truly passionate kiss.

Even if this was not quite what Melanie had in mind, it would probably have proved just as efficacious, for the slimy penis immediately stirred its head. But the precocious Nikki had understood perfectly. Falling on the mattress, she inclined her head over Darcy's lap. Because her straight brown hair was cut short, it left her face and mouth exposed as she slightly lifted her head. There could be no doubt that she was fellating him with relish, drawing in and then releasing her rosy cheeks as she sucked that supple cock, and sliding her lips up and down a slippery shaft that grew visibly thicker as she did so. The appeal of this spectacle was further heightened for the Captain by the fact that she knelt at the work with her knees straddling Darcy's thighs and her little bottom thrust up towards the camera. Again the photographer felt an urge to sink his stiff cock into a girlish orifice, and either of the two splendid little specimens before him would have done nicely.

But it was not to be. Afraid that Nikki's mouth was about to bring the lad to yet another emission of the precious fluid, Melanie ruined the picture by squeezing the Captain's arm, and suggested that he should remove the girl from the scene of combat. So he reached his hands under her smooth armpits, placed the palms on her flat chest and hauled her to her feet, distinctly hearing a sound like that of cork being drawn from a bottle as her lips were pulled away from the now fully erected organ. She seemed reluctant to part with it, and wriggled forwards in the grasp holding her to bend over it as far as she could. The firm hands of her captor slid down to her narrow hips and hoisted her up so that he was able to shove his throbbing prick between her buttocks and hold her riding on it as if it had been the crossbar of a bicycle. In her bent-forward position she could see the knob projecting beneath her hairless pussy; with this temporary addition to her charms she must have looked even more like a boy than usual, although a front view was denied the Captain. When she applied her forefinger and thumb to it, though, he felt things had gone a bit too far, and dropped her on to her feet with a friendly pat on the behind.

'Later?' she pleaded, turning her head and gazing wide-eyed at him.

'Let's wait and see,' he whispered.

He returned to his photography, just in time to catch Darcy on the very point of consummating his union with the eager Mrs O'Flammery. He had raised himself over her on straightened arms and with legs braced as if doing a press-up. It looked as if he had posed especially for the camera, although the way he held his head indicated that really he simply wished to view their two bellies and his rigid cock before insertion. There it quivered, almost horizontal – long, slender and hard as an iron bar. The whiteness of all that surrounding flesh contrasted with the dusky mauve of the glans, the little chestnut bush of his pubic hairs and the darkened yellow of hers, still plastered down with the rapidly drying product of his recent spending.

At this juncture, Melanie positioned herself behind him to direct the operation, while the wedding guests crowded together at the foot of the bed, their eyes bright in the candlelight, and their faces rosy with anticipation. She made Susie spread her thighs as wide as they would go, while she herself placed her knees outside Darcy's legs. Her hands reached round on either side of his flanks so that one of them could hold open the girl's cuntlips while the other guided the straining prick to its goal. Once the head was securely lodged, she dealt his bottom a sharp slap and ordered him to shove.

The lad needed no encouragement. Seemingly a born fucker, he rammed away with a vigour that many a tender bride would have found too much for her on her wedding night. But Susie responded with equal enthusiasm, and only her closed eyes and blushes hinted, albeit very ambiguously, at sentiments of outraged modesty.

Of course, it was no time at all before their union was sealed with the first eruption of the boy's loins deep inside her vagina. They lay trembling in a tight embrace, and Melanie instructed

173

them to keep the penis sheathed until full erection could be reachieved. To hasten that end, she parted his thighs a little, and summoned the junior bridesmaid.

'Kneel here,' she commanded, 'with your right knee between his knees and the left one on the outside. Now rest your cheek on his bottom – that's right – and gently feel his balls. Got them? While you do that, see if you can reach forward with two of your fingers so that you grip the base of his cock between them. Give a little squeeze now and then to help excite him. And if you wriggle your fingertips about, you may be able to tickle Susie's pussy lips.'

To judge from the tremors of the couple as they lay there, Darcy in postcoital bliss and Susie yet to be satisfied in this bout, the bridesmaid was an apt pupil. Until this moment the Captain had paid her scant attention, her expressionless face being insufficiently distinctive to arouse his interest. But he realised now that she was not unattractive, her most striking feature being the long black hair which cascaded over the fair bodies of the lovers. Her own skin was beautifully tanned and shiny, almost as if it had been oiled, and rather surprisingly this tan covered the whole of her lithe body. Maybe, he speculated, the expression was not one of mulish blankness but of disdain for these licentious proceedings.

Was there no end to Melanie's inventiveness? She now grabbed Nikki and got her to lie flat on her back at right angles to the others, with her head resting on Darcy's right thigh. This meant that her face was located directly beneath the other bridesmaid's smooth little cunt. Nikki was then made to place her hands on this colleague's buttocks and draw them down a fraction so that her pubis was brought into contact with her own mouth. As usual, the randy girl knew exactly what to do, and the ministrations of her tongue spurred on her suntanned mate (whose expression rapidly lost its blankness) to titillate the newlyweds with ever-growing enthusiasm.

Meanwhile, the Captain's own enthusiasm was being titillated to such a pitch that immediate relief was imperative. He placed his hands on Melanie's shoulders, lowered one to her bum and drew her tightly towards him so that she could feel the hardness of his member. Then he stooped his head to her ear. 'Melanie, you sexy bitch, I've never been so ready for it,' he whispered hoarsely. 'My balls weigh a ton. If you don't let me screw a cunt right now, you're going to be soaked with my come.'

'Well,' she answered, 'it's a busy schedule, but maybe we can slot you in somewhere.'

'What about your own slot?'

Instead of replying, she mounted the mattress and stood facing him, with a foot on each side of Darcy's calves. With impressive athleticism she first raised her hands above her head and then leaned right back until they touched the mattress above the couple's head. Her whole body was now bent backwards to form an arch under which the marital ritual was being conducted; her buttocks, their sides quite concave with the muscular exertion of this posture, were just in contact with the kneeling bridesmaid's behind. From his position it was obvious to the Captain that she was offering him her cunt, still covered with the little black triangle of cloth, which he rudely pulled aside. As he did so, the pink cleft pouting out from its growth of gingery hair released the rank, gamey odour of sex to inflame his nostrils. He was rampant.

Letting the front of his gown fall open, he bent his knees slightly to bring his tool to the right level. As soon as its head was nuzzled between the lips, he grabbed her buttocks and drove hard into her until his crotch was wedged against hers, which she thrust up even higher to meet it. Joined together in this way, leaning forward with his knees slightly bent, there was little scope for him to move inside her, but she made up for this, partly by wriggling her bum up and down as much as she could between him and the bridesmaid, but mainly by exerting the most amazing vaginal contractions. The pressure mounting within him, he allowed his hands to drift down from Melanie's firm buttocks to the hips of the younger girl below her. First stroking and then pinching them, he felt himself rising to an uncontrollable climax.

At that moment, Darcy and Susie must have reached their own orgasm. An enormous heave of their loins lifted Nikki's head and jammed her mouth so violently against the other bridesmaid's shaven cunt that she, too, bucked in the bliss of what she later admitted to be her first time ever. Her convulsions threw

Melanie off balance, and all four attendants collapsed on top of the honeymooners. In what seemed an unending series of explosions, the Captain's sperm gushed and gushed into Melanie's tight channel. Too long delayed, it was his first fuck of the evening, and in his view absolutely necessary.

Panting, giggling and laughing aloud, they all started feeling each other as they lay there in that collapsed heap of flesh. His fingers had no sense of who they were touching, but wandered delightedly from silky skin to tufts of scrubby hair to well-lubricated mucous membranes. A little of this promiscuity, however, was enough for Melanie, who broke up the party and suggested that the couple whose union they were supposed to be celebrating ought to be allowed to enjoy themselves undisturbed for a few delicious fucks while the rest of them paired off to flirt by themselves.

'Oh yes!' cried the delighted Susie, who was certainly warming to her new marital status. 'Handling and holding, frigging and fucking, just like we promised. Come on, Darcy, stick your thing in me again.'

'It's gone all soft,' he murmured bashfully.

'You kiss me between my legs,' she replied, 'while I lick that gooey stuff off it. Let's see if that makes it go stiff.'

While Susie and Darcy toyed, kissed, cuddled and screwed, the others present withdrew to the shadows surrounding the bridal bed and subsided on the cushions scattered on the floor, disturbed only by the flashes of the Captain's camera as he prowled among them, snapping their pleasures. First, his attention was attracted by the youngest couple, the two charming bridesmaids. They had adopted a sophisticated classical embrace, lying on their sides, each with a thigh raised and tongue stuck out, about to lock into each other in what had to be a well-rehearsed sixty-nine. Their conduct certainly belied their innocent looks.

Having captured them on film, he moved on to Cathy and Heini, more developed physically (as Miss MacDonald would surely have pointed out), yet nevertheless possessing a beautifully innocent appearance. At the moment the flash illuminated them, they stood facing each other, their heads slightly inclined and gazing downwards. Heini was unbuttoning the front of his girlfriend's nightdress and had allowed one of her lovely, ripe breasts to find its freedom in the candlelight. Her hands were on his shoulders. She had already unfastened his buttons, all except the top two, and the focal point of her gaze seemed to be his superbly well-grown organ.

They looked up, surprised out of the self-absorbed rapture of young love by the dazzling flash. Heini whispered a few words in his girlfriend's ear, and the Captain was the one to be surprised by her next move. She turned her back on the photographer, hoisted up the nightdress to her waist and bent forward, displaying her bum. Taking what he assumed to be a strong hint that she was hoping to be served by him, he opened the front of his gown, behind which a massive erection had already reared itself up. But even as he laid his hands on the luscious flanks and made to drive his penis home, her well-endowed partner snatched her from him and, while she remained bent forward, spun her round so that not her cunt but her mouth received its pulsating length. For an instant the Captain feared she was about to bite it off as Heini shoved into her from behind. Her contorted expression suggested that the rough handling she was being subjected to was causing her some pain, and appearances favoured the inference that he was buggering her. But the discomfort only lasted a moment and was replaced, judging from the lecherous treatment the Captain's prick now received from her tongue and lips, with deep enjoyment. His hands and her boyfriend's both struggled to find and handle her pendulous boobs, and they tacitly settled on one each. Her older partner discharged in her mouth just as Heini shot his hot load up her arse. Instantly she stood up straight, threw her arms round the Captain's neck, and clamped her lips to his mouth. His own seed slid copiously from her tongue on to his, and he swallowed it. Cathy and her Heini then turned away from him and sank down on the cushions to engage in a bout of serious lovemaking.

Melanie and the Captain were now the only ones left to be paired with each other. She stood there half-smiling like a streamlined, slimmed-down version of the goddess of love, clad in nothing but her white neckcloth with its starched bands, her black sandals and the black G-string, now thoroughly soaked following the screwing she had so recently received. Already the edges of its wetness were giving way to a white stain as it dried. Down the inside of her left thigh, slow and sticky, flowed a mass of whitish jelly. One of his hands on the small of her back, he wiped the other one up the thigh to collect as much as he could of the reeking juice, which he immediately rubbed all over her chest, working it with relish into the hardening nipples. All that then remained was to push her down on her back so that he could kneel above her and let his lips pasture on the salty snouts.

Soon he felt her wriggling her bottom, and realised that she was discarding the ruined G-string. She turned away from him on her side and lifted her upper thigh, caressing its length in an invitation which was not refused. His hand took over from hers, its stroking of that soft, shining skin moving ever closer to the groin, until her damp hairs brushed his knuckles. At once he drew the lips apart and pushed his hard prick into her from behind. Instead of thrusting in and out, he let it rest there, growing even thicker and longer, while he frigged her clitoris with nimble fingers. It was not long before the tensing of her muscles heralded the onset of her climax and gave him the signal to start rogering her with all the vigour and rapidity he could summon up. 'Yes, yes, yes!' she gasped, throwing her limbs about as if a high-voltage current was being passed through her. He responded by smothering her ear, neck and cheek with delighted kisses as he met her convulsions by pouring a torrent of spunk into her vagina.

After this invigorating fuck, Melanie went off to make up a threesome with Cathy and Heini, who were romping on the cushions over on the far side of the marriage bed. The Captain was not left alone for long, though. Very soon the two brides-maids joined him, lying down on either side of him and snuggling up for a cuddle. Nikki was hardly able to control a fit of giggling, but her suntanned colleague, whose name was never disclosed, remained as solemn-faced as usual.

Nikki spoke, trying to fit the words into the gaps between her giggles. 'My, my mate here (he-he-he) says you, says you (he-he) promised to, to screw her (he-he-he) later on. Are you, are you (he-he) ready?'

'I can't tell if I'm ready till I try. But you bet I'm ready to try, especially if both of you can help to make sure I really am ready.'

178

The Captain winked at them both in turn, and conveyed Nikki's hand to his limp prick.

'Listen,' she replied, rolling it between her thumb and forefinger. 'When we say, when we (he-he) say "screw", we don't really mean going (he-he), going the whole hog. We're both, both virgins, see.'

'I might be able to change that for you.'

'No! We don't want to get in, involved with that, that stuff (he-he-he). I helped Sue, Susie with the finger exercises Melanie made (he-he) made her do before the wedding. It really hurt her, and we both, both got our fingers all bloody. But can't you (he-he-he), can't you sort of pretend and still make her, make her come?'

The Captain replied in what were meant to be avuncular tones: 'I'll see what I can do if you help me to bring her on, as well as me.'

This scheme was now put into practice. The girl and man embraced, lying facing each other. The top of her head was tucked under his chin, her mouth nuzzling his chest. Her thighs gripped his upper one, so that about halfway down its length it pressed into her smooth, damp crotch. His hands clasped her bottom, and his cock was squashed against her tummy.

With an apparently spontaneous lechery that still left him wondering how far it was the product of hours of experimentation, the hot-tailed Nikki Culpepper knelt astride them both as they lay there, her giggles having now subsided. She insinuated one hand between his legs, to play with his testicles, tease his pubic hair and tickle the root of his penis, already beginning to swell up yet again. Her other hand was on his partner's mound, with a finger working away at the clitoris.

As she performed these offices for both of them simultaneously, she leaned forward to kiss the Captain, an action which involved a good deal of sucking and slurping. His passion rose. Suddenly he became conscious that they had an unexpected audience – Cathy and Heini, their nightshirts unbuttoned and hanging completely open, were standing above them watching intently. Even as the pressure to ejaculate became intolerable, this inseparable pair seized the surprised Nikki and threw her down on her back at right angles to the Captain and his partner. Her

179

knees were raised and spread wide, her feet prevented from stretching forward by the suntanned bridesmaid's side, up against which they were pushed. This, of course, gave the Captain a fine view of her cunt, and its aphrodisiac effect was as powerful as that of the manipulations she had been engaged in when the intervening couple tore her away.

The two young lovers, who must have planned their assault in advance, lay down on either side of Nikki, their heads level with her loins. Their own genitals were positioned so that, almost instinctively, she reached for them with her hands and toyed with them, turning her head from side to side to lick and suck the stiffening cock and moistening cunt alternately. Under the stimulation of this treatment, they made bold with their fingers, exploring and mauling her pubis. In a short time the smooth, youthful vulva had been pulled open.

This can have given but little direct satisfaction to Cathy and Heini, as the Captain was the only one to whom the inside of the glistening pink gash was visible. But the sight brought him to an instant climax, and he felt the hot sperm spreading between his belly and the one it was pressed against, seeking places where it could run out at the sides and flow down to drench the cushions.

Reluctant to disappoint his partner, who must have gathered from the evening's scenes that such bouts were expected to end with both (or all) participants in throes of ecstasy, he slid down her body, which was slippery indeed and reeking with his tangy effusion, and tongued her to a rapid conclusion. How fresh and clean her cunt juices tasted! Rising from her, he was unable to resist pushing Cathy and Heini's hands aside and kissing the open lips of Nikki's cunt, which tasted just as nice as the other one – indeed, hardly distinguishable from it. Nikki writhed with lust, and exploded. Then the Captain collapsed among all that young flesh and fell instantly into a heavy slumber.

He awoke to a sharp odour of greasy smoke. All the candles save two had burnt out, and everyone appeared to be asleep, covered with the blankets that had been thoughtfully provided by Melanie. He stretched himself, and stumbled around until he located an unused candle, which he lit from one of those still burning. Kneeling at the foot of the bridal bed, he let a little puddle of wax drip on to the floorboards and stuck the candle upright in it.

The newly broken bride lay sleeping peacefully under an old cover, with her thumb in her mouth. On the pillow beside her, he noticed her torn and discarded velvet choker, the rosebud crumpled. Beginning at her feet and working cautiously upwards, he lifted the cover, delighting in every inch of flesh as he exposed it. In the flickering light cast by the candle her skin shone pale and silvery, reminding him of the moon. Closer examination, however, revealed that much of her body was crusted with crumbling, flaky dried sperm. Her ravaged cunt swelled out between her slightly parted thighs. It looked puffy and was oozing quantities of slime, as if she had been debauched by the great garden-god Priapus himself. And her bottom rested on a large damp patch spreading on the purple sheet.

How could the gallant Captain not be moved by such a sight? First he sneaked a quick snapshot, and congratulated himself that everyone slept through the flash. Then he slipped his gown from his shoulders. Stealthily, so as not to disturb the spent youth sleeping beside her, he laid the length of his body alongside hers and pulled the blanket over both of them.

He must have been colder than he realised, for his proximity woke her up, and for a moment she stared at him without recognition – even, perhaps, with alarm. Then she smiled, and pressed her warm, firm body against him. He removed his mask, and her smile widened.

'How are you feeling, Susie dear?' he inquired.

'Not too bad. Sort of stiff.'

'You made a lovely bride, you know. You really got all of us going. I envy your husband – look how shagged out he is.'

'Yes,' she replied, 'I do seem to have drained the last drop of – of sperm from his balls.'

'And your lovely little cunt is certainly overflowing. I had a peep at it before I got into this bed, and I've never seen such a flood. How many times did he squirt it in?'

'I lost count,' laughed Susie. 'Every time he went soft I, you know, frigged him with my mouth, like Nikki did, till he got hard again. But in the end his willie was just like a wet shrimp, and he went to sleep. He's awfully sore.'

'You seem to have taken quite a battering yourself, my darling. Be thankful his cock's still not very thick when he gets it up.'

'But he wasn't the only one,' she admitted. 'When he'd finished, that rude Heini had a go at me, and his gets much bigger. I thought he was going to split me.'

The Captain was on the point of protesting indignantly, but remembered that Melanie had promised everyone present a share in the bride's treasures, and that this was in fact his own excuse for intruding on her slumbers. 'How do you feel about being an unfaithful wife so soon after your wedding?' he inquired, trying to suppress the hint of irony in his tone.

'Oh, Melanie said it doesn't count. It's just like kissing the bride – all part of the big occasion.'

'But suppose you have a baby. You won't know who's the father.'

'Oh, no, you don't understand. Melanie's been giving me these pills. And anyhow, Heini's thing was so fat he couldn't get it into me properly, only that big plum on the end.'

'He must have been disappointed!' commented the Captain.

'Well, not all that disappointed. He got up on my chest and wanted to stick it in my mouth.'

'Did you let him?'

'I wasn't sure if I wanted to. It looked a bit frightening, all blue and bulging. But it happened while I was staring at it.'

'You mean he came?'

'Yes. The end of it got bigger, and went all dark and shiny. Then I thought it had burst. All this sort of creamy, sticky stuff came shooting out of it. It went all over my face. A little bit of it got in one of my eyes, and some of it splashed my lips. I was glad it hadn't gone in my mouth when I tasted it. It felt really warm and had this strong smell like fish, much stronger than Darcy's.'

'What about the girls – did they do it with you too?'

'You bet. First it was Cathy. When she saw Heini trying to do me, she jumped on him and started kissing his bottom, and when he pulled it out and climbed up on my chest she got down and kissed my thingie. She got a bit rough, and pinched me. I suppose that was when she was having her – her orgy. But afterwards, after Heini dirtied my face, she was really nice. She told him to go away, and licked me clean. Then she just cuddled me, you know, and sort of squashed my face between her bosoms.'

'And your bridesmaids?'

'Oh yes. They wouldn't leave me alone. They sort of made a sandwich of me. Really I think they were making love to each other, and using me to help them get excited. They were reaching across me and round me, doing things to each other. But at the end they did sort of bring me into it a bit more.'

'How did they do that?'

'Well,' she explained, 'it was like a kind of triangle. Nikki had her head between my legs and started licking me and kissing me and all that, and I had to do the same to the other one while she was doing it to Nikki, if you see what I mean. And we used our hands to play with each other's tits. That was fun.'

'And Melanie? Did she get a share of the action?'

'Oh, she was helping us all the time. She was the one who got us into this triangle thing. And she kept spanking Nikki's friend and calling her lazy and telling her to go at it faster.'

'I'm surprised Melanie didn't join in herself.'

'She couldn't. Heini and Cathy were doing something to her. I think he'd stuck his thing in her bum, and Cathy was down there licking her tummy and her furry part. But she came to me a bit later.'

'Was that nice for you, my pretty one?'

Susie considered. 'She's really wild, isn't she? Once she gets going she throws herself about and makes noises and sort of works you up with her. I went all giddy with the stuff she was doing to me, and I can't really remember what happened. She put her tongue everywhere, and made me do things to her with mine. I was so tired when she finished, but I feel a bit better now.'

Slyly, the Captain drew her to him, planted a kiss on her forehead and remarked that she had done well to give pleasure to so many of the company.

'Yes,' she said bashfully, 'you're the only one who hasn't had me.'

This, of course, was his own thought precisely. Ever since he had first caught sight of her in her saucy wedding outfit, he had been longing to force that tight, juicy cunt. No, ever since that

183

snatched glimpse of her through his binoculars, romping with Nikki in the long grass. To be sure, on first turning back the blanket he had been somewhat deterred by the quantities of spent sperm defiling her pussy and thighs. In the normal run of things he had little stomach for 'buttered buns', to use the jocular expression he was familiar with. Even he, after all, could lay claim to a certain measure of fastidiousness; he didn't relish the idea of paddling in the scummy secretions of other men. But, in the light of Susie's detailed account of what had been done to her, he felt much better about it. Only the virginal Darcy had actually discharged inside her. The prospect of enjoying her while her vagina was awash with fresh young seed newly broached and mixed with the sweet juices of her own body was distinctly appealing. As long as she didn't turn him down because of his age or some other stupid reason. He pondered what to say, but she cut in.

'I want you more than any of them. You're the only real man, aren't you? And I don't care how big your thing is. I know you'll be gentle and we'll get it in somehow. Please make love to me. Go on, do it now.'

'Very well, my dearest one,' he replied, 'but be sure to let me know if I'm hurting you.'

His penis stiffened and lengthened as he spoke the words, and he let it press against her belly. Instead of responding to her invitation by ramming straight into her, he went for the option of reviving her spirits with gentle foreplay.

One of his arms cradled her golden head, the pigtails now loosened and unplaited, and his free hand fondled the firm little bottom. Beginning with a kiss that he thought of as chaste and friendly, he waited for her lips to part and the tip of her tongue to dart out wetly. Even then he kept his own closed, but signalled his approval of what she was doing by pressing the length of his middle finger into the warm cleft between her buttocks. This caused her to wriggle slightly, and he now went to work with his own tongue in and around her mouth. She gazed at him and blushed, then closed her eyes, opened her mouth wide and, just as he pushed his finger down to a lower position so that the tip hovered at the sodden entrance to her cunt, she clamped its length tightly between clenched buttocks.

The finger was held, enveloped in soft but muscular flesh. Even so, he found that the tip still had some freedom, and was able to agitate it backward and forward and from side to side against the slippery lips. Before long he could tell he had succeeded in sheathing it up to the second joint.

With the tip of his tongue he traced a path over her chin, down her neck to one of her nipples, and teased it into full engorgement before lowering his whole mouth over the tiny breast to suck it rhythmically. Susie, who had been reclining facing him on her side, now stretched out on her back, limbs extended, so that his hand had to be withdrawn from its position of attack from the rear. He brought it smartly to the other breast and pinched the nipple between thumb and forefinger.

She was pulling at his cock, dragging it in the direction of her gaping vulva. But forgetting the gallantry that was in fact no more than part of his stock in trade as a self-proclaimed 'feminist ladies' man', he resolved to teach her who was master. He would reject her unspoken pleas to be instantly skewered flat on her back. Instead, he rolled her over quite roughly, thrust a hand under her belly while kneeling behind her, and dragged her up on to her knees, her head hanging limply on the mattress. With his other hand he tugged at one of her breasts, letting the inflamed head of his cock find its own way down between the silky buttocks towards the hot portals of desire.

As soon as he felt it nudge the cuntlips open at the right place, he shifted both his hands to her hips to give him a good purchase. He was just on the point of shoving in his prick with all his strength when Susie, not humiliated but delighted by the turn these proceedings had taken, thrust powerfully backwards, impaling herself with a scream of joy that would have awakened any normal sleepers.

But they all slumbered on after their exertions, leaving the field to the triumphant Captain and his temporary darling. He hugged her bottom to his lower abdomen and let his rigid cock grow thicker and thicker as that delicious young cunt tightened its loving grasp. Then, reaching both hands around her to press her upper thighs and groins while frigging her clit, he began, slowly at first, to move his whole throbbing length out and then in again. Every movement he made was met with a corresponding one from Susie, whose desire was as rampant as his own. The powerful contractions of her vagina by themselves could have brought him to his peak, but as he felt the critical moment approaching, he increased the pace and rammed in and out with a violence that set his partner's buttocks quivering.

The strain on her braced muscles was too much for her – she fell forward on her tummy. So tight was her cunt-grip and so hugely erect his prick that their fierce copulation continued uninterrupted. Her head being turned sideways, he was now able to press passionate kisses first on her ear and then on the corner of her mouth. But the full-length contact of their bodies in this position was too much to be borne. Just as Susie hammered her fists on the mattress and tensed every muscle in paroxysms of fulfilled lust, the Captain's bursting loins erupted and poured forth their scalding lava into the innermost depths of her pulsating love canal.

Thus began the most glorious night of pleasure of the Captain's life. What wedding guest had ever enjoyed such hospitality? They fucked and fucked until, outside, the birds began to sing and a shaft of sunlight penetrated the dusty window hangings to fall on their still coupling loins.

THIRTEEN

NYMPHS AND SHEPHERDS

After his exertions on the wedding night, the Captain found it necessary to take a day off. He slept until mid-afternoon and stayed indoors until opening time, when he biked down to the village for a few swift jars in the Green Man. Then back for another protracted night's sleep.

On Saturday morning he was aroused by a persistent rattling at the door of the Lodge. It was an excited Melanie, charmingly attired in skimpy white shorts and a loose-fitting blue sweater. Her hair was tied back with a matching blue ribbon.

Not bothering to cover his nakedness, the Captain let her in, and she followed him upstairs. She took her cue from him when he slipped back into his warm bed. Off came her shoes and socks, then the shorts and little white panties. She took a couple of turns round the room in her sweater, showing off her slender, well-shaped legs and affording glimpses of the undercurves of her bottom and of the golden tuft that winked where the thighs met beneath the loose hem. Then she, too, got into bed and clung to the Captain.

'Doing anything today?' she inquired.

'I'm doing whatever you want me to, my pet.'

'Well, I remembered your suggestion about a nymph hunt. I've organised one for this afternoon. No sweat.'

In acknowledgement of his delight, the Captain's member stretched out and wormed its way between Melanie's warm thighs. He felt her breasts through the sweater, and then ran his hands up her body inside it until they rested on the hardening buds.

'You're great,' he said. 'You'd do anything for me, wouldn't you?'

She was silent for a moment, and drew back her head to gaze into his eyes before speaking. 'I don't belong to you, and you don't belong here. OK, it's good to have you around, but all good things must come to an end.'

Rather than press her on this point, the Captain pressed the points of those lovely breasts as he brought his lips to her mouth. The knob of his prick swelled out from the foreskin, and bedded itself in the mushy warmth between her slackened labia. He reached down her back and squeezed her buttocks, pulling her tightly towards him. Melanie rolled on to her back, taking him with her. Her knees parted and were drawn up as high as they would go, opening an easy highway for her partner's lust. The actual penetration was so easy that he could almost imagine someone had recently been up there before him, filling her cunt with slippery spunk. True, her juices had always flowed copiously under arousal, but as copiously as this? Something to do with her cycle, perhaps.

He felt a small hand reaching behind him, and then another. The first one probed his arsehole while the second one lighted on his testicles, applying the lightest pressure while he squirted his semen into her. Whatever juices had lubricated that delicious cunt were now enriched with the effusion from his reservoirs, replenished by rest.

'Meet me at the Secret Garden at three,' she whispered, pushing the Captain off her and leaving him to a few more hours of restorative sleep.

Three o'clock found him waiting outside the hidden door to the garden, which he had unlocked. After the succession of thunderstorms that had marred the latter half of the week, it was again bright and sunny, though fresher than before. He didn't have to wait long. Subdued chatter announced the arrival of Melanie and her party, wearing weekend attire and carrying sports bags. The Captain pushed the creaking door open to admit them one by one: Cathy, Gina, Nikki, Carla, and Melanie herself, accompanied by Heini, Joker and, perhaps rather surprisingly, Darcy, who might have been expected to devote all his free time to his bride and her sexual requirements.

Although the Captain knew all these lads and lasses by name and had actually fucked Carla Merryweather on the occasion of the dorm feast, he had never spoken to his coveted Gina Wootton, or to Joker Jennings, and Joker had never set eyes on the Captain. Melanie introduced him to these three, and he pressed Gina's hand to his lips. Greeting Joker, the Captain asked how he had come by his name.

'I wasn't always called Joker, was I,' the youth replied. 'At 'ome me mum and dad called me Wanker, but I didn't reckon that, so I knocked 'em abaht a bit till they started callin' me Joker. Funny, innit?'

'Yes, but you do make us laugh in other ways too,' said Melanie, adding for the Captain's benefit, 'He may not be a wit exactly, but he's up to all sorts of merry pranks and practical jokes.'

'Like what?'

Joker stood sullenly dumb, while Melanie explained that it was he who had defaced the Cunlip College sign out on the main road. 'And not knowing the MacDonald had already taken care of the problem, he got up into the loft, didn't you, Joker, and tried to make us safe from the local yeomanry by putting a load of contraceptives in our water supply. Used ones.'

'Drinking water comes straight from the mains, though,' the Captain pointed out.

'That was certainly a blessing. But we still had some nasty experiences washing and brushing our teeth until old Muttock sent Derrick up to drain the tank. It was like frogspawn flopping out of the taps.'

Melanie then got the eight of them to gather round her while she expounded the ground rules of her nymph hunt. These were simple. The males of the party were to be shepherds, apart from the Captain, who was Zeus, king and father of the gods. They were to retire to the farthest limit of the garden, two or three hundred yards away at the top of the hill. When the nymphs had hidden themselves among the undergrowth and plesaunces of the lower slopes, a blast on Melanie's whistle would be the signal for the hunt to commence. Each shepherd would take as many nymphs as he could handle, hunting either singly or in groups. Each nymph would have a white ribbon round her ankle. These were to be seized as trophies and tied to their captors' weapons; in the case of a multiple rape, the nymph would yield her ribbon to whoever had pleased her best. Zeus, the father of the gods, would also participate, in the guise of a mortal visiting his favours upon the daughters of (professional) men. But his

189

supremacy over the mere shepherds was to be reflected in the licence he would enjoy to usurp the position of any of them he caught *in flagrante delicto*. Even if penetration had already been effected they were to withdraw at his bidding and allow his godlike sceptre to assert its authority in the shrine of love. And that nymph's trophy, as well as any others already adorning the shepherd's crook, would be taken as a tribute to the godhead. Finally, nymphs who had already surrendered their ribbons were to be fair game for all comers, but a shepherd deprived of such a prize by Zeus would have to forfeit all his trophies in tribute.

This Arcadian scenario was greatly to the taste of the Captain, who had always longed

> To sport with Amaryllis in the shade,
> Or in the tangles of Neæra's hair.

The girls now withdrew to a sheltered greenhouse abutting the wall, where they were to change into the drapery they had brought with them in their bags. Melanie dished out loincloths (or maybe dishcloths) to the shepherds, and Miss Muttock's leopard-skin rug to the Captain, who refrained from suggesting that this costume might be more suitable for Bacchus than for Zeus. Quickly they changed, and left their own clothes by the garden door. The Captain – great Zeus himself – then led his lithe-limbed crew along winding paths and through the neglected growth of many years to the very top of the Secret Garden. Whereas the shepherds, almost naked though they were, had their genitals concealed by the small rags Melanie had issued, the Captain's appearance was more aggressively masculine. The fangs of the moth-eaten leopard skin gleamed on his forehead, its front paws hung over his shoulders and the mottled body covered his back and buttocks. But the whole length of his shaggy torso and belly, together with the well-tried equipment slung between his thighs, was nakedly displayed for the mere mortals to marvel at. This made it a matter of some concern to him that his manly member was now reduced to dimensions scarcely more impressive than those of his little finger. He took care to stride on ahead of the three youths, and hoped that he would not be at a loss when the time for action was at hand.

At the top of the hill they waited under the high brick wall, and Zeus drew one of the leopard's hind legs majestically around him. He cast an eye over his young rivals, who stood around impatiently. Heini, his white loincloth contrasting starkly with the red fuzz that covered his entire body, was visibly salivating. Joker scratched his groin and picked his nose. Darcy, blushing, looked down at his slender, pale trunk as an unmistakable erection stretched up inside his flimsy garment. At this moment, the whistle shrilled, and these amorous shepherds vanished into the bushes.

The Captain blundered after them, but soon decided that his interests would be better served by quiet stealth than by breathless rampaging. As he worked his way forward through the tangled foliage, occasional flashes of flesh or the glimpsed white of a loincloth indicated the position of one or another of the hunters. Where were the nymphs hiding? Would they be cornered and pinned down, or would they break their cover and streak through the undergrowth before his eyes?

The inspiration for this afternoon's sport had been a passage recalled from Keats, and now the Captain remembered another. Like the poet, he aspired to

> Catch the white-handed nymphs in shady places,
> To woo sweet kisses from averted faces,
> Play with their fingers, touch their shoulders white
> Into a pretty shrinking, with a bite
> As hard as lips can make it.

He rounded a huge laurel bush. There, in a small clearing beyond it, lay Heini Hintenburger with the nobly endowed Cathy Condon mounted atop him, jockeying furiously up and down. No pretence of a struggle here – it was more as if the nymph had been lying in wait for her swain and had sprung out on him.

'Stop!' cried the Captain, his sceptre springing to godlike life. Roughly he rolled the girl off Heini's wet, red prick. She lay on her back, resentful, and her new captor admired the taste with which her simple white drapery had been arranged to leave one firm but ample breast free. Then, in a flash, he was on her, his great ram swollen almost to bursting point as it stretched the tender cunt.

Heini lay beside them, foaming with rage, and the Captain was moved with compassion. He remembered the touching devotion of this couple, and with Jovelike magnanimity withdrew from Cathy without ejaculating. 'Take her,' he commanded her red-haired lover.

'*Danke, Herr Kapitän*,' the youth replied, hurling himself between her thighs. 'You are ze chentlemen of ze olt school tie. *Wahrhaftig!*'

His member now fully erect and glib with Cathy's love juices, the Captain cut an imposing figure as he stood there over them in his leopard skin. He stooped to fondle the German's balls as he bucked up and down, but his own lust was now growing too urgent for its satisfaction to be long delayed, and as the crimson-fringed orifice between Heini's buttocks held no charm for him whatever, he charged off in search of tastier game.

Here his knowledge of the Secret Garden's layout proved a decisive factor. True, his previous explorations of its labyrinthine pathways and secluded arbours had been brief and superficial. But as far as he knew, none of the others, apart perhaps from Melanie, had ever been there. He made his way diagonally upwards, pausing every now and then to listen. Each time, squeals and screams from lower down the hill testified to some good sport. And now, as he covered one ear and pointed the other towards the far corner of the garden, he heard the snapping of dead twigs followed by breathless panting. A white apparition, glimpsed through the leaves, flashed across his vision.

The Captain pressed forward. It seemed that this girl was lost, wandering aimlessly through the dense shrubs. Easy enough to keep up with her and close in until she stood, trapped and quivering, with her back to the angle of the great brick wall.

Carla Merryweather: the dappled sunlight rippling on the dishevelled hair which fell in dark tresses over her shoulders. The gauzy white covering Melanie had devised for her was clasped in a kind of Empire line just below the convexities of her budding but still unripe bosom. It fell in fluted folds, and its hem was artfully contrived to rise from above her knees on one side to the hip bone on the other, affording an unobstructed view of the whole length of her slim right leg. This time it was a verse

192

of Robert Browning's that flitted through the Captain's consciousness: Panlike, he was 'Ready to twitch the nymph's last garment off'.

This flimsy *chiton* was indeed Carla's last garment. No longer did her ankle sport the sacrificial ribbon. To take possession of her would gain the Captain no points in the contest, but would be purely a labour of love – a labour, however, which the condition of his procreative organs now compelled him to put in hand. Bursting into the open, he advanced on her in the pardlike majesty of his divinity.

Carla whimpered. For her molester the encounter held the illicit thrill of a rape, and yet, as she had consented willingly to participate in the fun and games, he felt no scruples as he placed one hand on the back of her neck and with the other drew aside the hanging folds of gauze to expose her darkly furred delta. Semen had started to run down the inside of her left thigh.

'Who's had you already?' the Captain demanded as he licked her ear and kissed her cheek.

'That dreadful Joker,' she quavered. 'He's so rough and rude, sir – I thought he was going to split me open. Oh, I was so frightened I nearly had a heart attack.'

The Captain's response was a stock one: 'Don't worry love. I'll go slow past your heart.'

All the time, Carla, who had lost the balletic grace which usually distinguished her movements, was trying to back away from his embrace, but now he had her right up against the wall. His yard rammed up stiff into her bellybutton. Grasping her under her black-tufted armpits, with his fingers on her shoulder blades and his thumbs on her hard little nipples, he lifted the girl bodily and lowered her on to his slick, purple spike. Under these circumstances it was not difficult for the Captain to put aside his aversion to sounding recently plumbed depths. Indeed, it was the copious lubrication of her sexpot, and its prising open by Joker's tool, that made it possible to slip her so easily into place on his throbbing rod. Instinctively, she wound her pale legs round his hips. The sobs now ceased. She closed her eyes and sighed as a hot fountain jetted vertically up into her soft flesh. He squeezed her buttocks until every last gobbet of sperm was wrung from his loins, then kissed her and set her gently on the ground. Carla just managed a smile before slinking off to find a hiding place from the other hunters.

Resuming his search, the Captain proceeded slowly downhill, straining his ears for telltale sounds. But this time his eyes rather than his ears led him to his quarry. A flurry of whiteness betrayed the presence of two youthful forms, and he burst from the thicket just as Darcy O'Flammery threw himself on Nikki. Darcy had evidently mislaid his loincloth. Nikki's tunic was a diaphanous length of muslin with a central hole for her head and a girdle loosely tied round her waist. Her assailant simply ripped this off her as she sprawled on her back, kicking frantically against him as he guided his long, slender stem towards her sex.

Before the violation could be consummated, the Captain seized Darcy by the scruff of his neck. 'I'm surprised at you, young man,' he chided. 'You're supposed to be enjoying your honeymoon, not fucking your chief bridesmaid.'

'I am enjoying it,' the lad retorted, 'but Susie's a bit sore. She said I could come here and have some fun.'

'In that case, let's all have fun together,' replied the Captain. But even as he spoke the words, he realised that his own manhood was not yet quite ready for the task he contemplated, so he devised a preliminary diversion to restore its vigour. He got the three of them lying on their left sides in a triangular formation. Nikki, who seemed game for anything and had engaged in a similar but all-female threesome with Susie and the other bridesmaid on the wedding night, played with his testicles and took his drooping penis into her mouth. Darcy was directed to lick her anus and penetrate it with his tongue, using his fingers to urge globs of lubricant from her cunt and rake them back to mingle with his spittle. The triangle was completed by the Captain, who wetted his lips and closed them over Darcy's cock. But instead of sucking and pumping the lad to orgasm, he was careful to avoid rhythmical movements, allowing the saliva to well up in his mouth and flow right down to the root of the rigid organ.

A few minutes in this position brought his own prick back to stiffness. He broke up the triangle, stretched out flat on his back and got Nikki to straddle him. 'Hold her open for me, Darcy,' he ordered. 'Keep her sexlips wide open while she spikes herself on me. Oh, and go on licking her arsehole at the same time.'

The operation was performed successfully, except that as the girl's sheath slid right down to the Captain's pubic hairs, no room was left for the play of Darcy's tongue. The Captain reached up to grasp her ribs beneath her arms and pulled her down towards him, so that her arse became available once more. Without being told, she kissed his mouth. He swirled his tongue against the inside of her teeth, and then pushed her gently upwards, just enough to slip his hand between their chests, but not far enough to obstruct Darcy's access to her arse.

'I want to feel those tantalising breastlets,' he murmured, as his cock grew even longer and thicker within her.

'That's a funny thing, mister,' the girl replied. 'When you say "breastlets" you mean little tits, don't you? But in *Adventures of a Naked Girl* the word means a small bra. I'm so much into the book now, you're getting me all confused.'

At this point, verbal definitions and slippery etymologies were far from the Captain's mind. He called to the boy. 'Bugger her, Darcy,' he ordered. 'Really lay into her bum and bugger her hard.'

Even now, the slipperiness of language was not to be evaded. Somewhere between the transmission of this urgent message and its reception, the signified skidded away from under the signifier that was meant to hold it in place. 'Right,' said Darcy, and rained a series of blows on the girl's buttocks that almost threw her out of her saddle. 'Bugger you, Nikki!' he yelled. 'Bugger you, you little tart!'

Although the surprise of this development nearly brought on his crisis, the Captain had enough self-control left to correct the boy's misconception and persuade him to plunge his well-lubricated tool into the orifice Nikki was presenting to him. As the stiff instrument was forced home, the older ravisher could feel its hardness moving against his own prick; it was almost as if they were both encased in the same tight sheath. Stimulated by the extra constriction produced in his way, he was moved to immediate orgasm at the same moment as his two young companions.

All three of them lay panting for a while, before the Captain made Darcy remove the white ribbon from Nikki's ankle. 'You can tie it on my prick,' he smiled. The tying, however, presented a slight problem, and had to be repeated several times before he felt sure that the bow was neither so tight that it would inhibit further erections, nor so loose that it might slide off his slippery member in the heat of the chase. When at last it was secured, the Captain stood up and readjusted his leopard skin, which had come quite adrift in the throes of copulation. And then, his new adornment flaunted proudly at the base of his belly, he launched himself once more into the undergrowth.

His next kill took place in the lower reaches of the garden, not far from the old greenhouse. Face down in long grass sprawled the lovely, auburn-haired Gina Wootton, the shreds of what had been her white tunic up round her neck and shoulders. She was being held in this position by the rampant Heini, who sported Cathy's ribbon in a saucy bow, while Joker, the knob of his penis enormously distended by the pressure of Carla's tied round its root, was attempting to enter her from the rear. Gina kicked, struggled and bucked up and down, her heaving bottom a beautiful sight in the flashes of afternoon sun which the few unbroken panes of the greenhouse reflected on to it.

'This ain't no good,' puffed Joker. 'Roll 'er over, you clumsy kraut.'

Remaining in the shadows, the Captain watched with bated breath as both youths forced the reluctant Gina over on her back. Apart from the tangle of drapery concealing her throat and armpits, the full length of her delectable person was now exposed to his view and to the cruel attentions of her captors. The white skin was piquantly decorated with constellations of freckles, although these had not colonised the globes of her breasts, the curve of her belly or the insides of her thighs. Her nipples rose hard and red from their puckered areolas, and her coppery bush flamed out in subtle contrast to the German lad's carrot-coloured one. The ribbon on her ankle was intact. Intense longing raced through the Captain's arteries, but he forced himself to hold back and watch as Heini stifled the girl's cries by cramming his thick cock into her mouth while Joker wrenched her thighs open and lowered himself between them, his buttocks clenched.

Gina was surely the most desirable of the nymphs in the Captain's eyes, but as he understood the rules he would not be entitled to cull Joker's ribbon until the yob had penetrated her. Therefore, although he knew the violation to be distasteful to her, he was obliged to stand by, his cock quivering, while Joker rammed home. But as soon as the girl's gasp indicated that she had been entered, he rushed forward to her rescue and tumbled the youth off her, sideways. Heini, whose member had been ejected from her mouth by her shocked gasp, cringed away. He had lost face undoubtedly, but at least he retained his trophy.

To assert his triumph over Joker, whose case was different, the Captain now addressed his bronze-haired darling. 'Untie his ribbon, dear,' he instructed her, 'and put it on me.'

Without speaking, Gina complied, and without being bidden she removed her own ribbon from her ankle and added it to the other two that decorated her deliverer's pole. 'It's lucky that your thing's so long,' she remarked. 'But what'll happen to these bows when it gets small again?'

'When will that be, you cute kid?'

'Oh, when you've fucked me, of course. And you're certainly a welcome change – I can't stand that low-class git of a garage hand.'

Joker and Heini had by now disappeared into the bushes. Any further conquests they made would be purely for pleasure, as the great spotted deity had already proved himself *victor ludorum venatoriorum*, champion of venery, by securing three of the five trophies. But the third of these, although so willingly bestowed, still had to be earned.

He pushed Gina gently back on the grass, and she spread her thighs, clasping her hands round the neck of the leopard skin to draw him down on her. The first touch of her vulva against the tip of his prick felt cold and wet; a little push, effected simultaneously by both of them, brought it into a region of hot stickiness. The girl's tongue forced itself with a fucking motion into his mouth in time with his own thrusts as he churned his way inch by inch up her cunt. Before he reached the limit of his ingress, Gina informed him that both the ribbons had made contact with her tender love lips and were being dragged into her.

197

How regrettable, thought the Captain, that he had not become intimate with the girl earlier. Still, it was the unfamiliarity of this new pussy flesh that added zest to the present fleeting encounter. 'Oh, Gina,' moaned the Captain, wrenching back his head to interrupt the kissing for a quick breather. 'I've seen your loveliness on the netball court and outside the Palace of Sweethearts. I've always longed for you, and now I'm lying on top of you fingering your tits and all set to shoot off inside that adorable pussy of yours. I want to . . .'

He was unable to complete his sentence. Gina pulled his head down again and stuffed her tongue back into his mouth, just as the passion welled up in his heaving loins and spilt incontinently into her lustful sheath. They lay entwined for some moments. When he withdrew, the bows of the white ribbons were sadly bedraggled and stained with the mutual effusions poured out in this love bout. The Captain took his leave of her with kisses applied to the lips of both her mouth and her cunt, and loped off to see what could be done about claiming the prize due to him for his sporting prowess.

Shrieks and whoops led him to a bower fragrant with wild roses. In the centre stood Melanie, clad in transparent yellow chiffon that matched her hair. The sun was behind her, revealing the clean lines of her limbs. It appeared that she was now at bay, cornered by Heini, Joker and Darcy. Hunting in a pack, all three of them had been determined to save their honour by winning the last remaining trophy, but now that they had caught her, cooperation was at an end. All three flew at her, and she went down under a mass of flailing arms and legs. The Captain's nostrils caught the arousing odour of sex mingled with that of sweat. His own lust began to stir yet again.

Partly because he was smaller than his rivals, and partly as a matter of sheer chance, it was young Darcy who got stuck into her while Joker and Heini were still struggling for supremacy. But the Captain tugged all three of them off her, snatched away the remnants of the yellow tunic and fucked her soundly before declaring himself outright winner of the contest.

The others took this rather unfair triumph in good part. Melanie blew the whistle hanging round her neck to summon the girls from their hiding places, and reminded her ravisher that he could now do whatever he liked, or was capable of, to all or any of them.

'Right,' said the Captain, when they had all gathered around, stretching out on his back with his legs wide apart. 'You girls are to take it in turns. Each of you must kiss me, rub your pussy on my mouth, suck my cock and then wipe it against your cunt while the next one's already kissing me, and so on. And while two of you are busy with my mouth and cock, the other three waiting their turns must use their tongues and fingers all over my body any way they can. Heini, Joker and Darcy, I want you to kneel round us and work on the girls while they're busy with me. Oh, and when I'm really stiff and ready, whichever girl is playing with my prick must sit on it and let me shoot my load into her. Any questions? No? Go!'

The ensuing orgy was conducted with much confusion, fast and furiously. So rapidly did the performers of the various tasks alternate that the Captain lost all sense of their separate identities. At length he felt he had been coaxed back to a state of tumidity, but when his member finally squirted out what resources remained after the day's exertions, he had no idea which cunt he was being drained into. It was as if he was servicing all five simultaneously, with just enough seed to satisfy them. His mind went blank and he . . .

Mary Muttock was taking an evening stroll between the lengthening shadows of the avenue, pausing at intervals to raise her silver hip flask to her lips. All was quiet in the grounds. Seized with an urge to masturbate, she headed for the walled garden she occasionally used for just this purpose. From her handbag she took the key she always carried, and let herself in, steering tipsily towards the rose bower.

Suddenly she froze in her footsteps. A bestial form loomed, obstructing her path. A leopard, proudly rearing itself up on its hind legs, displaying the lewd baggage of its masculinity, loaded down with white ribbons. The beast staggered towards her, a gin-summoned visitant from that monstrous, monster-infested *terra incognita*, the realm of dreams. She dropped her flask, turned with a scream, and fled from the enchanted garden.

199

FOURTEEN

SNAPS AND SLAPS

It was Monday morning, and most of the girls were taking exams. Miss Muttock locked the door of the dormitory, raised the corner of the rug and nearly broke a fingernail in her haste to lift the loose floorboard and extract the diary. Perching on the edge of Melanie's bed, she flipped through the pages until she found the latest entry.

Sun, June 10

This morning the Captain knew I would be waiting for him by the plank bridge below the Lodge. A lovely day and I had on my pale-blue summer dress and a pair of sandals. Considering it's just a uniform this dress is quite sexy, especially for the likes of the Captain. And to make it even sexier, nothing on underneath. On a day like this he was sure to get randy, even after all the bonking in yesterday's nymph hunt, and I was itching to be fucked myself.

Just starting to get bored with watching the stream, and worrying in case some of the other girls not doing exams came down and joined me, heard door of Lodge opening and shutting and looked up. The lecherous beast came loping down the hill with big grin on face. He was in shorts and T-shirt, and carried a plastic bag.

CAPTAIN (*glancing all round before giving me a wet peck on the forehead*): Hi there.

ME (*looking wide-eyed at his thighs and giving his ballocks a quick squeeze*): What's all this, then, Hairylegs? Taking me to the seaside?

HIM: No, I'm taking you somewhere a bit more private than that. (*Holding up bag*) Here – I've got a surprise for you.

Reached to grab it from him, but he pulled it away and whacked me playfully on bum. 'Not yet,' he said.

Well, we strolled along stream, past pool and through woods

till we came to the old brick wall. At a point where thorny shrubs pressed close up against it, he forced a way through for me to a little door.

'After yesterday, you know all about my secret garden,' he said, producing key and turning it in freshly oiled lock.

Didn't tell him I'd been climbing wall and mucking about in there for last two years. He was as excited as little boy with new toy. Let him take my hand and he led me through tangled undergrowth to a clearing, where he got an old blanket out of bag and spread it on ground. We threw ourselves on it, face down, and turned our heads to look at each other. I kicked off sandals.

'Where's that surprise, then?' I demanded.

He reached into plastic bag and brought out an envelope. 'The wedding pictures – I've not looked at them myself yet,' he grinned, breaking open sealed package, yanking them out and setting them in a pile in front of us. As he did so, he wriggled his right side up against my left one and laid his right hand lightly across my bottom. 'Oh good,' he said, 'all twelve seem to have come out.' Going through them was likely to be a slow business, I reckoned. Wished I'd brought my Walkman with me.

On top of pile was general view of ceremony. Reminded me how exciting it had been, and what a buzz it had given me to organise wedding and take control of everything. Maybe I'll be able to do something like that in real world, after I leave.

Captain stroked my side through cotton of my dress. Horny look told me he'd just discovered what should have been obvious from start – nothing at all under it. He kissed my ear, and turned over next picture.

This showed pretty little Susie and Darcy hand in hand, waiting for the service to begin. I'd been through all the words with them, and rehearsed the moves, but they couldn't have had faintest inkling of what was going to hit them when we did it for real. Captain was having a good old gloat at this one, I could tell. After all, he'd really screwed the tail off her while I was pretending to be asleep. Poor kid wouldn't want to be leaping about netball court again for a while.

Then he kissed nape of my neck, and slid his hand down

thigh to hem of dress. A tug needed to loosen it from under my legs. Although I had no intention of helping him by shifting thighs, let him work away at it till he got it free. A cool hand crept up under skirt to its previous position on bum, but this time caressing bare skin as it moved to its resting place.

But it didn't rest there very long. He moved his palm to centre of my bottom, and gently played with buttocks. I closed my eyes. After a bit of this kneading treatment, he kept hand in place on my soft behind while running tip of middle finger down groove between buttocks. I wriggled my hips, and lazily uncovered next picture.

Bride and groom facing each other, exchanging vows. To frig and to fuck. Wow, that got them going!

Captain took hand off my bum. Then I felt him lift hem of dress right up to hips and lick my left buttock lightly for a moment (sun would soon dry it, he said). God! He tickled my arsehole while we both looked at next picture.

'I liked this bit,' I said. 'I was consecrating the chalice, remember? Just before the part when Darcy pushed me over and stuck his nose in my pussy.'

As we chuckled over incident, my demon lover moved down to bury face in softness of my left buttock. At same time he was stroking backs of my thighs and – help! – parting them. Then I felt him kissing and nibbling at left thigh while pulling open bumcheeks and no doubt having a good close look. Obvious when he shoved a hand under his belly that he was sorting out a stiff cock caught up in shorts. Glad it wasn't my blanket we were lying on. Felt him caressing and gently parting inside curves of my buttocks, playing with place where they border my pussy. Ooh! He made his fingernails tickle tiny hairs which I've seen in mirror just encroaching on those smooth curves. I imagined him staring goggle-eyed at dense, damp bush of mature hair on either side of central slit lurking there below my arse. From the warm feel of it I was pretty sure it had begun to pout open. To begin with it would only have been a line of silky pink, really tempting for fancier of young cunt like him. Next thing he was kneeling beside me and trying to get his hand, palm upwards, under my pussy. How it made me squirm! He slid it higher until the whole fanny was cupped in his hand. Then he did something really wild. Opening his fingers, he arranged two of them on each side of my outer lips, squeezing them together and then releasing pressure, slowly but repeatedly. At same time I could feel him teasing my cunthairs and then my inner lips with tip of what must have been his thumb, before pushing it right into my wet slit where he wriggled it from side to side. Without letting up at all, he worked his body upwards alongside me till he was kissing my cheek. 'Let's see the next one,' the sly devil suggested.

Next one disappointing. Had been taken fraction of second too late. Susie had just been licking Darcy's cock, and he'd spunked in her face. Captain had meant to catch that spunk flying — to catch it in picture, I mean — but all we saw now was Darcy's wet little dick dangling down with some of that white goo still oozing out of it. Would have been better if he'd got photo of her face, all wet with it.

He was frigging me steadily now, and I couldn't help squirming on blanket and moaning. The bastard got up on his knees. He pulled out sticky thumb and replaced it with three fingers, which he thrust in brutally. I suppose he did that so his thumb could be free to poke about in my arsehole. After using other hand to slap my buttocks and set them quivering, he shoved it between my left boob and blanket, roughly squeezing nipple through material of dress. I could tell nipple was hard as a dried pea. His sharp teeth pinched flesh of my behind. Suddenly I was on the point of coming. Had to throw myself over on my back. Doing that forced his fingers out of me. But he brought a hand down on each thigh and wrenched my legs wide apart. Then he buried his face in gaping wetness of my cunt, just as I lifted bottom high off ground and exploded in climax. Must have squashed his ears with pressure of my hot thighs as my honey flooded into his mouth.

We still had a few pictures to drool over, and Captain said that, speaking for himself, he didn't want to come too soon. So gave me a quick kiss on forehead and rolled me back on my tummy, dress still up to my waist. For greater comfort, as randy bugger put it, he slipped off own shorts and got down beside me again. Bet the blanket was getting damp under him now! I turned over next photo.

As it caught Captain's eye, he sort of whiplashed as if an electric charge had blasted through his privates.

'Just look at this,' he gasped. 'This picture captures one of my most vivid memories of the occasion.' That's the way he talks, even when he's got a hard-on. True enough, it had been a high point for me too.

There was Susie, or rather Susie's bum, stuck up at the camera. Her clothes had been pulled up to give full view of her arse and tight little cunt, all lovely and smooth. No wonder I'd got idea of making Darcy feel her up – that was just what I'd wanted to do myself.

Just looking at picture made me hot and shaky. With my fingers I started scrabbling at Captain's upper thigh, trying to work them underneath to grab prick. He playfully patted my arse and shifted up so close to me that my hand couldn't get at him that way.

'I know what the next one's going to be,' he laughed, gently tugging pigtail.

It showed me standing in profile, the huge rubber dick strapped to my pussy. We were both getting worked up as we gawped at it. I forced a hand between his thighs, worked two fingers up under him from behind and felt root of his prick thicken as they gripped it. But he squeezed legs together, trapping wrist. I knew he was trying to put off big moment. Meanwhile, we examined next photo.

In close-up, we saw faces of the two kids, now officially married, and looking even more gobsmacked than most newlyweds. And in this case, *gobsmacked* isn't a bad word for it. This was where the threefold kiss business began. Susie had turned her head sideways and was trying to break away from her horny husband, who had managed to get tongue in her mouth for a moment before she turned away. Her cheek all wet with his spittle, and you could see from look in his eyes that he really had the hots for her.

While we gazed at this lovely wedding portrait and relived occasion in our minds, my fingers were hard at work, even though Captain still held my wrist trapped between upper thighs. Had brought him on so far by tickling balls and squeezing prick that he told me in very urgent tones he was now on point of flooding blanket. To avoid messing it, he knelt up and climbed between my open legs. He grabbed me by hips and roughly dragged me up so I was kneeling in front of him. My head stayed down on blanket and my bum was forced up against bottom of his belly. Felt him bursting his way into my wet love tunnel. Then he gripped my hips even tighter and shook me like dog shaking bone. From wet stuff running down inside of my thighs I could tell what a load of spunk he was pouring into me. He was still pumping it in as it came bubbling out again, just like when my dad overfills tank of our car, standing there with nozzle thing stuck in hole and eyes all glazed over. We fell forward, Captain on top. Didn't bother to pull out – in fact I daresay his sperm was still gushing out of cock – as he reached forward to pile of pictures and turned next one over.

As I said, the last shot had shown us the happy couple's faces in close-up. This next one just as close but pointed lower down. They had been specially decorated for our benefit. Susie's clit was covered with lovely red carnation, hanging down from silky little tuft I'd left just above it when I shaved her. And Darcy's dick was standing up like a coat peg, but instead of a coat it was holding up that daisy chain. Chain looked a bit wimpish, but you couldn't say that of his cock, which must have been busting for first-ever fuck.

We'd now got nearly to bottom of pile, and number ten turned out to be a proper shocker. Close-up view of poor Susie's cunt, in sharp focus, taken from between her legs as she lay flat on back. Some contrast with tasteful shot we'd just been enjoying! Looked as if she'd been gang-banged or badly mauled by overaffectionate gorilla. Not actually bruised or bleeding, but you got impression it was just short of that state, kind of swollen and beaten up. The inside lips were sticking out, sagging open and really bright red, except where they were clogged with the thick white muck draining down on to sheet. And you could see the little tuft was all clotted with great dried-out cakes of it.

Write it down like that, of course, and you want to feel

sorry for the kid – makes her seem such a victim. But in fact that brutally manhandled cunt was really pretty, and I could tell we were going to get off on it again as we looked at it – Captain's cock, which had nearly slipped out of me, was beginning to stretch and climb up my insides already. After all, I'd watched everything we did to her, and she'd loved almost every minute of it. The only bits that really made her howl out *not* for more were when Heini couldn't jam his great sausage right into her, and then again, after he'd jerked off over her face to get himself smaller, when he stuck it in her bum and buggered her silly. I reckon that was mostly psychological – she kept yelling out it was dirty. OK, although it went in without too much hassle it must have got pumped up quite a bit while he was doing it to her. Dragging it out of her arse was nearly as hard as trying to stuff it into her cunt. That's why I said no when he wanted to give it to me. Let him have me from behind on all fours, with Cathy licking my clit, but I made sure he only did it in cunt. 'I'm not a fucking animal,' I screamed at him. 'I don't vont an enimal to fuck,' he snapped back. 'Vot I vont is a machine vot fucks, vot fucks vizzout stoppink. *Vorsprung durch Technik*, as zey say.' And his cock sprang forward into my open pussy.

By this time Captain's thing was rampant again inside me, and he'd started to slam it in and out. What with all these porny pictures and his hands working away under me like the clappers on both tits, which he grabbed through dress, I was ready to climax. But just as the waves began to surge through me, bastard pulled out, forced me over on back and made me take his boiling come in mouth and swallow it. Shock of unexpected made me come myself anyway, and I got him to kiss me and lick out mouth.

Rolled off me to my right and lay exhausted for about a minute. Then he started snoring. Was quite glad myself to stretch out and relax in sun. Pulled dress right up to let it warm belly and not-so-privates. Held photos we'd already looked at up over face and went through slowly once more. As I did so felt my juices run down to dry in fresh air. This gave me itch, so put a hand on his balls.

In no time at all he was up again. Up? I mean both that

he had another hard-on, and that he was sort of sitting up beside me. Of course, he didn't want to know he'd been sleeping. They think that makes them seem clapped out. He turned me over and unbuttoned dress all the way down front. His mouth went to work on right nipple, first tongue and then, very gently, teeth. Not biting, but just the slightest scraping of the sharp edges, dripping with his spit. Each time teeth passed across nipple, they dragged it towards him and then let it spring back before he did same again. While he was exciting me like this I felt fingers of his right hand idling through my pubics.

Then he cupped whole pussy in palm, using heel of hand to press gently but firmly on area just above upper end of slit. At first hardly noticed anything when he flexed his wrist so he could apply the pressure in circular motion, working away to stimulate hooded clit. My own hands played with my nipples. He grinned at me lecherously.

This delicious frigging was making me come. Suddenly I melted in warm juices, so his whole hand sort of sank into the flesh. I grabbed wrist and snatched hand away. Next I lifted my bum off ground. He knelt between thighs and took my buttocks roughly in both hands, forcing them up and clamping face to wet cunt. Plunged his nose between the slippery folds, and then his tongue, first wriggling it about in entrance to vagina before sliding it up cleft to settle on clit. But not for long. I came with jerking shudder. Think he could tell I was on point of coming again. Anyway, he backed off, got up on his knees and slipped bursting cock straight into gaping opening.

'Yes! Fuck me!' I yelled. 'Fuck me like there was no tomorrow, as they say.'

My thighs tightened round his hips – luckily no need for him to be free to thrust in and out, as we both thrashed about in ecstasy, drowning in simultaneous climax at the instant his pubic hair rammed against mine.

Still joined together, subsided on blanket and kissed hungrily till his prick got back its full thickness and stiffness inside tight twat. Flattering old fucker said just looking at pretty face could have this effect on him. But I'm sure feeling my tongue darting about in his mouth while my fingertips tickled his bum can't have been bad news exactly for him. Before he knew what had hit him he lost control, and shouting out how 'maddeningly desirable' my cunt was, he once again flooded it with spurting cock juice.

As he tried to withdraw, I forced finger up his arse and pressed him to me even tighter. Kissing grew more and more frantic, and our mingled saliva flowed down my chin and neck. With both hands he groped for and found my nipples to tease and squeeze them brutally. Well, after a while I pulled finger out and rolled us both over, our sexual parts still linked. When I pressed myself up so my pointed tits hung down for him to play with, I felt cock hardening again. Somehow, without letting it escape its tight sheath, I managed to bring my knees up on either side of him so I could ride him. This position gave him full view of front of my 'lovely body', including shoulders, from which he now slipped the open dress. It also let me control speed of screwing while his hands wandered all over my front. Moved up and down slowly, slowly, each time lifting my pussy so high that tip of his prick almost escaped, letting me see its whole shiny wet length as the spunk of his two recent climaxes ran down it. Then, after a dozen or so of these slow heaves, I sped up and bonked away for a few minutes like jockey riding hard to finishing post. This galloping made my small firm tits shake like little jellies. And every now and then, made a complete pause to lean forward over him and force tongue into his mouth. In this way made sure that at last we enjoyed a long, slow fuck. Yes, it lasted long enough for us to drool over last two pictures.

Number eleven was a rude one of the bridesmaids, just about to lick each other out. They made a pretty contrast – Nikki with her fair colouring and her little friend with dark short-cut hair and unmistakable overall tan. This suggestive pose brought us straight into home stretch, at full gallop. I fondled my tits under Captain's hands and threw my head back. Thought I was on verge of coming. But no, I pulled up panting, and slowly down again while we marvelled at randiness of these innocent-looking kids.

Last shot was of Cathy and Heini. As Captain said, their

own rather innocent look showed up in photo. We could only see them from waist up, looking down at each other as Heini dragged one of her boobs out of nightie. She was staring down, presumably at his ever-ready cock.

That got Captain going – what's more, it got both of us *coming* amd no mistake. Buckets of spunk spouted up me just as lightning exploded inside my head and my whole body screamed SEX! SEX! SEX!

And that was our friend the Captain's lot. I pulled my cunt up off him.

ME: Hope the earth moved for you, because that's got to be the last time.

CAPTAIN: Come again?

ME: No, that's what I'm telling you. We can't screw again and I'm not going to let you come again. End of the affair. *Finito*. That's why I told you to screw like there was no tomorrow. You won't want to hear this, but I've never been your property, your exclusive piece of meat. There's someone else, and he's always been *Numero Uno*.

HIM (*going white*): That's great. Great for you, I mean. So you want me to get on my bike and bugger off?

ME: You don't have to do that, big boy. Listen, you had a surprise for me when you brought me here, and I've got one for you.

HIM: You've already surprised the shit out of me. But it's true – you don't belong to me.

ME: I knew you could take it. Easy come, easy go, isn't it? Listen. I've fixed up another live show for you in the Palace, with your own partner. It's not quite true there's no tomorrow – just no tomorrow for you and me as a couple. Everything's ready for tomorrow night. You game?

HIM: Which partner?

ME: Your lovely Gina.

That clinched it for him, and his disappointed face lit up a bit. Then I explained what was planned.

I'd got the idea for show from dirty book the MacDonald had lent me, *Fanny Hill*. Great book, except that whenever you think someone's naked it turns out they've still got something on. Mr H enters Fanny's bedroom in nightshirt and cap. 'Hurries off his clothes' and leaps into bed. Then kneels between her legs, and what happens next? 'He drew up his shirt, and bared all his hairy thighs (how many? Is this really the tale of little Ms Muffett?), and stiff staring truncheon, red-topped.'

Anyway, what I had in mind was that bit where Fanny gets initiated at a 'public open enjoyment' in Mrs Cole's brothel. I'd made six friends read up their parts in it, with the MacDonald helping. They didn't have to learn like for a play – we were just going to sort of improvise, following lines of story as far as possible. Gina to be Fanny and the Captain her 'particular', as he's called in book. I was getting costumes from Drama, and already had nice highwayman's suit for him.

Idea seemed to tickle his fancy. Could see he was embarrassed. He didn't know whether I'd let him kiss me now. I didn't. Put our clothes on and left Secret Garden. He slunk back to Lodge.

Miss Muttock snapped the diary shut. Instead of returning it to its place of concealment, she put back the floorboard and covered it with the rug. Then, clutching the notebook to her bosom, she hurried to her room and switched on the intercom system.

'Melanie Winspur to the Principal's study,' she intoned into the microphone. 'Immediately.'

Twenty minutes later, a flushed and apprehensive Melanie knocked on the study door and entered.

'Do sit down, dear,' said the Principal, in a voice anything but endearing. 'I'm sorry to say you are exposed,' she continued, as the girl sprawled in an easy chair.

Melanie straightened her back, snapped her knees together and tugged down the hem of her dress, which had indeed ridden up high on her thighs.

'I said you are exposed.'

Melanie's hands went to her breasts, which she found almost but not quite completely covered by the top of her dress, provocatively unbuttoned halfway down to her waist.

'You misconstrue me, girl,' Miss Muttock proceeded. 'Did you write this?' She held up the yellow notebook.

'That's private, miss.'

'I'm not interested in whether it's intended for publication, but in its authorship. I can see perfectly well that it's an intimate journal.'

'Yes, miss,' conceded Melanie, casting around for a plausible explanation, 'but it's not what it seems to be. It's part of a novel I'm writing.'

'Oh, so it is for publication after all, is it? I doubt whether you will find a publisher sufficiently depraved and corrupted to accept it. What's it to be called – *The Secret Confessions of a Teenage Whore*? Bodice ripper's hardly the word. Listen, my dear, I'm old enough to know the difference between fact and fiction. You have abused the trust your excellent father placed in me by having sexual intercourse on the college premises.'

'Why should he want to do that – isn't that sort of thing unprofessional?' asked Melanie, deliberately pretending to misinterpret the ambiguous utterance and be scandalised, but actually rather worried.

'Insolence will not help your case, you rude girl. You will pay for it. But first, account for your lewd behaviour during these crucial weeks of the examination period.'

Cringing, Melanie did her best to keep up the pretence. As Miss Muttock read out lubricious passages, she acknowledged that they offended against the standards of decency and taste Cunlip College strove to uphold, but insisted they were nothing but the product of an overheated imagination.

'It's the time of year,' she explained. 'I get sort of worked up in the summer, what with the clothes we wear here and the – the games some of the girls get up to. I need an outlet.'

'Well,' replied the Principal, 'you certainly seem to have found one. Regrettably, this has involved the abuse and defilement of an *inlet*, a sacred inlet if I may say so, and not just one. Our girls have always been taught to keep themselves pure for their husbands.'

Even under pressure, Melanie was unable to resist such an invitation to a display of impudent wit. 'I haven't got a husband,' she retorted, grinning smugly.

'Which brings me,' her interrogator went on, 'to the material evidence.'

211

'Evidence? What evidence?'

'Proof that you are lying to me, you wicked girl. Of course *you* are not married. But what do you say about the case of Susan Freemantle?'

'Susan Freemantle – who's she? Oh, Susie. How could I be married to her?'

The Principal fumed. 'You think you can run rings round me, young lady. It's time to teach you you've met your match. Watch that screen.'

Melanie turned her head slightly to confront the small TV monitor on one of the shelves. Using remote-control units, Miss Muttock first caused the screen to light up and then set a video-tape cassette in motion. The picture was black and white, poorly lit and taken from some distance away from the action. But the occasion depicted was instantly recognisable to the dumbfounded girl, whose defences were quite broken down by this concrete proof of her diary's authenticity as a record of actual events.

Scantily arrayed in white, Susie and Darcy stood demure before a profane altar, their movements directed by a priestess of lust whose identity could not possibly be mistaken. Miss Muttock kept fast-forwarding the tape and returning it to normal playback speed at selected points of interest, denouncing the lascivious proceedings while at the same time betraying signs of arousal: shortness of breath, flushing, crossing and recrossing of her thighs, and other little indications which did not escape Melanie's experienced eye.

She was aware of the Principal moving round behind her, but when she turned her head to see what she was doing, was sharply ordered to pay attention to the screen, on which she herself could be seen, armed with the ridiculous dildo and preparing to violate the kneeling girl's cunt. She heard sounds of activity behind her chair, and a rather breathless voice: 'Melanie, you have been up to some wicked, wicked pranks. I cannot imagine what Dr Winspur would have to say about the depravity of his own daughter.'

Melanie gasped. 'Oh, please, miss,' she mumbled, reduced to the moral stature of a little girl, 'you can do anything to me, but *please* don't tell him about this.'

She heard Mary Muttock getting closer, and felt the hands lowered on to her breasts, which they clasped firmly through the thin dress. And then that voice, close to her ear: 'Anything?'

'You can do anything to me, miss. And I'll do anything for you.'

'Is it correct that you are planning a lewd performance tomorrow night, based on Cleland's *Fanny Hill*?'

'Well . . .'

'Have you found someone to play the part of Mrs Cole, the brothel keeper?'

Melanie sensed trouble, but felt she had no choice but to tell the truth. 'Yes,' she replied, 'Miss MacDonald.'

The Principal laughed a thin laugh. 'Very apt casting, my dear. In that case, I must curb my own Thespian ambitions. I will settle for a ringside seat. A concealed one. You understand?'

Melanie nodded. 'Is that all?'

'Not quite. There is something else, something you are going to do for me here and now, you little trollop.'

The hands resting on the girl's breasts gave her nipples a sharp tweak before pulling the front of her dress wide open to toy rather roughly with their nakedness. Miss Muttock's loosened hair fell over her face; under it, cheek pressed against cheek. Involuntarily, Melanie flinched, but thought better of it and twisted her head, presenting her open mouth to receive the older woman's kisses.

'Get up!'

Melanie rose from the easy chair and confronted Mary Muttock, standing naked save for black shoes, black silk stockings, and a black suspender belt. She was quite surprised to find herself sexually aroused at the sight, and felt the warm dampness spreading between her legs. The Muttock took her victim's place in the soft chair. Reclining back, she pushed her bum well forward, right to the edge of the cushion, and opened her outstretched legs. Below and between luxuriant light-brown curls, a delicious pink cunt pouted open, the insides of its slack lips glistening moist in the sunlight which fell on them from the window.

What was required was obvious, and as her own interest had been sufficiently awakened, the eighteen-year-old needed no prompting. She took her place kneeling on the leopard-skin rug, the disappearance of which over the weekend had been attributed by Miss Muttock to a slight ocular disorder that had troubled her lately, gripped the unprincipled Principal's hips, and stooped her mouth to the slippery blisses gaping to meet it.

'What are you doing to me?' cried the delighted woman, rubbing her own breasts. 'Ah! Lick and suck, lick and suck!'

She felt the vigorous young tongue slide up and down the groove of her sex. It paused at the upper limit of its play and flickered over a clitoris now engorged and throbbing. She writhed in ecstasy as the girl's lips tightened over it. The sensation of suction drew it right out of its fleshy hood. Then it was released naked to the cool air, while Melanie continued her tonguing between the oozing lips. This time the tip paused at the lower end of its travel. Mary Muttock moaned at the sudden pressure as Melanie, her face squeezed hard against that yearning vulva, thrust her flickering tongue right into the vagina as far as it would reach.

The stimulation of the rapid tongue-fucking which then ensued was bringing on an urgent crisis, and she held her breath, trying to delay it as long as possible. She lay there rigid. The hands on her hips now worked their way down under her buttocks, and pulled them apart to open the way for a titillating attack from the rear. Nor was the rampant clitoris neglected – the tip of the girl's nose was pressing hard against it and rubbing it, so that she was simultaneously thumb-buggered, nose-frigged and tongue-fucked.

When she recovered conciousness, it was to find herself huddled on the carpet, panting and trembling, quite oblivious of the rapturous spasms that had hurled her from the chair. Melanie stood above her, grinning, and helped her to her feet.

'Oh, you wicked young beauty!' she murmured in a strangely deep voice. 'How you need to be punished for this impudence! Stand with your back to the window and bend right down over my desk.'

Melanie complied, and moving the clutter of books and papers her stern lover made sure that the girl's thighs were pressed close against the side of the desk and her upper body flat on its top, arms extended forward to grip the far edge. She leaned over her and kissed her cheek.

'This won't hurt too much, darling,' she hissed. 'I don't want to mark you so much that it spoils your partner's fun tomorrow evening.'

'Or mine, I hope.'

'Or yours, and not just tomorrow but now as well.'

Miss Muttock raised Melanie's dress over her thighs and bottom, and tucked it up round her waist. She stroked the smooth white cheeks admiringly and parted the legs wide enough to reveal her plump, inviting vulva.

'No panties, of course. Not even a flimsy wisp of lace. You know our rules. You get an extra six lashes for that, you slut.'

She marched across to a cupboard, from which she fetched a slender cane, flexing it to test its pliancy. Her victim was surprised to feel it laid lengthwise in the cleft between her buttocks.

'I will at least spare you the smart of having the rod applied to raw flesh,' said the Principal. 'My mercy knows no bounds short of those set by religion and the demands of corrective justice.' And bending over the exposed behind, she licked it energetically all over until it was bedewed with saliva that winked wetly in the morning sun.

When it came, the main assault was administered briskly but not too brutally. A torrent of blows stung the tender flesh into crimson weals. The skin remained unbroken; indeed, the lashes were inflicted with such a practised wrist that the marks would fade away within the hour. And yet they were quite sufficient to encompass their object. After howling in agony for some minutes, her knuckles white on the edge of the desk and her bum tensed against the cruel onslaught, the abused girl began first to relax and then to squirm voluptuously as pain was overtaken by a rising tide of pleasure.

Even now the disciplinarian in Miss Muttock remained in command. Instead of allowing nature to take its course, she desisted just as the wild gasps of lust heralded the approach of orgasm.

'Stand up, girl!' she shouted, and as soon as the teenager stood dazed before her, seized the front of her dress, already open to the waist, and ripped it apart with both hands so that everything

215

– thighs, belly and gingery-tufted mound – was exposed to her hungry gaze.

'Down!' she snapped.

Melanie subsided to the floor, followed by the passionate Principal. In a flash their limbs were intertwined in an acrobatic embrace. They sat on the leopard skin with their upper bodies clasped, breast rubbing on breast and mouth pressed to mouth. The older woman had her right leg curled round the girl's bottom so that the foot was tucked under her right buttock. Melanie's right thigh was raised sufficiently to allow Miss Muttock's left one, resting on her own, to pass under it.

In this posture, it will be appreciated that their cunts were locked together, lip between lip, their fast-flowing juices intermingling before spilling down on to the rug. It will also be appreciated that the clinch could not be maintained for long. Their crisis hit them both at the same time, and as their bosoms fell apart their heads flopped down to the floor. But for many minutes nothing could disengage their loins, the muscles of the Principal's inner thighs having tightened on those of her struggling young partner in a vicelike *rigor amoris*. So intense was her ecstasy that she was not even aware that the leopard's fangs had pierced the skin of her right buttock.

FIFTEEN

PARTICULAR PLEASURES

That same night, the Principal wrapped her black academic gown around herself and hurried down to the pavilion about half an hour before the time designated for the revels to commence. Melanie had already seen to it that a couple of cushioned chairs were in position in the small side room. Using tools left there by the Captain, she had pierced the wooden partition between this room and the main one in several places, to give a full and clear view of the lascivious transactions she had planned.

The half hour passed slowly. Even the battered hip flask Miss Muttock had brought with her in place of the one she had mislaid in the walled garden failed to help it slide past faster as she sat, rocking backwards and forwards, in the dark. But eventually she became aware of sounds outside on the veranda, and after a while a group of dim figures entered. The lights in the changing room were switched on, revealing a trestle table laid with a clean cloth, tall candles, plates of sandwiches and bottles of wine. Four chairs were arranged on each side of the table, and another at the head.

Momentarily she suspected that she was hallucinating again. Apart from the bare bulb of the light, she seemed to have been transported to the eighteenth century: three foppishly attired rakes-about-town and a bold highwayman were seen in the company of a handsome woman, resplendent in the costume of the period. The woman set about lighting the candles on the table and others placed in every convenient position, and then stepped over to switch off the electric light. Now the scene took on an even more authentic appearance, bathed in the glow of flickering candles.

To break the spell, the voice of the woman, who was thus identified as Miss MacDonald, rang out. 'OK, boys,' she said, 'why not take off your hats and wigs to cool down a bit before you get stuck in?'

Off came tricorn hats and powdered wigs, recognisable as

belonging to the wardrobe of last term's spirited production of *The Beggar's Opera*. Miss Muttock, who was far more aware of what went on within the Cunlip purlieus than her colleagues and students suspected, immediately identified three of the males as Heini, Joker, and her trusty friend the Captain. The features of the fourth one were concealed by a black mask, and although there was something familiar in the way he carried himself, she could not place him.

'I think, lads,' Miss MacDonald proceeded, 'we could dispense with those hats altogether. But you'd better put the wigs on again for the proper effect. Now remember, you're supposed to be gentlemen, or even noblemen, and you're visiting this high-class, genteel brothel run by me. You call me Mrs Cole, by the way. Tonight you've come here on a special occasion. As well as our usual girls, a new one's being initiated, and you're all going to do your coupling together, watching each other. Try to remember these girls' names, would you, although really it'll be better if you don't speak to them too much. Melanie Winspur plays "Louisa", Catherine Condon is "Harriet", Emily Capstick's easy – she's just "Emily" – and Gina Wootton will be the new girl, "Fanny", who doesn't know what's going to happen. Captain, it'll be your task to take her in hand. To use the author's slang term, you'll be her "particular" for the evening. The rest of you can have your regular girlfriends or anyone you like.'

Miss MacDonald stepped over to the door and admitted Emily, Cathy and Melanie, who were waiting out on the veranda. These three had been artfully rigged out to look their parts. The *Beggar's Opera* costumes were brashly suggestive, but now the outer garments had been left off to create an impression both more revealing and somewhat demure. Cathy and Melanie wore petticoats, stays and white shifts adorned with coloured ribbons. Cathy's legs looked pretty in maroon stockings, and Melanie's in sky-blue ones. The well-grown Emily's get-up was slightly different: instead of the tightly laced corsetry of the period, her breasts were only just contained in a tight but flimsy bodice secured down the front by four buttons. Her black stockings, as Mary Muttock noted, emphasised the truly elegant lines of her legs. All three girls wore white mobcaps on their heads.

On entering, they were greeted with the utmost gallantry by

their well-briefed young men, who led them directly to the table. Heini and Joker held the chairs for their partners, Cathy and Emily, and sat down with them on one side with their backs to Miss Muttock, while Melanie and the masked stranger took their places facing her. The MacDonald and the Captain remained standing for a moment, apparently groping for suitable dialogue. They both spoke at once, stopped, began together once more and stopped again.

'La, sir,' cried the handsome whoremistress, 'I pray you, continue.'

'Futtocks, madam, I thank you,' rejoined the Captain, who cut a dashing figure in the highwayman's outfit which the MacDonald and her classes had run up for Captain Macheath in the opera. 'I am pleased to see your young ladies have been able to join us for our supper and sport. They are all of them tasty dishes, and my mouth waters at the recollection of past encounters with them. But had not you promised to acquaint me with a gamesome novice fresh to your establishment?'

'Indeed, sir,' came the reply. 'Fresh from the country and a stranger to the rites of Venus, e'en now Miss Fanny Hill waits to be presented to you. Fanny, my dear . . .'

At this point the outer door opened to admit Gina, dazzling in the white morning gown thrown loosely over her dishabille. Her auburn tresses were swept up under her mobcap, leaving her slender neck bare, and the bottle-green stockings contrasted beautifully with her colouring.

'Ah, Fanny, my dear, pray be acquainted with this gentleman. He has undertaken to treat you most tenderly, and to be your *particular* during your first essay of the pleasures of the house.'

'Sir,' stammered Gina with simulated modesty, 'I am at your entire disposal.'

The Captain kissed her hand, chucked her under the chin and kissed her mouth, before leading her to the table, where Gina bent over each of the company in turn to receive a wet kiss from them, too. The couple then took their places next to Melanie and her masked gallant. Miss MacDonald sat down at the head of the table, and the party devoted itself for some time to the business of eating and drinking.

As the cheap wine flowed, tongues became looser, as did the

costumes of the young ladies, wantonly toyed with by the wandering hands of their gallants. Kisses were snatched between bites of sandwich, and gales of laughter indicated that the girls were not at all dismayed by the liberties taken. Miss MacDonald, in the guise of the indulgent Mrs Cole, wagged a finger and uttered the odd reproof when the decencies of the table seemed threatened with lascivious excesses, but her reprimands were neither meant nor received too seriously. Mary Muttock judged that all present had worked themselves up, or been worked up by their partners, to a high pitch of arousal. They certainly seemed pleased when the Captain spoke.

'Well, Mrs Cole,' he said, 'I propose that we waste no further time, but commence the country dances forthwith. I fancy,' he added with a lewd wink, 'that the instruments are in tune.'

All present nodded their assent and rose from the table. Miss MacDonald curtsied, excused herself tactfully and withdrew at once to the side room, where she was horrified to stumble into the seated form of the Principal. 'I can explain everything,' she gasped. 'Just an idea for next term's production. I'm going to stop them now.'

'No, Muriel,' replied Miss Muttock. 'Sit down. I insist on seeing it through. We can watch together.'

'But Principal, I'm afraid their horseplay is likely to get out of hand if . . .'

'Silence, woman,' the Principal hissed. 'Just relax and enjoy yourself, can't you?'

By this time, the gentlemen had moved the table and chairs to one side of the room and had lifted into their place an old couch draped with a scarlet cloth and furnished with a red velvet cushion, before retiring to the chairs on the sidelines. Gina looked up inquiringly at the Captain. 'Pray, sir,' she whispered aloud, 'what purpose will be served by this rearrangement?'

He rested an arm on her shoulder and attempted to reassure her: 'Do not be alarmed, my dear. Tonight's pleasures have been devised on your account, as a novice in Mrs Cole's academy. 'Tis the wish of these our friends to enact an open, public enjoyment, and to see you broke of any taint of reserve or modesty. For I may tell you, my dear, that they look upon modesty as the very poison of joy.'

'But sir, I had rather die than see my maiden modesty outraged!'

'Fear not. Our friends have no desire to shock a young beginner with transactions too violent and abrupt for her stomach. They have elected first to set an example, which I dearly hope you will not be averse to follow, since it is to myself that you have been devolved in favour of the first experiment. Nevertheless, my dear young lady, you are at perfect liberty to refuse the party. Its very nature is one of pleasure, which supposes an exclusion of all force or constraint.' And in a louder voice: 'Let Louisa and her beau open the ball.'

In the darkened side room, both spectators had settled with their eyes at spyholes and their hands between their legs. Melanie, in the guise of 'the amorous Louisa', rose to her feet and was led to the couch by the masked stranger, supposedly a 'cornet of horse', who tumbled her roughly down on her back. The others followed them and stood by the scene of action, fortunately leaving an unobstructed view on the side towards the peepholes.

Without ceremony, Melanie's mettlesome assailant drew her petticoats and shift right up past her waist. Melanie lay there grinning, her sky-blue-stockinged legs spread wide on the scarlet coverlet, and her white, exposed flesh gleaming in the light of more than a dozen candles. Everyone's eyes, however, were surely fixed on the pink cuntlips, delicately soft and pouting, displayed in their bed of gingery curls.

While Melanie sprawled there, gently teasing apart the petals of her sex with her fingers, her partner was stripping off his own costume. The turquoise coat was flung aside, the long, pink waistcoat with its endless row of buttons to be struggled with, the silver-buckled shoes, the white silk stockings and cream-coloured knee breeches. At last he stood before her in wig, mask, and long, voluminous shirt, frilled down the front. This final garment was removed, and the company gasped at the size of the throbbing weapon momentarily exposed to their view.

But only for a moment. Instantly he was on her. Hard prick engaged with soft cunt, and the spectators were left with the sight of his hairy bum and thighs slamming away at the girl pinned beneath him. There was no tenderness in his relentless rogering, yet it was evident that Melanie was in raptures. His fierce lovebites were returned with equal zest, and her nails raked bloody tracks up his quivering buttocks. Her active limbs kept wreathing and intertwisting with his, and finally she raved out, 'Oh sir! Good sir! Pray do not spare me! Ah! Ah!'

Simultaneous orgasm overcame the lovers, and they relaxed panting in a close embrace. Mary Muttock removed her hand from her vulva, eased her knickers down to her ankles, and edged her chair up beside the other one. Gently she took the Mac-Donald's hand from that woman's privates and placed it on her own. She reached into her companion's damp panties, and they both returned their eyes to the peepholes, just as the second couple entered the lists.

These were Cathy, playing the part of the charming 'Harriet', and her Heini, stripped to his shirt, as the young baronet who was shortly to remove her from the brothel to be his kept mistress. The fact of their real and long-standing love affair was apparent at every stage of the present encounter. In the midst of this 'public open enjoyment', he was seen to dote upon her to distraction, so that the spectators, both those beside the couch and those in the adjoining room, felt truly privileged to witness a scene of such tender intimacy.

Cathy blushed as her spark led her to the couch. Eschewing violent approaches, he made her sit down beside him, laid an arm around her neck and began with a kiss fervently applied to her lips to give her courage to go through with the performance. As he kissed her, Heini eased her backwards until her head rested on the cushion. The kissing continued as he carefully bared her well-formed bosom.

Miss MacDonald explained to her superior. 'According to the author, he means "to gratify both his pleasure and his pride in being the master, by the right of present possession, of beauties delicate beyond imagination".'

And indeed the twin beauties of her breasts were a sight to inflame the coldest libido. As he kissed their exquisitely white skin and licked the nipples into hard snouts, he reached down with his free hand and by degrees, so as not to alarm her too suddenly, stole up her petticoats until the pale flesh above the maroon stocking came into view. No sooner had he begun to delve among the dewy moss between her thighs than Melanie and Emily, as if a signal had been given, grasped her legs in pure wantonness and held them wide open.

Everyone in the room, as well as the two concealed witnesses, feasted their eyes on the delicious display. Even while they watched, the lips of the pussy, fringed with the softest fur, puffed up and fell apart of their own accord as drops of thick and sticky fluid began to ooze from them. On cue, the truly enamoured Heini drew his shirt over his head, revealing a cock poking up rigid along his belly from his flaming bush. He stood between the legs which Melanie and Emily held for his convenience. With one hand he gently eased her luscious sex mouth open still further, and with the other he forced his mighty machine down from its upright angle so that he could nestle the broad, shelving head just within the lips.

The girls now placed Cathy's thighs against his hips, and withdrew, leaving her clinging to him. Slowly, to spin out his pleasure, he passed up his instrument into her, inch by inch, until the pubic hairs of each met and intertwined. Heini now applied the fingers of both his hands to the mossy region where they were conjoined, and began to massage her mound vigorously. The girl's expression grew less and less innocent, and more and more lustful, and she visibly increased the pressure of her thighs around him as her passions rose. Her lover now transferred his hands from her pussy to the magnificent breasts, kneading them and tweaking the nipples, already as hard as leather tags. Cathy's thighs fell apart, allowing him to sweep in and out in long, slow strokes, which gradually rose to a crescendo paralleled by the accelerating rapidity of her moans and gasps. At last, to the delight of the company, the male members of which were showing signs of impatient tumidity, her climax just anticipated his own, and he threw himself upon her to cover her embarrassment and to plant a fervent kiss upon her mouth.

'I'm glad I didn't encourage him to speak,' Miss MacDonald whispered to her trembling companion. 'It would have spoilt the effect. Cleland knew that no words were needed here. In the book, that kiss is enough to express "satisfied desires, but unextinguished love".'

As soon as Heini rose to find his shirt, Gina hurried to Cathy's

223

side with a restorative glass of wine. The girls embraced until Heini separated them and led his sweetheart from the couch.

And now Joker brought Emily forward for her share of the dance. As they stood before the onlookers, he lost some time fumbling with the buttons of her bodice.

The MacDonald's commentary continued. 'She's got lovely, pear-shaped boobs,' she remarked, fondling the Principal's prominent ones as she spoke. 'I hope the boy's not making a cockup of this operation. All he has to do, according to the book, is "disengage her breasts and restore them to the liberty of nature from the easy confinement of no more than a pair of jumps".'

Just then, Joker succeeded in disengaging them, and they sprang out to view in all their shining whiteness. First he let her stand there, and turned her round so that the sight could be enjoyed by all. Then he began to touch and handle them, gently at first so that the glossy smoothness of the skin eluded his hand, and then applying firm pressure and letting them rebound as he drew back. After some minutes of this sport, the publicity of which caused Emily to blush charmingly, he stooped to raise her skirts. These he tucked up round her waist, exposing the full length of her black stockings, held up by red garters, and the contrasting whiteness of the plump thigh-tops and buttocks. These pale, silky parts in their turn provided a foil in both texture and hue for the yellow curls adorning her pubic mound.

Emily stood in such a way that most of her pussy was concealed between her thighs. For his own benefit and that of the spectators, he first tried to force her legs apart and then, despairing of securing the best view in this manner, made her bend forward and rest her head on the end of the couch. She was now standing with her legs apart, her bum and puffy sex pouch fully displayed to the lecherous voyeurs peeping through their spyholes, as well as to the participating bystanders.

Unbuttoning the flap at the front of his mock-buckskin breeches, Joker drew out his upward-curving tool, ready erected, and drove it into that inviting cunt. He reached forward to caress Emily's tits, every now and then letting his hands wander back to fondle the smoothness of her buttocks and then passing them round her hips to tickle her lower belly and clitoris. The girl was in ecstasy. She shook her bottom in time to his thrusts, hiding her scarlet face in the cushion. Joker drove her fast and furiously. Each time he backed away from her bum, the thick piston he was working in and out of her cuntlips glistened more wetly with pungent foam. Emily screamed and collapsed on the couch with her gallant on top of her, and it was obvious to everyone that the moment of this collapse was also the moment of his discharge into her vagina. The other girls helped her to rearrange her clothing.

It was now the turn of Gina, as 'Fanny', to be initiated into the customs of the house. The Captain addressed her tenderly. 'The frolic is come round to you, my dear. But let me assure you that if all the force of example has not surmounted any repugnance you might have to concur with the humours and desires of the company, although the play was bespoke for your benefit and great as my private disappointment might be, I would suffer anything sooner than be the instrument of imposing a disagreeable task on you.'

'I thank you, sir,' she replied, 'but even had I not contracted to be at your disposal without the least reserve, the example of such agreeable companions would alone determine me. I am in no pain about anything but my appearing to so great a disadvantage after such superior beauties.'

The company applauded, complimenting the Captain and openly envying him for his acquisition. He took her by the hand and led her to the centre of the floor, where he set to work undressing her to spare her the confusion that would have attended the forwardness of doing so herself. First divesting her of her flimsy morning gown, he took from Melanie a pair of scissors and saved time by snipping through the lace of her stays. The open bosom of her shift now gave everybody's eyes and the Captain's hands all the liberty they could wish, but the stripping did not stop short there. At the desire of the others, he tenderly begged the auburn-haired beauty not to suffer the small remains of a covering to rob them of a full view of her whole person. Gina complied, and her mobcap came off with the shift as it was pulled over head, allowing the coppery ringlets to tumble over her freckled shoulders without restraint.

The onlookers caught their breath in admiration, helping to stifle her simulated shame by remarks of sincere flattery. 'My dear Miss Fanny,' protested the Captain, 'I declare that this figure infinitely outshines all other birthday finery whatever.' And to prove his point, he devoted some minutes to posing her in every attitude he could think up to entertain himself and his companions, accompanying these proceedings with kisses planted on every portion of her body, and manual liberties which brought a soft flush of desire careering down from her throat to her belly. Finally, coaxing her to place one foot up on the couch, he inserted a lewd finger and addressed the party triumphantly. 'Mistress Cole has not imposed upon us,' he said. 'This young lady has not the least reason to be diffident of passing even for a maid, on occasion, so inconsiderable a flaw have her preceding adventures created here in her centre of attraction, and so small is her natural make in this part.'

Her 'particular' threw off his clothes, leaving to the last his breeches, which now gave up their contents to view. For a moment, Gina quailed before the enemy she had to engage with, stiffly bearing up its head unhooded and glowing red. He stepped forward a pace, embraced her, and stuck the swollen instrument between her thighs. The girl reacted bravely, canting up first her left leg and then her right one, so that her thighs clung round his naked hips as every inch of his standing cock slid home. She hid her face in his neck as he carried her once round the couch and then, without dischannelling, laid her down on it. Both the lovers were so overheated by the scenes they had witnessed that one or two thrusts were sufficient to draw from the Captain a shower of hot spray which was received by Gina's convulsing cunt.

This relief, however, had not satisfied the pair. After the briefest pause for fondling and kissing while still coupled by means of the Captain's pleasure pivot, their wrigglings and writhings grew more and more turbulent as his manly vigour returned in full measure and waves of lust swept once more through her whole being. At length they both expired in orgasmic surrender as the member which so deliciously plugged and choked up Gina's stretched receptacle injected a second flood of vital juices into its deepest recesses.

The Captain withdrew, exhausted, and staggered to the table for a glass of wine. Standing there already was Melanie's mysterious partner, who handed the glass to him, bowed low, and with a swagger removed the mask that had concealed his identity. This unknown spark was now exposed as the objectionable Derrick, whose fully reciprocated attentions to Melanie showed that, whatever might have passed between her and the Captain in the last couple of weeks, these old-established lovers clearly had no intention of relinquishing each other.

Miss Muttock caressed Miss MacDonald's inner thigh, well pleased at this turn of events, for she had not welcomed her senior student's attentions to the new odd-job man she had appointed for her own reasons. But her satisfaction was replaced by panic when her companion, thinking the Principal was in complete control of the evening's activities, dropped a remark which brought her smartly to her feet.

Still wearing her academic gown, but with the front of her blouse open, her bra pulled up to her throat, her skirt halfway down her thighs and her knickers completely abandoned, Mary Muttock burst into the main room of the Palace of Sweethearts. She stormed past the astonished revellers and threw open the outer door. There she found, kneeling on the veranda, a sinister figure in flat cap and raincoat, his eye glued to a spyhole and his right hand frantically wanking away at a huge, semierect dick. Taken by surprise, this clapped-out voyeur struggled to his feet, clasping the raincoat around him. It was none other than Hardbuckle, the deputy chief constable. 'Oh, sir!' gasped the distraught Miss Muttock, 'I'm so sorry, sir. I don't know what to say.'

After his initial shock and disappointment at finding Melanie still involved with the short-arsed (and now, after her scratching, bloody-arsed) Derrick, the Captain was relieved to find that the vibrations emanating from the latter seemed to be not hostile but merely sullen. No fists and no objections were raised when he drew Melanie aside to express his surprise at her preference. She explained, laughing high-spiritedly, that, with her connivance, Derrick had been spying on them ever since his official expulsion from the Cunlip domain, and she had been getting off on the knowledge that her intimate moments with the Captain had all provided secret thrills for his younger rival.

In fact, this reversal was much easier to bear than it would have been a couple of days earlier. Fucking Gina Wootton in the course of Wednesday's nymph hunt had confirmed his feeling that this girl, with whom he had been infatuated since first seeing her on the netball court, had truly supplanted the promiscuous Melanie in his affections. As the party broke up, he approached Gina, and resuming the part of her 'particular', begged her to accompany him back to the Old Lodge. An angry Joker intervened, having overheard the whispered suggestion. 'Giddorf!' he shouted. 'I mean, she don't fuckin' belong to you. Jus' piss orf, Jack.'

Life is short, the Captain reflected, and it was pointless to waste too much of it in vain regrets when there would always remain more delights than could be fitted into the days of the year. So he laid hands on the not unwilling Emily Capstick, and led her home to his bed.

Tues, June 12

Have had a fucking good time the last couple of weeks. He's a good sport, the Captain, but not really my kind of a hunk. I like a bit of rough, which is why that prick Derrick suits me better. But Captain appreciated me for my mind, and I do get on with educated people like him. Hard to imagine what he's doing farting about in a place like this. Suppose I rather regret giving him up. And his cock was bigger than Derrick's.

What was left of the previous night had not passed uneventfully for the Captain. He and Emily had torn off the remnants of their eighteenth-century costumes and fallen on the unmade bed in a leisurely embrace. Although neither could be sure, they both had the impression that they had slept for some time when they once more found themselves linked together in the act of copulation. It was not clear whether they had been roused to consciousness by the heat of their rising passion or by a hammering at the door of the Lodge. In any event, the Captain stopped his pumping but remained encased in his current sweetheart's love canal and pulled the grubby sheet up over her as a distraught Miss Muttock burst into the room, switching on the harsh light.

It would be as tedious for the reader as it was for the interrupted lovers to have to unravel the import of her garbled utterance. A summary will suffice. Her urgent message was that an investigation had been set up at 'the highest level' into the running of the college, as a result of which she would have to resign and probably leave the country. Explaining that events were moving too quickly for delay, she advised the Captain to do the same, and departed as abruptly as she had arrived.

She had, of course, left the light on. To mitigate its savage glare, the Captain crept down under the sheet to complete his intercourse with the quivering Emily, who first needed to be calmed with kisses on mouth and breasts. His prick felt as stiff as a bone as he jigged it in and out. He licked a finger, slipped it up Emily's arse, and bathed in the warmth that flooded under pressure from his bursting cockhead and seeped out to soak the intermingled hairs adorning both their genitals. When they awoke in broad daylight a few hours later, their bushes were cemented together by the dried flakes of come. They tore them apart with some discomfort as the Captain's flaccid member took its last leave of Cunlip cunt.

Pulling on jeans and a sweater over his aching joints, he descended the stairs and stepped out into the pallor of a chilly morning. No doubt the Principal knew what she was talking about, even if she had had difficulty saying it. He would have to go, and go a long way from here. But this was not the end of the world. He would not have to renounce the pleasures for which he lived and which he had found so freely available in and around the Palace of Sweethearts. He would take off on his motorbike and seek out a warm beach somewhere in the South. There he would recruit his forces to their full vigour, surrounded by the gleaming bodies of girls yet unseen – young, slim, and cock-stiffeningly pretty.

NEW BOOKS

Coming up from Nexus and Black Lace

The Cloak of Aphrodite by Kendal Grahame
November 1994   Price: £4.99   ISBN: 0 352 32954 8
Having completed the quest for the Golden Fleece, Jason must
embark on an even more demanding mission: the recovery of
a mythical cloak with aphrodisiac powers. Medea has the task
of bringing back the world's most gifted athletes. Kept apart
on their respective missions, the lovers vent their desires on
the men, women and gods they meet en route.

His Mistress's Voice by G. C. Scott
November 1994   Price: £4.99   ISBN: 0 352 32961 0
Tom can't believe his luck when Beth picks him up and takes
him home. Her proclivities become clear when she ties the
young man up – but when her dominant friend Harriet ar-
rives, things get even kinkier.

Melinda and the Countess by Susanna Hughes
December 1994   Price: £4.99   ISBN: 0 352 32957 2
Everyone's favourite blonde submissive has arrived in Paris to
meet her new Master – or in this case, Mistress. Beautiful and
capricious, the Countess wastes no time in demonstrating just
how cruel, and how loving, she can be.

The House of Maldona by Yolanda Celbridge
December 1994   Price: £4.99   ISBN: 0 352 32962 9
Deep in Andalucia lies a world all its own: a world devoted to
discipline. A group of women calling themselves the House of
Maldona act out all kinds of bizarre erotic rituals. Interference
or disobedience earn severe punishment – as Jane, on holiday
in the area, finds out.

BLACK
lace

Wicked Work by Pamela Kyle
November 1994   Price: £4.99   ISBN: 0 352 32958 0
All her life, Suzie Carlton has been in control. Now, as a jour-
nalist on a major women's magazine, she holds as much power
as ever. But a meeting with the masterful Michael shows her
that by nature she is sexually submissive. Will her budding
masochistic impulses undermine her career?

Cassandra's Chateau by Fredrica Alleyn
November 1994   Price: £4.99   ISBN: 0 352 32955 6
Cassandra has been living happily and sinfully with the Baron
for eighteen months. Now a friend's daughter has come to
stay, and there is a familiar gleam in the Baron's eyes. The
dark, erotic games look set to begin again ... This is the sequel
to the hugely popular *Cassandra's Conflict*.

Dream Lover by Katrina Vincenzi
December 1994   Price: £4.99   ISBN: 0 352 32956 4
Film producer Gemma de la Mare is holidaying in Brittany
when she feels a powerful presence nearby. While she is unable to identify the source of this overwhelming sexual aura,
her desires begin to boil within her. Can she find her dream
lover before she loses control?

Path of the Tiger by Cleo Cordell
December 1994   Price: £4.99   ISBN: 0 352 32959 9
India in the 1850s: Amy Spencer, a ravishing young English-
woman, is exploring this land of exotic pleasures. One of the
many exciting people she meets is Ravinder, handsome son of
the Maharaja, who shows her the great wisdom he has acquired – chiefly from the Kama Sutra.